THE WATER'S EDGE

THE WATER'S EDGE

A NOVEL

Beverly M. Rathbun

Library of Congress Control Number:		2011913495
ISBN:	Hardcover	978-1-4653-4453-3
	Softcover	978-1-4653-4452-6
	Ebook	978-1-4653-4454-0

This book was printed in the United States of America.

To order additional copies of this book, contact:
Xlibris Corporation
1-888-795-4274
www.Xlibris.com
Orders@Xlibris.com
102094

For Charlie

ACKNOWLEDGEMENT

What began as a day dream about the perfect place to reflect and relax blossomed into a four year journey to complete the story of Fern's retreat to, and return from the Water's Edge.
I would like to thank my family and friends for listening patiently while I shared my process with them, and for encouraging me without judgment.

Beverly M. Rathbun
2011

"We shall not cease from exploration and the end of our exploring will be to arrive where we started and know the place for the first time."

—T. S. Eliot

CHAPTER 1

T HIS CAN'T BE right. I glare at my GPS. The destination star blinks in place with maniacal surety. I grab the brochure off the dash: *The Water's Edge—Luxurious accommodations set on an expansive lake surrounded by hundreds of wilderness acres.*

I stare at the cinderblock building set back in the tall woods. Two motel-style wings stretch out from either side of a stark gray cube like the arms of a man being fitted for a suit jacket, or more likely a straitjacket.

It is official then, my loving family has checked me into an institution for the mentally deranged.

"It will be good for you, Fern, dear." The same line my mom had used to convince me to attend summer camp. If I remember correctly, it had rained the entire week and I'd been miserable.

"It's about time you vacated that convent you work at and come out of seclusion." My dad was in the habit of siding with Mom.

To be fair, Eva and Ted DeGiulio had always wanted what was best for their little girl, even if she was now fifty-four years old. My twenty-two-year-old daughter Maria—'Ria—concurred.

"You've reduced your life down to a pinhead," she'd told me. "You are still young and attractive, and you need to meet some new people."

I knew she really meant that I needed to meet another man. I wasn't sure about that, but I appreciated her assertion that I was still young and attractive. I had tried to maintain my aging body, and with the exception of a few extra creases here and there, I'd always entertained the notion that 'Ria and I could pass for sisters—maybe—on a foggy day.

Like a three-way firing squad, Mom, Dad, and 'Ria came at me from every angle until I finally gave in to their nagging and agreed to go.

"I only hope you're not sending me to some far-out cult where they make you strip naked and roll around in body paint."

'Ria had rolled her eyes. "Oh, Ma, just give it a chance."

*   *   *

An arrow of Canada geese flies over my head, pointing the way into the dense, shadowy forest. *Honk, honk, honk,* they mimic the comments made by my fellow teachers on that last day of school. "Have fun meditating with the hippies and communing with nature." By now my esteemed colleagues had jetted off with their families to some posh resort in Saint Thomas, Saint Croix, or Saint Disney.

And where was I on this beautiful July day? I was alone, in the middle of nowhere, about to share my vacation with a bunch of total strangers.

I thought about decamping to the nearest hotel, but I knew I couldn't handle the guilt. My family had paid a small fortune to give me this three-week creative arts retreat at the Water's Edge. It was my own fault. If only I hadn't mentioned my desire to take a drawing class, they might have sent me to someplace more exotic—like the Greek islands.

From my open window, I watch a black-capped chickadee flit along a cluster of Queen Anne's lace. A Carolina wren calls out, *teakettle, teakettle, teakettle-tee*. I lean back into the worn bucket seat and catch the warm summer breeze across my face. I look into my rearview mirror; weary hazel eyes stare back at me, and strands of tawny brown hair fall randomly over my freckled face. I clip the fugitive locks back into a barrette at the base of my neck.

Regardless of where I am, summer is my favorite time of the year. The cessation of work, the sensation of all things bursting forth into bloom. But instead of hiding out in my beat-up Toyota hatchback, I'd much prefer sitting in my own garden, sketching butterflies and tulips. But my garden has been plowed under, the flowers churned into shallow graves, and if someone handed me a sketch pad right now, I'd tear it into shreds.

I look down in my lap and see that the brochure is torn in half. What other details had been embellished? The five-star hotel accommodations? The gourmet cuisine? I picture a padded cell with nothing but a creaky camp cot to sleep on and a grimy chamber pot to pee in. The gourmet cuisine? Probably a crust of stale bread and a tin cup of water pushed under my door each day.

I gaze out at the windows on either side of the entrance expecting to see prison bars, but instead I see someone waving at me. A moment later the front door swings open, and a very large, very dark man with a salt-and-pepper afro and a bushy gray beard hustles his way toward my car.

"So sorry, ma'am," he says in a lazy southern drawl. "There was a meetin' goin' on." As if that explained everything. He opens the car door and offers me his jumbo-size hand, hoisting me out of my escape vehicle.

"Welcome to the Water's Edge."

We pass through a square vestibule lined with coat hooks, umbrella stands, and an empty boot rack. I am instantly Alice stepping through the looking glass. The room we enter radiates warmth and comfort. My feet sink into a plush green carpet, and my eyes are drawn to a magnificent fieldstone fireplace. The cream-colored walls are trimmed with rough-hewn woodwork, and the exposed ceiling beams ascend cathedral style over my head. Pillows in brilliant hues lounge on upholstered chairs, and fresh cut flowers splay forth from a giant pedestal vase. In one corner, water cascades playfully into a small pool. The place looks like a center spread in *House Beautiful*.

Shaking both of my hands—I can tell he really wants to hug me—Jonas introduces himself.

"Have a sit down, put your feet up, and relax." He checks his clipboard. "Sonja will show you to your room in a few." He ambles off.

I settle myself into one of the chairs by the fireplace. There are embers still glowing in the hearth, and a soft smoky scent permeates the air.

A woman, thirtyish with short spiky orange hair ejects from another door. "You must be Fern," she nearly sings. "I'm Sonja with a *j*. Off we go."

I follow Sonja with a *j* back outside and up one flight of stairs. We stop at door number 11. She hands me a key and a thick folder of information.

"When you hear the gathering gong," she tells me, "meet us in the dining room." Gathering gong? I plop my bags down on the comfy double bed. There's a mint on the pillow—nice touch. The pale peach walls are decorated with framed wildlife photos—a doe and her fawn peak out from behind a spruce tree, an eagle perches on a jagged cliff. I inspect the vacant hooks with a frown. I'm sure they are there to display the Fern originals I'll be inspired to create during the retreat. The pressure is on to produce. Some vacation.

I'm delighted, however, to discover a Jacuzzi tub in the bath and a well-equipped kitchenette. The bay window on the far wall transports the breathtaking view of the lake and the woods so near that it's difficult to tell if I'm inside or outside. I open the french doors and step onto my own private patio. Inhaling a deep breath of fresh air, I imagine a morning ritual of sipping a steaming mug of coffee at the bistro-style table while I watch this panorama of beauty unfold before my very eyes. "OK, 'Ria, I'll give it a chance."

"The creative process is very therapeutic." Her words. "Not only will you be able to explore your artistic nature, you'll have a chance to meet some interesting people."

A self-proclaimed introvert, I'm in no hurry to meet my compatriots, interesting or not. Maybe I'll just stay right here and order up room service. Do they have room service? A long low tone sets off some kind of symbiotic vibration in the pit of my stomach. The gathering gong.

Jonas, still carrying his clipboard, directs us into the dining room. Tables and chairs are strategically placed so that everyone can access the view of the lake from the three sets of sliding doors that open out onto the stone terrace. Sprawling grassy lawns slope down to the edge of the woods.

Sonja greets us and gestures behind her with a smile. "My number one competition for your attention; if nothing else, we know you won't complain about the view." She explains that we'll be sharing our meals and attending classes with a different group of people each week.

"Hopefully by the end of the retreat, you'll have had the opportunity to get know everyone, whether you want to or not."

There's a smattering of nervous laughter. Sonja continues to brief us on the history of the Water's Edge.

The original mansion was owned by a wealthy woman named Bet, who considered herself a patron of the arts. She spent her life supporting struggling artists by inviting them to live in her mansion—for weeks, months, even years—rent free so they could work their craft. Unfortunately, about ten years ago, while Bet was traveling in Europe, a metal sculptor was careless with his torch and the place burned to the ground. A more modern facility with additional wings for lodging was built to replace the grand house. Bet arranged for a board of directors to continue her philanthropic venture after her death.

"You're welcome to browse through the scrapbook in the foyer. You'll see photos of the mansion and some of the colorful characters who crashed here over the years." Sonja turned to Jonas. "You may even notice a familiar face."

"Nice segue," Jonas says. "Bet was like a mother to me, God rest her soul. I miss her every day." He clears his throat. A petite young woman, about half his size, moves to his side, pats his arm, and introduces herself as Lucy—our spiritual counselor.

"I would just like to mention a few of the house rules," she says. Her smooth Indian accent is so pleasant, her voice so soothing, that her recitation of the house rules sounds more like lyrical poetry. They are the acronym REST. We are to gift each other with respect, empathy, space, and time.

I study the faces of those I'll be empathizing with over the next three weeks. They're all grinning and bobbing their heads like marionettes on invisible strings.

"While you are here, we hope to offer you the very best for your body, mind, and spirit," Lucy finishes.

There is a murmur of approval when she introduces Chef Julian, an attractive Mediterranean type who assures us that he'll do everything possible to make our stay a culinary delight.

To begin the tour, Jonas leads us into the soundproof music room and plays a rousing rendition of "We Shall Overcome" on his baby grand piano. There are stacks of music scattered about the room and one entire wall is banked with an intimidating array of African drums. I believe him when he promises us a musical experience we'll never forget.

The art room is Marc's domain. He's a twenty-eight-year-old Buddhist monk who has just finished his bachelor's degree at the Rhode Island School of Design. He jokes that today is the only day we'll see him in his long, flowing alb. "Jeans and a T-shirt are much easier to move around in," he chuckles, running a hand over his smooth bald head. He acquaints us with the fully stocked shelves of art supplies and challenges us to try something outside of our comfort zone. "If you're used to painting modestly, consider sculpting extravagantly," he says.

He's speaking to me, I think, looking at the huge jugs of paint and enormous frames of stretched canvas. Maybe it's my reluctance to waste large amounts of paint, or maybe it's my diminutive living quarters, but in the three years that I've been dabbling with acrylics I still haven't graduated to anything larger than an eight-by-ten-inch canvas board.

Sonja merrily dances us into her studio. Wearing a chartreuse version of the "little black dress," she chatters on about how we'll rediscover our bodies through yoga, tai chi, and interpretive movement. Mine is not the only expression of anxiety reflected in the floor-to-ceiling mirrors that cover the walls. I may enjoy hiking and low impact aerobics, but there are certain body positions I respectfully refrain from discovering.

Our footsteps hush into the rich red carpet when we enter the inner sanctuary of the library—Lucy's domain—a quiet place to read, write, or just *be*. The wall-to-wall shelves, lined with hundreds of books, are a deep mahogany brown. The same dark shade as the long, neat braid draped down the middle of Lucy's back.

In the half hour before dinner, some folks opt to return to their rooms to freshen up, but most of us spill out onto the terrace. The summer sun is just above the tree line, and I watch it sink into the forest. I'm so overwhelmed by the sweeping beauty before me that, for the moment, I can think of nothing at all.

Once again I scope out the people around me. Who are they? Why are they here? Most of them are at least twenty years younger than I am. What could we possibly have in common? I glance over at Sonja. She's talking with a woman who could be about my age. The woman has silvery-white hair framing her tanned face in soft ringlets. They lean toward each other in a familiar, almost intimate way, like they've known each other for a long time. The woman with the silver curls plays with the beads around her neck as if they are part of the conversation. She's wearing slim-cut jeans and a tailored white blouse, and she exudes the confidence of one who could easily take command of both a boardroom and a barroom.

I self-consciously smooth out the wrinkles from my plain cotton shirt. I bring my hand up to the knob of brown hair behind my head, chestnut number five, a salon solution, applied regularly to help cover the traces of dull gray. I guess I'm staring because she catches my eye and smiles. I smile back.

"Time for dinner!" Jonas's voice rings out nearly in unison with the gong. "Don't forget, we'll be eating with our assigned groups this evening, so please look for your names on the place cards."

We walk through the serving line and fill our trays. Tonight's menu: a fresh salad and a spicy rice and bean dish with the option of broiled steak tips for those who must have meat.

Lucy directs me to her table. As we munch away, Lucy asks us to share a bit about ourselves and why we've come on retreat.

Sue, a computer programmer, was working seventy-hour weeks until the day she smashed her desktop computer with a baseball bat. The company determined that she was due for some vacation time.

For Karin, an operating-room nurse, this retreat was part of a sexual harassment settlement—a doctor who couldn't keep his hands to himself.

Ben is a college professor on sabbatical hoping to find the inspiration for his next book. He leers about the room making no secret of his propensity for the ladies.

And then there's Davy. His mom sent him on retreat to find himself. He's an unemployed interior designer who's so flamboyant that he doesn't need to tell us he's gay, but of course he does several times. "Black, gay, and proud of it!"

During dessert, strawberry shortcake with real whipped cream, Lucy explains the basic daily schedule. Monday through Friday a full breakfast is served at 9:00 a.m. Julian will have tea and coffee set up for any early risers who want to go for a walk, a canoe ride, or participate in morning stretch with Sonja. After breakfast we attend an art, music, or dance class until lunch. We have free time until midafternoon when classes begin again. After dinner there is usually an evening program planned. Tonight's offering is a wine and cheese party.

"Take full advantage of this time you've given yourselves," Lucy says. "Savor every moment."

Maybe I've had too much to eat. Probably I've had too much chitchat, but I've developed a whopper of a headache and I make my escape to savor the next few moments by myself in my room.

"See you later," Ben reminds me.

Maybe, maybe not.

CHAPTER 2

THE TWILIGHT SETTLING onto the lake has a calming effect on my nerves, and after twenty minutes of quiet I feel more like myself. Still in no hurry for wine and cheese, I decide to finish my unpacking.

I transfer my clothes from bag to closet and arrange my books and painting kit on the desk. From the bottom of my suitcase, wrapped tightly in a T-shirt, I extract a wooden bowl. I try not to dislodge the handful of small stones resting in the belly of the bowl as I carefully unfold the shirt.

Buffed by generations of love, as familiar as my own body, the cherry bowl was a gift from my dad on my tenth birthday. He'd line the inside of the bowl with a swatch of black velvet cloth and in the center he'd place a piece of milky white quartz. "The entire story of the earth is embedded in these sedimentary monuments," he'd tell me. Over the years, Dad and I had collected a legion of specimens: paper-thin bits of slate as black as ink, moss-stained chunks of granite as cold as ice. The treasures in my bowl had accumulated and overflowed. I'd sort and cull them many times until what remained were only a precious few.

It had been suggested that we bring something familiar to the retreat, something from home that gave us joy. I remove the stones one by one and place them on the desk. In many ways they marked the paleomagnetic study of my own life. I hold the heart-shaped stone 'Ria had found on the beach when she was five. "I heart you, Mommy," she said when her little fingers had placed it in my hand. It was warmed through by the summer sun, and now, as I cradle it in my palm, I imagine I can still feel the radiant heat of her love.

Missing from my cherished collection is the river-worn rock my ex-husband, Ed, had presented to me the day we met. Twenty years later, it had left a sizable dent in his car door the day I'd thrown him out.

The marriage had been nothing but a sham. We'd met in college, and I think the biggest thrill for him was that I was still a virgin. He was the first man I'd even dated. My high school years had been spent solely with my best friend Vicki. I think back to those carefree days as I run my thumb over the irregular bit of granite I'd found in her driveway.

We'd been inseparable. Her mom and dad were divorced and her mom worked the second shift, so we spent many happy afternoons after school at her house free from parental supervision. The activity of choice was to practice our limited cooking skills for imaginary husbands.

Our cooking skills were sadly lacking, and at first we were lucky we didn't burn the house down. Progress was made when Vicki took a home economics class and discovered a real passion for cooking. It was about the same time that I began my obsession with plant biology. Eventually we outgrew our fairytale fantasies. Vicki's mom and I became willing guinea pigs for her culinary creations, and they in turn marveled at my ability to resurrect even the deadest-looking plant in their atrium window. When Vicki and I were accepted at colleges on opposite coasts of the country, we vowed to write or call every day, but that was before e-mail and texting, and we lost touch not long after I met Ed. Ed became the human catalyst that transported me into a life I thought was expected of me—marriage and a family.

Our daughter, 'Ria, was the precious gift from that life. At first I was content to be a stay-at-home mom, but when she entered the first grade, I decided to go back to college and get my master's degree. I found my niche teaching earth science at the local junior high school. My desire to work with teenagers usually baffled people. "How can you stand those hormonal monsters?" they'd ask. I don't think they believed me when I told them that I found teens, with their flailing pheromones and raw approach to life, refreshingly honest. I think my students also appreciated the way that I never tried to be clever—just genuine. The boys thought it was cool that I wasn't squeamish when dissecting things, and the girls followed my lead because being cool was a good thing. My greatest achievement was the garden I'd cultivated in the school's courtyard. With cuttings from my own garden, I'd taught the students how to nurture them into robust flowers and vegetable plants. The Grub Club I initiated became quite popular, and each year we raised enough money for at least one field trip by selling the seedlings and plants to family and friends.

The only thing not growing in my life at the time was my marriage. Separated by the parallel universe that sometimes comes with the mundane routine of married life, we hardly recognized each other. I was the one who had suggested counseling.

After the divorce we sold the house. I think it was the depression that prompted me to change jobs. Working at the private school was a substantial cut in salary, but they provided housing—a studio apartment on the campus. 'Ria had been right about reducing my life to a pinhead, but that was all I could cope with at the moment.

That was three years ago. Three years of working hard to adjust to my new situation. Three years in shock, my dad would say. *Maybe I have been insulating myself*, I think, dropping the rocks back into the bowl; another good reason to get off my duff and sample some wine and cheese.

*   *   *

Because the evening is plenty warm, the single log fire in the fireplace is more for ambiance than heat. Like pack animals, the twenty or so people milling about have gravitated into their assigned groups. Ben, the leering professor, is waving me over to our little group on the far side of the room.

"Fern!"

The arm that slides through mine is adorned with multi-colored bangles—Sonja. She propels me away from Ben—thank you, Sonja—all the while chattering in my ear about how she hopes I'm settling in. She introduces me to Flo and Jean.

"Y'all will have lots in common, being in the field of education," she gushes, momentarily adopting Jonas's southern drawl. And then she's gone—off on another hospitality mission.

As it turns out, Flo and Jean are preschool teachers and plan to spend the retreat brainstorming clever projects for the little ones. Why do preschool teachers talk in such high-pitched voices? When I tell them I teach earth science to teenagers, they give each other a *thank-god-it's-not-us* look, and exclaim in unison, "Good for you, Fern!" their voices rising up three irritating octaves.

"Hello, ladies." We've been shanghaied by the ominous professor. As he introduces himself to Flo and Jean, I manage to slip away. Have I lost my mind? I'm not sure I can survive these people for three days, never mind three weeks. I pour myself a glass of wine before I remember that I don't drink wine. My social beverage of choice has always been a tame cranberry juice with a twist of lime, but tonight I suddenly crave something stronger. The noise around me is reminiscent of free-range chickens—*cluck, cluck*. They cluck out inflated versions of their life stories, trying to impress or outdo each other. I notice a couple of people heading in my direction, so I raise my glass in some kind of salute and bolt out into the night. Well, actually I end up in the dining room, then onto the terrace, and then out into the night. I cross the lawn and somehow stumble across a path that I hope will lead me down to the lake.

Fragrant blossoms tickle my nose as I push along the trail overgrown with honeysuckle and high bush blueberries. The sliver of moonlight—God's thumbnail, my dad called it—gives off only the tiniest beam of light, and as I approach the water it occurs to me that I haven't any flashlight to help me find my way back. *Who cares*, I think. I'm certainly in no hurry to return and mingle with that bunch of egomaniacs. I perch on a flat rock at the lake's margin and peer out over the glassy expanse. With no breeze to ruffle the water I can see my reflection. Not very flattering. I listen to the frog's deep-throat croaking, and the eerie warble of a loon calling to its mate.

"Here's to me at the water's edge." I gulp down more wine.

The aroma of wildflowers and wet, earthy smells induces a homesickness that I've tried to ignore for the past three years. Ed and I had bought our house new with a perfectly groomed lawn and professionally landscaped flower beds, but over the years I'd turned the yard into a country garden overflowing with wild colors and textures that blurred naturally into the woods beyond. I welcomed the goldenrod, the Queen Anne's lace, and the wild geranium that migrated into my yard each year. They were gifts freely given. I can still see the small pond surrounded by the clusters of cinnamon ferns. The garden had become my sanctuary. When I'd installed the shed, Ed had remarked snidely that if I set up a cot I could sleep out there.

"I should've moved my bed out there," I spout aloud, chugging the last of my wine. Angry tears well up in my eyes as I brood over the greenhouse I had planned to add to the shed. Bile rises in my throat as I recall the insipid voice of the new buyer prattling on about bulldozing the backyard to make room for a pool and play structure for the kids.

The roar in my head amplifies with the surge of the night sounds. *It's time to go home*, I think. I mean, back to my room. As I eyeball the bank of trees for the mouth of the path, I hear a rustling sound. Something is moving toward me. I blink, but everything is a bit blurry. Is that a pair of shiny eyes I see bobbing along? I stand up and nearly fall over. I haven't had a buzz like this since my cousin's wedding.

The creature of the night is the woman with the silvery curls; the eyes—the beam from the flashlight she's carrying. "Need any help?" she asks.

I wipe my eyes. "I don't know my way back."

Gently she guides me up the path to the safety of the lodge.

"Deep breaths," she says every time I wobble. I keep apologizing and insisting that I don't usually drink.

"Sit." She leaves me in a chair on the terrace.

I sigh and look out over the placid lake reflecting the millions of stars in the sky like sequins on a blanket. Silent tears slide down my cheeks.

"You need something to eat." She pushes a plate of food into my lap.

"Thanks."

Other people have filtered out onto the terrace, their distant voices naming various constellations. I hear Ben pontificate on the difference between a planet and an ordinary star, and I wonder if there is such a thing as an ordinary star.

My guardian angel's name is Dannie, short for Daniella. When I finish the cheese and crackers, she suggests that a good night's sleep might be helpful. She offers to walk me to my room, but I shake my head and thank her again.

"I'll see you tomorrow then."

*   *   *

Perhaps it is the fresh air or Dannie's act of kindness, but by the time I'm back in my room I no longer feel like collapsing into bed. I sort through the books on my desk and find my journal. The leather-bound book I'd bought especially for the retreat had been an extravagant purchase considering that, despite my best intentions, I've never been able to fill more than a page or two in all my other diaries. I stroke the supple cover, lifting it to my nose, inhaling the earthy aroma. I crack open the crisp new binding to the first clean white page. With pencil in hand I write a few words, but after several minutes I begin to doodle. An oval-shaped face edged with curlicues. Daniella? I gaze out the window. My eyes begin to close. The exhaustion of the day finally catches up with me. I close my sketch pad and lug my weary body off to bed.

CHAPTER 3

I T IS DAYLIGHT long before any reasonable person would venture out of bed, but for some reason my eyes pop open, and the fatigue in my body has vanished. From my balcony, I spot a lone canoe cutting across the tranquil lake. Someone is rather ambitious. I try to make out who it is, but all I can see is the top of a wide-brimmed green hat. Hoping that I can get a cup of coffee, and maybe a glimpse of our handsome chef, Julian, I throw on a pair of jeans, tank top, and hoodie and head down to the dining room.

Too early, the dining room is empty. The kitchen door is locked but I can hear the commotion of pots and pans clattering away to the rhythmic beat of Earth, Wind & Fire. I walk outside and around to the door marked STAFF ONLY. Also locked. I knock, but doubt I can be heard through the heavy door. When I turn to leave I'm distracted by a familiar smell.

"Be careful where you're stepping!" Chef Julian's voice booms out. He's standing at the door waving a giant spoon at me.

"Sorry."

"If you want to be helpful, you can grab me a handful of sage. It should be over to your right. It's the plant with the purplish-gray fuzzy leaf."

"Oh, I know what sage looks like." My voice crackles as I try to clear the sleep from my throat.

Down on my knees gathering the sage, I'm overwhelmed by the plethora of aromas—sweet, savory, spicy. I close my eyes. A spray of mint, a sprig of rosemary, a stalk of chive can transform the simplest dish into something special. The herbs I'd planted in my own garden had rarely seen the inside of my kitchen. Ed was strictly a meat and potato man. He didn't like any funny-looking stuff added. When I did try once to sneak in a dash of rosemary, Ed had asked me why there were pine needles floating in his soup.

"It smells so good," I whisper.

"Do you need any help?" Julian whispers back.

Ah. Julian is squatting right next to me, so close that I can almost taste the scent of the freshly baked bread emanating from his apron.

"This is an amazing kitchen garden," I say, managing to stand up and regain my composure.

"I suppose." He frowns. "But the mint is out of control, and I don't have time to weed, and . . . Oh my god, the biscuits!" He grabs the sage from my hand and dashes back into the kitchen, his apron strings fluttering behind him.

I study the door as it slams shut, and then look more closely at the herbs growing around my feet. He's right about the mint. I'll just thin it a bit. Mint spreads on a continuous root system, so when I try to pull up one stem I end up with a fistful. The oils from the leaves saturate my skin. I bring my hands to my nose and remember how my dad would tuck a mint leaf from my garden into his pocket. "Better than the most expensive perfume," he'd say.

Last year I had asked the head master at Saint Barnabas if I could plant a small garden on the grounds, but he vetoed the idea, citing the fact that it might spoil the meticulously manicured lawns. My stubborn response had been to haul large pots of soil into my classroom so my students could learn how to plant container gardens. The janitor had immediately filed a complaint.

I bundle up the pile of weeds into the red bandanna I retrieve from my back pocket. Again I hear another one of Dad's ruminations: "Always carry a bandanna. You can set a broken leg with one if you need to."

"Looks like you've been busy," Dannie says, appearing at the mouth of the path, her green fedora swinging from her fingers.

"It was you out on the lake." I wipe my hands on my jeans. "So early."

"Early is when you see the sights." She smiles. "Turkey buzzards playing around on the air currents, beavers dragging logs to their den. You'll have to come with me next time."

"I'd love to."

The gong interrupts us.

"Oh no, is it time for breakfast already?" I knock some of the dirt from my knees. "I'm a mess."

"Relax, you have plenty of time. That was only the eight o'clock wake-up call." Dannie brushes a leaf from my arm and laughs. "You wear the earth well."

We walk into the lodge together.

"See you at breakfast."

"Too bad we have assigned seats," I say, disappointed that we don't have more time to talk.

"That rule never lasts more than the first day," she assures me.

"How do you know?"

"This is my third retreat."

*　　*　　*

Three retreats, I ponder as I rinse the shampoo from my hair. How can she take that much time off from work? I scrub the dirt from my nails. There must be something good about these retreats if she keeps coming back.

I put on clean shorts and a tank top. I place the sprigs of mint I'd brought from the garden into a glass of water, set it on my desk, pick up my sketch book, and sit out on the patio. I open to last night's drawing. It reminds me of an illustration in a bedtime story I used to read to 'Ria when she was little. On the opposite page I sketch in the scalloped leaves of lemon balm, the feathery fingers of dill weed, and one olive-green bay leaf. I doodle in a chef's hat and a canoe paddle. I entitle my drawing, *Elixir of the earth*.

*　　*　　*

A breakfast buffet fit for a king is laid out in the dining room, and I'm greatly tempted by the selection of bacon, eggs, and home fries. Instead I spoon out some blueberries, top them with low-fat yogurt, and choose a bran muffin. I commend myself on my healthy choices—not so sure

I'll be as disciplined tomorrow morning. My mouth waters when I sit beside Karin, whose plate is heaped with eggs, bacon, and home fries.

"I don't do breakfast," Davy explains, sipping black coffee from a mug the size of a soup crock. "It's my delicate stomach you know."

"Did you sleep well?" Karin asks me. "I hope your mattress was more accommodating than mine. My back is killing me."

"Didn't Sonja mention that she gives massages?" I ask. I don't say that Karin's weight might challenge any mattress because I'm trying to practice the rule of respect.

"I took an extra-strength pain killer," Karin continues. "But I have to be careful not to take too many because it will interfere with my other medications."

I don't ask how many medications she's on, but there's an immediate response around the table as others offer up their own pharmaceutical inventory. I feel slightly left out because I only take an iron supplement.

Sue, the stressed out computer programmer, proclaims her disdain for traditional drugs and describes her alternative homeopathic road to recovery. After the first doctor she went to had given her a stack of expensive prescriptions, she'd gone on the internet in search of other options. The online health coach had prescribed a few helpful dietary changes and a daily regime of meditation.

"So how long before you ended up popping pills?" Karin asks smugly.

"I'll put it this way," Sue replies with a gracious smile. "The company gave me two months to get my act together, and I was so much better after the first month that I decided to reward myself with this retreat before going back to work."

"Lucky you." Karin chomps down her last piece of bacon.

"I think I'll go get me an apple," Davy says with a guilty grin.

Sue mentions that she's also seeing a therapist. I try not to cringe. "He's a friend of Lucy's." We all look over at Lucy, who is just finishing her fruit, eggs, and blueberry muffin.

Ben saunters over to our table. "Good morning one and all." When had he developed the British accent? "Terrible hangover, what? A little too much of the bubbly. Cheers," he declares, chugging down a tomato juice. His plate is stacked with a tower of cheese danish.

*   *   *

After breakfast we join Marc's group for art class. It's the first day of school all over again, and the good students take out their clean new notebooks and freshly sharpened pencils. Since I thought everything was provided, I take out nothing. Not to worry. Marc gives each of us a bin of supplies. I breathe another sigh of relief when he instructs us to create an example of something we are most comfortable doing. I begin happily working on a painting of Julian's herb garden.

"I know this place," Marc says enthusiastically when he checks my progress. "A splendid rendition, but I am curious as to what you might add to make it uniquely your own?"

I paint a cast iron park bench in the center with a giant sunflower towering behind it.

"Lovely," Marc says. "Now close your eyes and imagine yourself just about to sit down on the bench, and you discover something unexpected."

I have no problem conjuring up the scene in my mind. The fragrant herbs, the heart-shaped leaves of the sunflower stalk, head bent toward the park bench. I gasp out loud.

"Don't say a word," Marc cautions. "Just paint what you saw. Trust me."

When everyone finishes their projects, we are asked to share them. Reluctantly I hold up my picture of the beautiful herb garden; the cheerful sunflower bows its petal-framed face, reverently observing the body of a dead bird lying prone on the bench, its one vacant eye staring back.

"Any comments?" Marc asks the rest of the class. There are murmurs of profound gobbledygook. He puts his hand on my shoulder. "What do you think?"

I think that the painting is ruined but I merely stammer, "I'm not sure."

*　　*　　*

Dannie waves me over to her table at lunch. She was right, the assigned seats have been totally abandoned. People are sitting wherever they want to.

"How was art class?"

"Somewhat disturbing." I tell her about my painting and my discomfort with Marc's prompting.

"That's what the leaders are trained to do—push us to the edge. I know I'm going to hurt like hell after some of the pretzel positions Sonja twisted us into at yoga this morning." She waves her hand summarily. "I try not to take it all too seriously."

"What are you doing during free time?" I ask.

"Indulging in a long, hot shower and reclining with a good book."

My own bed looks so comfortable when I return to my room that I postpone my original plan to go for a walk and lie down—just for a moment. The next thing I know I'm roused from a sound sleep by an incessant knocking at my door.

"Fireplace room in ten minutes!" Jonas calls out. "Wear your hiking boots."

*　　*　　*

"This will be a silent walk," Lucy explains when we've gathered on the terrace.

Quietly we pad our way along the very path I'd stumbled down the previous evening. Once again the potent fragrance of honeysuckle excites my senses. As we near the water, we cross a set of puncheons, crude planks that bridge over one of the natural springs feeding the lake. The clear water gurgles and clicks over the rocks and stones. I bend down and pick up a mossy-green pebble the size of a quarter and tuck it into my pocket; its cool wetness seeps through the fabric of my pants, leaving a chilly spot against my warm skin. Squirrels and chipmunks chatter and scold at us as we pick our way around the moose marbles, reminding us that we are not welcome on their turf.

We enter a pine grove and the earth softens beneath our feet. I brush my arm against a tree oozing with sap. I dab my finger at the tacky substance. It reminds me of the Christmas when 'Ria was five and we'd cut down our own tree from a local farm. She'd run to me with her hands covered in sap and said, "Look, Mommy, tree glue."

As we move further into the woods we seem to be picking up speed. The faster we move the louder we get. Less careful footsteps crunch and snap branches; quiet breathing becomes labored and distinctly audible. I hear someone moan and curse, and when I turn around I notice that there are several people who have dropped behind and are sitting down on the edge of the trail. Karin, who is just ahead of me, stops so suddenly that I nearly bump into her.

"Rest," she pants, her face a scary shade of white. "I have to rest."

The route up ahead is even more rugged, with rocky steps on a steep incline. Dannie looks at Karin, then at me. We both offer her a hand up and the three of us continue on.

"Brilliant," Ben gasps as we stand on the precipice of the ridge, puffing hard and viewing the world that has fallen away at our feet. The sun touches the trees with alpenglow and the lake stretches out—a wide ribbon of silky blue. All at once I wonder what the ledge looks like from the bottom up, and I have this insane desire to leap over the ledge and into the water below.

The descent is easier on the heart and the lungs, but brutal on the knees and ankles. Talking is once again permitted, but we are all either still in awe, or more likely, we're too exhausted to speak.

CHAPTER 4

A FTER JULIAN TREATS us to another mouthwatering dinner, I treat myself to a luxurious hot shower. The pulsing hot water massages away the muscle aches and pains from the strenuous hike; the steamy, moist air fills the room—a poor man's sauna. I wipe clean the full-length mirror on the door and scrutinize my reflection. *Not too shabby*, I think as I towel dry my arms, legs, and back. My breasts, having never aspired to being more than a handful, are still compact and perky, and thanks to my daily walking routine, my bottom and thighs are shapely and firm. I cradle my abdomen. With careful calorie consumption I've managed to ward off the thick waistline that threatens to conquer women my age.

What to wear? Pj's are an option for tonight's movie event, but I decide to dress in capris and a waffle pullover. I debate for a moment about wearing a bra. "What's the point?" I laugh. "Who's going to notice?"

Post divorce, there have been many times that I've wondered if anyone would ever want to touch me again. Not that Ed was all that affectionate. Our lovemaking had started off short and sweet, then short, and then after 'Ria was born we barely kissed each other. Regardless, I'd never felt self-conscious about stimulating my own body; there is no shame in the pleasure of *one*.

As teenagers, Vicki and I were intimately aware of our constantly shifting pubescent shapes, plotting out our periods on the calendar, giggling over the pictures in the *Playboy* magazine we'd found under the gym bleachers at school. We'd dare each other to leave our bikini tops untied when sunbathing in her backyard. I envied Vicki with her voluptuous body, and every once in a while I'd sneak a peek. Did she ever suspect? I hastily clip my damp hair into a barrette and grab a pillow.

*   *   *

The aroma of buttery popcorn assaults my nose from the threshold of the music room. Groups of people are arranging themselves on blankets and pillows on the thick area rug that has been rolled out in front of a big-screen TV. Karin, Sue, Dannie, and I crowd together in the doorway, scanning the early arrivals, surveying a very entertaining tableau.

Flo and Jean have parked themselves next to RJ and BJ—Ricki Junior and Bobbie Junior—cousins from Oklahoma who are at least ten years younger than the preschool teachers, and not at all happy about their close proximity. The cousins are more interested in the four sorority sisters who are celebrating their five-year college reunion from California State University. The "sisters" are flouncing about in rather revealing nightshirts, the sorority symbol plastered across their copious chests.

Davy is enthusiastically proclaiming the merits of Danish modern to an attentive Tony and Fred. Tony is considering redecorating his condo. Completing the group are Pammy and Tom, who have already found their own private corner.

"Glad we didn't miss the previews," I chuckle.

"And I almost didn't come," Sue says. "I generally don't do movies."

Karin, tented in a kelly green caftan and turban, agrees. "I brought my handwork in case I get bored." She holds up her bag of crocheting.

Dannie looks at me and winks. "Shall we find a seat?" She offers me her arm. "Bride or groom?"

"Bride please," I laugh and we promenade across the room, leaving Karin and Sue in our wake. We sit ourselves down just behind Ben, who is sharing fantastic tales of perilous wildlife photography with John, a criminal lawyer from Alabama.

"Gold stars on surviving your first day at the Water's Edge," Jonas congratulates as he turns down the lights. "Enjoy the movie. I'm off to meet with the other leaders to plot and plan tomorrow's trials and tribulations."

The flick is a familiar romantic comedy starring Steve Martin. At some point during the movie, BJ and RJ convince two of the sorority sisters to go out to the terrace for their own romantic comedy. I watch them leave and shift my position to get more comfortable. I rub at the kink in my neck.

"Allow me," Dannie offers. She gently massages my neck and shoulders. "Better?"

"Yes, thanks."

*   *   *

When I go to bed, I dream that Steve Martin is giving out free back rubs. When it comes to my turn I refuse, declaring that his back rubs could never compare to Vicki's, I mean Dannie's. "Who do you mean?" he asks. "I'm confused," I tell him. "I don't know." Laughter and applause explode as if I'm a character on some kind of situation comedy. The laughter crescendos, the applause becomes thunderous, and I bolt upright in bed, awakened by bona fide crashes of thunder and flashes of lightning. My room is as bright as day and I can smell the oncoming rain. I rush around closing the windows as the torrential downpour begins. In stiff sheets, it cascades off the patio overhang like Niagara Falls. A ferocious wind kicks up, power washing my windows and obscuring the view.

I can't get back to sleep and breakfast is hours away, so I make a cup of tea and open my journal. The painting of the dead bird from yesterday's art class slides out onto the floor. Ugh. When I'd moved into my apartment after the divorce, there had been a dead robin on the kitchen floor. He must have flown in through an open window and gotten trapped. I remember sobbing uncontrollably as I swept him into a dustpan and placed him under a bush in the backyard.

I squeeze paint onto my palette and shade the vacant eye closed. "Sleep in peace little guy," I whisper, brushing in a blanket of rosemary to cover his body. At least I could give this bird a proper burial.

When I'm finished, I tug on the pants I'd worn for yesterday's hike, hoping that the weather will clear so I can take a walk later. Slipping my hand into the pocket, I discover the greenish pebble from the brook. It has lost its wet sheen and is now dry and dull. Instead of adding it to the collection in my bowl, I release it into the glass of water with the sprigs of mint. It sinks to the bottom, wet and lustrous once again.

At breakfast Jonas announces that our group will join his group for a music class, Sonja's and Marc's will be dancing, and Lucy is available in the library for individual counseling sessions.

With the exception of the faint odor of stale popcorn, the music room is back to normal, a circle of chairs arranged in the center.

"We'll begin by experimenting with the most ancient of musical instruments," Jonas tells us when we take our seats. "The human voice."

"But I don't sing," RJ and Ben say practically in unison.

The two sorority sisters begin cheerfully warbling phrases from *Les Miserables* with Karin and Sue, who were also members of community choruses.

Davy leans over to me. "I'm a closet singer."

"Me too. And that closet would be my bathroom shower." We chuckle.

"Sorry I'm late," Dannie croons, careening into the room. "Tony is right behind me. He's been bribing Chef Julian for his raisin scone recipe."

"I got it!" Tony shouts. "Along with the ingredients for that scrumptious soup we had last night."

A chorus of conversation bursts forth extolling Julian's heavenly cuisine. The level of sound escalates exponentially until someone notices Jonas sitting quietly at his desk. One by one our chatter peters out.

"Whatever I cook comes out of a can and goes directly into the microwave!" Ben's voice blasts loudly into the suddenly silent room.

"Bravo!" Jonas exclaims. "Let me finish making a few adjustments on my miraculous mixing board and you can listen to your first vocal performance."

He manipulates the recording of our voices and we hear sounds from the ridiculous to the sublime. Then he passes around a box full of rhythm instruments that none of us have seen since kindergarten and we drum, jingle, slap, and tap like five-year-olds. By the end of our first music class we've even managed to learn a simple folk song that, thanks to the community chorus ladies, we sing in a three-part round.

*　　*　　*

The rain has tapered off to a light drizzle, so after lunch I'm able to go for a walk. I borrow one of the umbrellas from the foyer and a garbage bag from the kitchen.

It feels good to escape into the fresh air. The fragrant, damp earth rises up to meet me as I push my way through the dripping bushes along the path toward the shoreline. I drape the plastic bag over a rock and sit facing the water. A pair of mallard ducks paddles over, eyeing me expectantly. "I'll bring a couple of slices of bread next time," I promise. To express their disapproval, they dibble their heads beneath the water's surface, flipping their tail feathers up in the air like a couple of floating isosceles triangles. I reach into the gray water and plunge my fingers through the cool layer of new rain and into the deeper, warmer depth. I contemplate the last couple of days. Despite my initial reservations, the venue has certainly lived up to the brochure's description; and I admit that the classes are interesting—even fun. The new people I've met . . . well?

My dad had requested that I call and let him know how I was doing. Actually I think he'd secretly wanted to go on the retreat and was hoping to experience it vicariously through me. He definitely would have loved yesterday's hike and most certainly would have gotten a kick out of Jonas's electronic gadgets. If I call 'Ria she would probably inquire if I'd met anyone fascinating—meaning a man. I could tell her about Ben, or better yet, about Dannie. I shudder at the thought and massage the back of my neck. A warm sensation flushes over my body. It's the hot rays of the renegade sun, finally poking out from behind the clouds. Steamy ribbons of light embrace me as the world begins to bake dry. Reluctantly I stroll back to the lodge for the afternoon session—dance with Sonja. Oh, joy.

*   *   *

"Let's welcome back the sun," Sonja muses, handing out wooden dowels with multiple streamers attached. "Follow me."

As we parade through the dining room and out to the terrace, I notice that some of our group is conspicuously absent—chickens. Davy, Tony, and the sorority sisters are gamely skipping about, waving their streamers high in the air. Even RJ, who is conveniently positioned between the sisters, seems to be having a great time, although I'm not sure how pure his motives are.

Dannie, Sue, and I are trying to remain incognito at the rear of the line. We are doing our damnedest not to crack up as we gyrate and twirl around.

"Partner up," Sonja calls out. Everyone scrambles for the nearest desirable person. The sorority girls grab hands and poor Sue ends up with a crestfallen RJ. Dannie and I face each other.

"Now take turns mirroring your partner's motions," Sonja instructs. "Youngest leads first."

"That would be you," Dannie says.

"Not by much," I counter, wondering exactly what I'm supposed to do. At first my gestures are stilted and somewhat goofy, but as I watch Dannie watching me, my concentration increases. I become more creative and begin to relax in the dance. When it's Dannie's turn to lead, I find her graceful movements easy to follow and for one breathtaking moment it seems as if something of great importance passes between us.

*   *   *

"So how does this retreat compare to the others?" I ask her when Sonja has released us from our sun worship. We're resting on the terrace, sipping water from tall frosty glasses.

"I try not to compare," she says, flipping her white curls out of a ponytail and letting them float to her shoulders. "They're all so different: different people and different times in my life. The first two were during consecutive summers, but I waited five years before returning this time, and even then I almost didn't come."

"You must have a great job to afford, I mean, to take so much time off," I blurt out, shifting my eyes to the lake in embarrassment. "Sorry, none of my business."

"It's a strange and wonderful tale." She touches my arm reassuringly.

Seven years ago, Dannie was having her morning cup of coffee before clocking into her office cubicle at a financial conglomerate in New York City. She literally bumped into Sonja. After swearing profusely at one another for ruining their five-hundred-dollar suits, they discover that they work in the same building, separated by a mere ten floors. They order more coffee and bagels, start chatting about business, and decide they can be late for work.

"Turned out to be a life changing decision."

"9/11?" I murmur the date reverently, and neither one of us says anything for a moment; a prolonged moment for all those people, all that tragedy, all that hate that consequently altered the entire world.

"We didn't work in the towers," she continues, "but our office building was only two blocks away. Despite our differences, the experience created a strong bond between us."

Where business was concerned, they both made lots of money for people through risky investing. However, the risk that gave Dannie a thrill gave Sonja an ulcer. Sonja was only working the high-pressure job until she had enough money to open her own dance studio. Six months after they'd met, Sonja began having recurring dreams about empty cash registers and people disappearing from her office. Dannie knew that Sonja had a sensitive intuition but they were both shocked when the CEO of the company was taken away in handcuffs and the company ultimately went belly up.

"Sonja lost everything," Dannie adds. "I signed us up for the retreat hoping to give her a boost."

"Do you two plan to eat tonight?" Marc interrupts. We'd been oblivious to, or maybe just ignored, the dinner gong.

Unfortunately there are no two vacant seats at the same table, so we have to split up. I find a seat next to Marc, thank him for the dinner call, and dig into my four-cheese baked macaroni. He asks me where I'd learned to paint. When I explain that I'm self-taught, he graciously compliments me on my progress.

"You'll probably be disappointed to know that I modified my sunflower painting," I say apologetically.

"I doubt it." He smiles. "You have a keen sense of detail."

I explain how I'd closed the eye of the bird and covered up his body. "It was making me very uncomfortable," I say, not sure why it's so important for me to justify what I'd done, but Marc is listening intently, his understanding eyes never leaving my face.

"Should I bring it to class tomorrow?"

"Only if you feel you need to. In any case we'll be starting an exciting new project that I hope you'll enjoy." He stands up. "Which reminds me: I need to borrow some aprons from Julian. Please excuse me." He bows. "And Fern, thank you for sharing."

Jonas's voice calls out over the dining room clatter, "Can I have everyone's attention?" Standing next to him, dressed in black from head to toe, is a woman who could be anywhere between the ages of seventy and one hundred. "I'd like to introduce you to Geraldine. She's a very welcomed late arrival."

We all shout out a round of *hellos*, and Geraldine returns a friendly but exhausted wave.

"She's had a long journey, so Julian is fixing her a plate of food to take to her room. She'll join us in the morning, we trust refreshed by a good night's sleep."

CHAPTER 5

TUESDAY EVENING WE embark on a moonlight cruise in the canoes.

"You'll be my bowman, I mean woman, won't you Fern?" Ben nearly ambushes me with his enthusiasm. "I assure you that you'll be in very capable hands."

"So sorry, Professor." Dannie puts a protective arm around my shoulder. "She's already taken."

"But Dannie," Sonja begins, "I thought that you and I?"

"I'll be your partner, Sonja," Ben pipes up.

Sonja glares at Dannie, plasters a smile on her face, and climbs into the boat with Ben.

I look at Sonja, and then at Dannie, and I wonder what's up with that, and why am I suddenly glad Dannie chose me?

The night air is cool and clear, the lake as smooth as glass when we climb into our canoes and push off. Paddling quietly, we follow Sonja around the outskirts of the lake. We keep close to the shoreline, our eyes peeled for unsuspecting wildlife.

Perhaps I should be flattered to be so popular. If Ben wasn't so obnoxious I might even consider him attractive—*not*, to quote my students. He's what 'Ria would call a good catch, but I'm not at this retreat to catch anyone. I focus again on the lake. Someone points to a pair of furry heads that have popped up, and we watch their silent swim through the moonlit stretch. Beavers, otters, or maybe a couple of muskrats. *Blip*, they disappear under the water.

Sonja raises her hand, signaling for us to stop paddling and allow our canoes to drift. The evening breeze propels us aimlessly about like stray leaves on a fall day. Dannie and I float beneath the ledges and I get my wish to see how they appear from the bottom up. Tree roots cling to the base of the rugged shelf, straddling rocks on their tippy toes. A jagged overhang juts out above our heads, an ideal perch. We watch in fascination as a feathery creature of the night appears from the shadows. Its shiny orblike eyes reflect the moonlight as it scans the territory below and waits. Without the slightest sound, it dives gracefully over to the mossy land below and claims its meal. The owl then spreads its wings, talons tucked underneath, clutching its prey, and flies across the lake and out of sight.

"Wow."

"Probably the male," Dannie whispers. "This time of year the female is nesting."

"I read somewhere that owls are monogamous and mate for life," I say.

"A concept I find quite provincial," Danny states.

What does she mean by that? Before I can ask her, Sonja's low whistle calls us back to the group.

*   *   *

With pen and ink on a dusty-rose-tinted paper, I sketch the ledges, the tree roots, and the half moon. No matter what I think of some of the more esoteric schemes offered at the retreat, I'm thoroughly enjoying the huge amounts of time we're spending outside in nature. But then again, if I hadn't been forced to sell the house, I'd be spending these same summer days outside in my garden. Heartache and disappointment strike at my chest; my pen presses into the paper and I nearly ruin my sketch with a big blob of ink. After a moment of self pity, I transform the blob into a pair of rocks with the nose of a canoe resting between. Drawing people isn't easy for me but I manage to rough in Dannie's silhouette in the stern and mine in the bow, our paddles balancing on our laps.

I wonder again about Dannie's monogamous comment. Is she married? Maybe she doesn't believe in marriage. I'm not so sure I do anymore.

When Ed and I had gone for counseling, he told the counselor that I loved my gardens more than him, and maybe I did. When the counselor asked us what we had in common, we came up with a big fat zero. We tried. I watched football games with Ed even when I was aching to get out and prune the pear tree, and Ed attempted to help me weed. "You're pulling up my flowers," I'd scolded him. "But I can't tell the difference!" He'd thrown up his hands and walked away in a huff.

I kick myself for not recognizing the reason for Ed's metamorphosis when he suddenly began going to the gym after work. I was just glad to have the extra time by myself. Then came the day the counselor explained she couldn't work with us anymore. She and Ed exchanged a look that I didn't understand until a few days later when I saw them at the park walking hand in hand.

"Good riddance," I say out loud as I add the sharp points on the owl's talons. His body is taut with expectancy as he leans forward, ready to swoop in for the kill.

It's almost midnight when I finish my portrait of execution. My sleep is far from restful and when I wake up the next morning, I am drained. I'm not really hungry and I have no desire to see anyone, so I skip breakfast.

*   *   *

Instead of a morning class, I'm scheduled to meet with Lucy. She's sitting near the open glass doors in the library, admiring the view. The sunlight is showering the lake with a tiara of diamonds.

"It never gets old," she says, gesturing to a chair next to hers. I nod and sit. We remain silent for a moment; my weary brain threatens to shut down as I stifle a yawn. A red-breasted robin lands on the edge of the terrace with a fat, juicy worm hanging from its beak. "The early bird catches the worm," I recite to myself.

Lucy suggests we try a breathing meditation. "Choose a word to breathe in on," she says, "and then breathe out on the word *good*."

Ironically the first word that comes to my mind is *worm*, and I laugh out loud.

"It's OK," she encourages. "Just go with it."

And so I inhale on *worm* and exhale on *good*. After a couple of minutes, I let go of the words and simply breathe in and out.

"Fern?"

"Where am I?"

"You're in the library," Lucy says gently. "You've had a nice little nap."

"Oh no," I stammer. "Is our time up? I'm so sorry."

"Don't worry. You were sleeping so peacefully I didn't want to wake you. I'm curious though as to what the word was that made you laugh?"

"*Worm*," I chuckle. "As in *earthworm*. When I saw the robin I thought of that phrase, 'the early bird . . . '"

"Catches the worm," Lucy finishes with a smile. "Ah, those diligent little soil dwellers. Earthworms do have a tendency to churn things up."

"I know. I'm a gardener."

"Oh, tell me about your garden."

"There is no garden." My thoughts flash to the three potted plants in my apartment, probably dead by now. "Uh, I mean my current living situation isn't conducive to a garden."

Lucy waits for me to say more. When I don't, she asks, "Maybe you can tell me your favorite garden story?"

I tell her about the time 'Ria and I planted a patch of marigolds. We had started the seeds in Styrofoam cups, and she'd mixed up her words, calling them her cup of *miragles*. They were miracles to her—hearty green sprouts popping out of nothing but a feathery seed.

"Yucky," she said the first time I pulled a worm out of the ground when we were transplanting the seedlings. "I told her that the more worms there were the better her flowers would grow. Later I caught her lifting one of the wiggly creatures into her hand. She gave it strict instructions to invite all his friends to her garden party." My eyes shine with tears.

Lucy suggests that we take a walk through the herb garden behind the kitchen. I identify some of the herbs for her. She confides that she knows very little about growing things.

"I usually have my head in a book. A real bookworm." We both laugh.

Lucy returns to the lodge but I decide to stay in the garden and pick at the weeds choking out the fennel.

"At it again?" Julian asks. He's after some parsley for garnish.

"I hope you don't mind."

"Not at all." He flashes his beautiful smile at me. "In fact, if you're interested, and have a few minutes to meet with me after lunch, I have a gardening proposition for you."

"I'm interested," I try not to gush. "I only wish I had my tool basket with me."

"What kind of tools do you need?"

"A trowel, a claw, some gloves, maybe a kneeling pad."

"Right," Julian nods. "See you later."

*   *   *

I eat lunch with Fred, Karin, and Davy. They've spent the morning with Jonas learning to play the recorder. Davy blathers on about always wanting to play an instrument, and Karin spouts her frustration at not perfecting the song she learned so she can perform it for her husband when she gets home. They inquire about my session with Lucy.

"Did you enjoin in a deep spiritual discussion?"

"Actually we talked about earthworms." I ignore their puzzled expressions and ask if they've seen Dannie.

Karin shrugs, "She got a phone call just as we came into the dining room and took off in a hurry."

We linger over lunch. Most of us have sorted ourselves into comfortable cliques. Some have paired off for the inevitable summer romance, like Sue and John who are seated in the corner with their heads together, or Pammy and Tom who can't keep their hands off each other. It seems that RJ and BJ have finally made some inroads with the sorority sisters—the rumor being that BJ's family owns a chain of businesses and has money. We later discover that the chain consists of three Laundromats that are just about breaking even.

Geraldine sits down at our table. "Somebody over there might get lucky," she teases with a mischievous twinkle in her eye. "I'm not sure who though."

"Have you recuperated from your journey?" I ask.

"Much better, thank you." Geraldine's dark hair has flecks of gray and is pulled back in a thick plaited coil. Her long flowing dress is gathered at the waist by a belt decorated with intricate patterns of tiny beads.

Davy admires her belt. "That looks handmade. Is it Native American?"

"You have a good eye, young man," she answers, fingering the exquisite beads. "It was made by my mother, who is Cherokee and has devoted most of her life to the art of beading. At ninety-five she still teaches a class at the senior center."

"The detail is amazing. Do you do bead work as well?" Karen asks.

"I'm afraid I'm the renegade female in the family. My three sisters learned how to bead, but I was always more interested in stringing words together."

Geraldine explains that she would write down the old stories her mother told as she strung the tiny beads on moccasin, vest, or belt. When she penned them into an essay for school, her teacher had been so impressed that she encouraged Geraldine to submit the essay to a local paper.

"It was my first published work," she says proudly. "After that I began writing articles and stories for the paper on a regular basis. My humble roots as a journalist."

"You're G. Jones?" Davy exclaims. "I read your stuff in my high school humanities class. Right there, sister!" He puts his hand up and they high-five.

Even though I'd like to stay and hear more of Geraldine's story, I remember my promise to meet with Julian so I excuse myself. Julian isn't in the kitchen, but next to the staff entrance I find a basket filled with clean gloves, a shiny new trowel, a claw, and yes, a thick foam knee pad. I read the note attached: *Can't meet today. Busy with food order. Hope this will get you started. Thanks.—J.*

"All I need is my hat," I cry giddily, running up to my room to retrieve my straw hat. I'd packed the old garden hat as an afterthought, thinking it would protect my head when canoeing or hiking. Decked out in my familiar floppy friend, I spend the next hour scratching at the dirt, plucking up weeds, and disturbing the earthworms. I'm just about finished when Julian steps out of the kitchen.

"You look like you're having a great time," he says.

"Did you ever consider composting?" I ask, stretching out my legs and brushing the dirt from my knees. "We must generate plenty of vegetable waste, and you can use the rich mulch to beef up the soil."

"Whoa," Julian says. "I've no idea what you're talking about. I may know how to cook with herbs, but I'm no farmer." He laughs, a deep belly laugh, but unlike some cooks, he doesn't have a jelly belly. His body is what one would call solid and I can't help but imagine the ripples of strong muscles hiding under his chef's jacket.

"Thanks for the basket of goodies," I start to say.

"Fern!" Sonja yells out the window. "Stop flirting with Julian and get a move on or you'll be late for art class."

"You'd better go," Julian says. "We'll talk more about composting another time."

I dash to the nearest bathroom, splash water on my face, and rush to the art room nearly colliding with Marc.

"Sorry, I know I'm late. I was just cleaning up." I look down at my soil-smudged shirt.

Marc puts out his hand, "Slow down. Class doesn't start for another fifteen minutes, and there's no need to change because we'll only be making more of a mess."

"But Sonja just . . ." I begin, however Marc has already closed the art room door behind him.

Fifteen minutes? Why was Sonja so adamant about my being late? Is she jealous? Well she needn't worry, because Julian is at least fifteen years my junior, and no one that charming has ever given me a second look.

CHAPTER 6

U PON ENTERING THE art room, I remember that we're with
Sonja's group this afternoon. Darn it. That means fluttery Flo
will be gushing on about adapting whatever we do for the kiddies. I
steer clear of her, avoid Pammy and Tom, who are practically in each
other's laps, and find an empty seat next to Ben. Davy and Sue wave at
me from across the table. Sue beams as John sits down beside her. *We're
all in our places with bright shining faces . . .*

Sonja sails through the doorway. "Just popped in to check on my
little group." She flashes a bright smile around the room. It fades slightly
when she glances at me.

Marc is right behind her handing out aprons and balloons. There
are stacks of newspaper and plastic containers full of a gooey substance
already on the tables. Flo begins to clap her hands like a five-year-old.
"Papier-mâché," she cries. Not everyone shares her enthusiasm as we
don our aprons and blow up our balloons.

Marc shows us how to soak the strips of newspaper in the paste and
then plaster them evenly onto the balloons. At first we are tentative,
using only our fingertips to touch the sticky strips, carefully applying
them one at a time.

"Ooo, this feels so gooood," Ms. Sorority coos in an ooey-gooey sexy
voice. She giggles.

"I'm dripping all over," someone else sniggers.

"Reminds me of my ex-boyfriend." Davy holds up his balloon half
drenched in milky white slime.

The seemingly innocent look on his face cracks us all up; we relax
a little, and begin to slop the soggy strips on the inflated balls with a

little more joy. Flo tells us about a girl in her toddler class who talked to her balloon while she covered it with the papier-mâché strips. Like a doctor, she assured the patient that it would be as good as new when the bandages came off. Flo thought the little girl might freak out the next day when she discovered that the balloon had popped, but instead, she peered inside, looked up at the ceiling, and said simply, "He went to a better place."

"Ah, how sweet," Ms. Sorority sighs.

When we've cleaned up, Marc explains that we'll paint our plaster "heads" in the morning when they are dry. He grins at Flo. "And all the balloons have gone on to a better place."

*   *   *

I sit next to Dannie at dinner. "Where were you earlier?"

"Oh, I had some business to attend to."

She doesn't elaborate, so I continue, "You never did finish telling me what happened to you and Sonja after you lost your jobs and went on that first retreat."

"Let's get some coffee and dessert, and I'll catch you up."

There's a mass exodus from the dining room as people leave to primp for this evening's dance. Dannie and I settle ourselves near the sliding doors and enjoy the cool evening breeze.

"Like I said, I had hoped that the retreat would cheer Sonja up, maybe help her refocus, meet some new people, make some new contacts . . ."

"I've heard that one before."

"What?"

"Never mind. Go on."

As it turned out, Dannie had been the one to make the connection that ultimately gave them both career opportunities. The art instructor—not Marc—had received financing for his art studio from an eccentric entrepreneur who wanted art lessons. The entrepreneur invested only in businesses that gave him more than just a monetary return. When his computer had gone on the fritz, he found a computer whiz and set him up in business so he could have technological support 24-7; when his niece had wanted riding lessons, he financed a stable.

The idea intrigued Dannie. She sold one of her investment properties that was nothing but a headache anyway, and set Sonja up in her own dance studio.

"At first it was just a hobby but most of the ventures I took on were so successful that I was able to quit my day job and open my own consulting agency." Dannie was thoughtful. "It satisfied my need for risk, but I was surprised by the almost maternal pride I experienced when I helped 'birth' each project: watching it grow and then setting it free. An ideal solution to motherhood, don't you think?"

"I guess."

"Anyway, that was several years ago. Last month I set free my fifth 'child,' a used-book store owned by a very happy retired couple."

"Congratulations," I say, finishing my coffee. "So what's next?"

"I have some ideas cooking in my head but the secret to ultimate success is taking the time to do the preliminary research."

Sue and John poke their heads into the dining room. "Are you two coming to the dance or are you just going to sit there and talk all night?"

"No dancing for me," I say, making a futile attempt to tuck my windblown hair back into my barrette. "I'm a sight."

"Oh, you look just gorgeous." Dannie grabs my hand. "Let's go burn some calories."

Jonas had set up his sound system in Sonja's room. A rotating mirror ball hung from the ceiling, recreating a discotheque atmosphere. Dannie and I join a circle of people cavorting in the center of the dance floor, and do our best to boogie, bop, and twist.

Jonas, our DJ, keeps the music at a fast pace until Ben calls for a slow tune, and before I can stop him, the good professor takes my arm and leads me into a waltz. I have to admit that he knows what he's doing, and I do my best to follow him while still remaining at a G-rated distance. Davy, also an excellent dancer, cuts in. I loosen up and allow myself the pleasure of close human contact.

"My turn." Dannie twirls me away as the music picks up in tempo. We're joined by Karin and Geraldine and the four of us let loose like rowdy teens bumping about in a mosh pit.

When the sorority sisters insist that we should all learn the electric slide, I decide it's time for me to say good night.

*   *   *

Even after a hot shower, I'm still wide awake so I open my journal and pick up my pencil. The fresh new page stares expectantly back at me. Hoping for inspiration, I scoop up a few stones from my bowl and toss them like dice across the empty page. They shoot out over the rim of the book and onto the table. I gather them up, close the journal, and lay out a larger piece of paper. This time when I discharge the stones, they tumble out across the surface, scattered pebbles on dry sand. I trace them where they lay, then throw them a second and third time until I've filled the entire page with irregular circles. I use the edge of a black pastel crayon to create dark shadows around the spheres. I shade inside the disks with bright pastel colors until they pop off the page. *Dancing bits of earth*—so unlike my usual landscape or still life, it's the most abstract piece I've ever done. I prop it up on the desk and head to the bathroom to brush my teeth.

Someone knocks on my door.

"Who is it?"

It's Dannie. "I know it's late," she apologizes. "But I wondered if you would like to join me for an early morning canoe ride?"

"Sure. What time?"

"Can we meet at the canoes around 6:00 a.m.?"

"6:00 a.m.?"

"If you change your mind or oversleep, I plan to go anyway. Just thought it'd be fun to have some company."

"Oh, don't worry. I'll be there."

Charged up from my artistic endeavor and now Dannie's invitation, I need to use Lucy's breathing meditation to settle myself. Inhaling on the word *worm* and exhaling on *good*, I feel a moment of giddiness and then nothing more until the exhilarating breath of sweet morning air blows through the open window.

*　　*　　*

The night music of the crickets and katydids is succeeded by early morning bird song as I walk quietly along the path to the lake. I pause, aware of something about the size of a cat moving slowly through the trees. It turns and glances in my direction, showing me the black mask that frames its sleepy eyes. I watch it climb wearily up into a nearby tree for a well-deserved repose after a long night's prowl.

The cool air collides with the warm, tranquil surface of the water, kicking up a fine wispy fog. Through the mist I see Dannie's figure, holding our paddles. She puts her finger to her lips, and I nod in agreement. Making as little noise as possible, we turn over the canoe and lift it out into the lake. Gingerly I step in and Dannie pushes us away from the shore. We float on the smooth fluid plane, the haze lifts, and we scan for wildlife.

I see them first: a cow moose and her calf, wandering out to the water's edge for their morning constitutional. At first the calf is reluctant to leave the shallow margin, but Mom coaxes it with her nose until they are both deep enough to take a swim.

"Amazing," I whisper.

"Glad you came?" Dannie uses her paddle to maneuver the boat toward a wooden causeway at the far end of the lake. We climb out onto a footpath that connects the lake to an overgrown bog. She secures the canoe to a tree.

She offers me her hand as I stumble through some scrub brush. "This is where I found the beaver's lodge." I slide on a patch of wet moss and almost end up in the mud. She catches me around the waist. "Gotcha."

"Thanks."

We walk arm in arm until we come to an old fallen tree trunk. We sit on the center where its bark has been stripped clean; one end has been shaved to a point by a set of very sharp teeth. I run my fingers along the beaver's handiwork and then follow the pattern of grooves and holes made by hundreds of diligent insects.

Dannie breaks the silence. "You owe me, you know."

"Owe you?"

"I told you my story, now it's your turn."

"My story?" I wonder where I should I begin.

"Don't look so confounded. You don't need to recite your entire autobiography. I'll settle with why you came on this retreat."

So I give her an abridged tale of my career, my marriage, my divorce, and explain that this retreat is a mandate from my parents and my daughter. "They thought it would be good for me."

"And has it been good?"

"This is good."

We linger on the log a little longer, breathing in the savory bouquet of pine needles and wildflowers.

"Mm," I sigh.

"Almost sensuous isn't it?" she agrees.

I look at Dannie. You are sensuous, I want to say, but instead I say, "We probably should be getting back. Don't want to miss one of Julian's famous breakfasts."

She throws me the rope as we push away from the causeway. "I understand that you're helping him spice things up a bit."

At first I'm not sure what she's talking about. "Oh, you mean the herb garden." Am I blushing or having a hot flash? "Just doing some weeding." I balance the canoe with my weight as she settles herself into the stern.

We paddle back to the beach, flip our canoe, and stow our paddles.

"Thanks for the adventure," Dannie says.

"Any time."

*   *   *

There's a heavenly aroma drifting out from the open dining room doors.

"Wait till you taste what Julian has prepared for our breakfast," Karin greets us from the terrace. "It's positively decadent."

"Good thing we worked up an appetite," I say.

"Was that you two out there paddling around?" Ben asks. He's looking quite dapper this morning, like a poster boy for the Audubon Society, binoculars around his neck and a safari hat on his head. "I was up at the ledges hoping to spot an eagle when I noticed your canoe. See anything interesting?"

Dannie and I share our encounter of the cow moose and her calf while we consume far too many of Julian's scrumptious crepes. Loaded with sweet berries, smothered in cream, they are the most wonderful thing I've tasted in my life.

CHAPTER 7

OUR PAPIER-MÂCHÉ "HEADS" have been cut in half lengthwise and are surrounded by jars of paint, tubes of glitter glue, and remnants of yarn. Our task is to transform our plaster shells into character masks.

"One mask will nest inside the other," Marc explains. "Design the external mask with facial features that you think people notice when they look at you—your outward appearance. The other mask will represent your inner self. Be as open and honest as you can, and don't worry," he assures us, "you won't be asked to share either mask unless you choose to."

I lather one mask with a creamy beige undercoat. Waiting for the paint to dry, I cut lengths of light brown yarn for the hair. I pink up the cheeks and dot in dozens of freckles. The long, curly lashes I line on my eyes lids are somewhat of an exaggeration, and I admit I completely leave out the worry lines that should be in the middle of my brow.

"Don't we all think we're dashingly handsome," Davy jokes, sparking a surge of banter about our more attractive features. The chatter diminishes abruptly as we begin to block out our inner effigies.

"Don't think about it, just do it," Marc reminds us.

And so with courageous abandon, I smear a blend of blues all over the naked mask. I highlight the cheeks with bright orange sunbursts. I trail a single vine-like strand of mossy green yarn from my chin to the middle of my forehead. I affix giant flower-shaped button eyes on either side of a pink pom-pom nose. The outline I loop around the eyes runs out of control, forming teardrop after teardrop that course their way down to a set of pursed black lips.

"Are you all right?" Karin asks.

I suddenly realize that there are real tears seeping from my eyes. I quickly wipe them away.

"Not what I expected either," she says under her breath. I catch a glimpse of bright yellow stripes marred by purple and black blotches on her mask as she whisks it out of sight.

Since no one wants to share their inner faces, we are all relieved when Marc lightens the mood by having us wear our outside masks in a mock beauty contest.

*   *   *

With my stomach still full of crepes, I decide to skip lunch and go on a solo hike to the ledges. I lace up my boots, slip a granola bar into my pocket, and fill up my water bottle.

The woods are cool and inviting but instead of taking my time, I speed along as if I'm being pursued by an invisible adversary. The incessant pounding of my heart finally convinces me to slow down. I veer off the trail and enter a pine grove where I stop to rest on the solid back of a massive boulder. Slowly I sip from my water bottle and take small bites from the granola bar until my heart rate returns to normal. Gingerly I lie back and stretch out on the cool, smooth granite, dangling my feet over the edge. I listen to the surround sound of melodious bird song and I lift my face to the tree limbs that intertwine above me. A scruffy red squirrel is tucked up against the trunk, munching on a pine cone, tiny bits of peel from his snack flaking down around my head. *Tiny, like my life*, I think, reflecting on how I'd peeled away all but the bare essentials after the divorce. Until now I thought I'd survived fairly well, but maybe that's all I'd been doing—just surviving. I stifle a yawn, my eyelids become heavy—perhaps merely surviving is no different than being half asleep.

The sharp cry of a hawk splits through the air. A deafening stillness embraces me as the woods go suddenly silent. We wait, the birds, the squirrel, and I, for the crisis to pass. The hawk cries out again, then soars away to find another feeding ground. One by one the birds resume their chirping and the squirrel scurries off, leaping from branch to branch, bouncing them up and down like rubber bands. A playful wind invades the space he's left behind, stirring leaves and needles into motion. Pine trees really do whisper.

The remainder of my hike is slow and steady, and when I reach the ledges, I stay at the top for a while and enjoy the view. There are several canoes gliding about on the rippled lake below, and I watch as two of them nearly collide. After a barrage of splashing and rocking, they manage to untangle themselves and no one gets swamped. I procrastinate on my way back down the trail, once again drinking in the beauty of it all. When I return to my room, I collapse on the bed into a sound sleep until the gong gathers us for music class.

*   *   *

"You can do it, Fern." Davy is coaching me in my attempt to play "Jingle Bells" on the recorder.

I shake my head. "Maybe I'll get it right by Christmas."

After a tortuous thirty minutes of squeaking and squawking, Jonas gives us all a reprieve trading our instruments of torture for djembes and tom-toms.

"I'm still vibrating," Davy giggles when we stop.

Karin starts to sing, "*I'm picking up good vibrations.*" She catches hold of Davy's arm and swings him around. Jonas sits at the piano and jams with Ben, who is still thumping away on the bass drum. Sue and Geraldine find tambourines and maracas and we all join in a free-for-all music fest. We explode out into the fireplace room.

"Is there a party goin' on?" Fred asks, jumping into the fray.

Sonja flings open her door. "Some of us are trying to meditate in here," she scolds.

"Oh, lighten up and join the fun," Tony says.

RJ peers sheepishly from behind Sonja. "Weren't we finished anyway?" The two sorority sisters are more indignant; they hug Sonja and flash us a look, then stomp off into the dining room.

"Some people think they own the place," Sonja says. I'm not sure whether she's glowering at me or at Jonas, who is standing behind me, his head over mine like the top of a totem pole.

We calm down, and Fred, the eternal peacemaker, apologizes to Sonja while the rest of us meander back to our rooms to prepare for dinner and the evening program.

*   *   *

I decide to bag the night hike and treat myself instead to a plate of peanut butter cookies and a glass of milk. I notice the pair of masks glaring at me from the top of my desk. "Not helpful," I say aloud and chuck them unceremoniously into the bottom drawer. Creasing back a clean page in my journal, hoping to paint the moose family from this morning's canoe trip, I begin to lightly brush in the blues and greens of the lake, sky, and trees. But every time I pencil sketch the mother moose, I cringe. I've nearly erased a hole in the page and am ready to fling the journal across the room when someone knocks on my door.

It's not Dannie, as I'd hoped, but Marc. He's concerned about my being upset during art class this morning. His eyes sweep around the room.

"They're in the desk drawer," I say, more abruptly than I intend.

"Who's in the drawer?"

"Oh, never mind."

He seems amused. Then he notices the pencils, paints, and journal strewn across the floor.

"I'm sorry. Looks like I've caught you in the middle of something."

"I think I've about given up."

"Mind if I take a look?"

Like a preschooler, I meekly show him my failed attempt at the moose tableau. "I just can't seem to get it right."

"Which animal do you identify with?"

"The young moose, I guess. Or maybe it should be the mother."

"Let's go with your first choice, the young moose. Draw only the young moose and try to fill the page with him or her."

"Her." Not sure why I'm so positive.

"Good. Now try drawing her posture, her position, her facial expression, to show what you imagine she's feeling. I'll be right back."

When he returns, he looks over my shoulder. "Excellent," he says, viewing my new sketch. He cranks open the easel he brought and props up a canvas a hell of a lot bigger than the size of a bread box.

"Now I want you to forget what you actually saw with your eyes, and concentrate on what you thought with your heart," he says. "Tell the story from the young moose's point of view. Remember that this is not about producing a 'fine' painting, but about responding to your experience."

I protest, "So much empty space. What if it's awful and I waste this beautiful canvas?"

He chuckles. "That's why God created white paint."

I can't say that I stay up all night trying to be Da Vinci or Van Gogh, but I make a genuine attempt to depict what I imagine the young moose is thinking as she wades deeper into the water. I try to capture her fear of the unknown depth, the unknown creatures lurking beneath the surface. With a graceful curve in her neck, she looks longingly back to the safety of the shoreline. I title it *Testing the Waters*.

*   *   *

It's finally Friday, the end of the first week. Last Sunday seems like it was just yesterday and at the same time an eternity ago. Since the philosophy of retreat at the Water's Edge is not to remain in seclusion, we are set free for the weekend. Lucy and Marc go home, while Jonas and Sonja hold down the fort. Julian has a gig at a five-star restaurant this weekend, so he leaves the walk-in refrigerator stocked full of leftovers that we can microwave if we choose not to scope out the local cuisine.

Sue and John have invited me to go into the town of Hanover with them on Saturday, and I'm looking forward to browsing through the quaint shops and taking in the evening concert on the village green.

As people make weekend plans, they disengage from the program and there is very little focus during our morning dance class. Sonja is not happy that we aren't more serious about the contra dance she's teaching us. All four groups are circled up in the dining room trying to work out the intricate steps, but BJ and RJ are behaving like clowns, and even I feel badly for Sonja when Pammy goofs off and breaks out into the "Hokeypokey". Somehow we manage to finish two dances without Sonja blowing her top. I try to soothe my own guilty conscience by thanking her. "What are your plans for the weekend?"

"Sleep, sleep, sleep in heavenly peace," is her curt reply.

*   *   *

After lunch I have another session with Lucy. This time I'm wide awake and we discuss the diminished size of my life. She asks why I think I've chosen this tiny life.

At first I try to deny that it's my choice. "I don't know, maybe I have this insane notion that the less I have, the less I have to lose," I say. She suggests that I make a list of all the things I'd given up after the divorce and then circle what I want back.

"But remember." She looks at me, her eyes full of kindness. "Have fun this weekend."

The place is deserted by Friday evening, so I wander into the library as I wait for my laundry to dry. While reading and taking notes on Japanese rock gardens, I jot down the things I don't have in my possession anymore: bird bath, front porch, closet space, tool shed, lawn chairs; I add sunny windows, a real bedroom, my job at the Jr. High School, gardening, someone I can share my life with.

What did I want back? Everything!

CHAPTER 8

S ATURDAY MORNING I enjoy a leisurely cup of coffee on the patio and reread the list of what I want back in my life. Remembering Lucy's advice about having fun this weekend, I tuck the list into the back of my journal.

I'm surprised when I see not only Sue helping John load stuff into his van but Dannie, Karin, and Davy as well.

"A child's car seat?" Karin asks curiously when she opens the hatch.

John explains that he has a four-year-old daughter and an ex-wife. "Both are out of the country at the moment," he tells us, his voice shaking a bit.

We all just nod our heads as if we understand completely.

The town of Hanover is a thirty-minute drive on a scenic back country road. We park in the municipal parking lot next to the historic town hall and split up into pairs.

"Sue seems to have made a full recovery from her breakdown," Dannie remarks, watching John and Sue walk down Main Street, arm in arm. Karin and Davy wave as they go off in search of a yarn outlet. Davy wants to learn how to crochet.

"I guess that leaves the two of us to explore," Dannie says.

We wander in and out of the specialty shops and I make some small purchases. "Very touristy," Dannie muses, observing my treasures.

"I can be touristy if I want to." I fan my flushed face. The midsummer sun radiating up from the pavement is hot enough to fry an egg. "Whew, let's find some air-conditioning."

"Here." She brushes against my shoulder, further inducing my hormonal molecules into a rapid boil. "Let's go in here."

India & Company. The glittery gold lettering shimmers on the beveled glass as the door closes behind us. A strand of temple bells announces our arrival. The shop was thankfully cool, but dimly lit, my eyes strain to make the transition. Prickles of sweat wick off my skin and give rise to goose bumps. A cloud of sandalwood incense emanates about the room creating an atmosphere both cozy and claustrophobic. From some invisible source, the ethereal timbre of a bamboo flute weaves an irregular melody around the syncopated beat of a hand drum. Like my companion, the shop is organic with mystique—frighteningly foreign but equally enticing.

"Ladies," a gentle voice intones, "I am Suzee." With delicate countenance, a petite young woman floats into view, her lithe figure swathed in a sarong of deep crimson. Rose-petal soft, it swaddles her body like a baby's blanket. She flashes her arresting eyes and perfectly white teeth, extending her cinnamon brown arms in welcome. "May I help you?"

Dannie is enthusiastically sifting through a rack of garments. "We'd like to try on one of these."

"We?" I ask, fingering the veil of feathery fabric.

"You two are close friends, yes?" It's more of a statement than a question. "Come with me." She leads us into a dressing room at the back of the shop. "Wait here."

"What have you gotten us into?" I ask Dannie as we stand in the middle of the brightly lit cubicle. Our reflections flash on the full-length mirrors that flank all four walls, and I feel immediately exposed.

"Oh, Fern," she laughs. "Don't look so pensive. This will be fun."

Our host breezes back into the dressing room, her arms trailing a mountain of texture and color. "Now ladies, you must strip to your underclothing." She trills the word *strip* so it sounds like *streep*.

"What?"

"No worries," she assures us. "I have many elder sisters, but if you are too modest . . ."

"Elder my ass!" Dannie kicks off her sandals and drops her shorts.

With a bit more caution, I remove my cotton top, thanking the lingerie god that the bra I'm wearing is not my usual hundred-year-old rag. I maneuver my way out of my capris and glance over at Dannie.

"Lollipop red." She snaps the bikini waistband of her panties. "A Victoria's Secret knockoff."

"Mm," I say, thinking more about what delights lie hidden underneath. "I didn't know Victoria's Secret had knockoffs," I stammer, my eyes traveling up to the luscious lacy fabric coddling her breasts. Her silvery hair dances on her bare shoulders and neck. Tanned and toned, she is Aphrodite—a fine wine, aged to perfection. I let out a nervous giggle. What am I thinking? I must be certifiably out of control.

"You have to know where to look."

"Pardon?"

"For the knockoffs."

"Now you must choose a sarong and I will wrap you up."

I'd forgotten that Suzee was still in the room with us. Obediently I reach for the sarong draped over her left arm—muted earth tones of burnt sienna and mossy greens.

"Absolutely not!" Dannie snatches the fabric from my grasp. She tugs at the corner of material on the bottom of the pile. It unfurls like New England sunshine on an autumn day; a palette of tangy tangerine, hot pepper red, and lemon yellow zest swirl into a leafy design. She sweeps it over my shoulder, the heat from her fingertips searing through the cloth and onto my skin. I am helplessly undone.

"Yes, yes!" Suzee claps excitedly. "Arms up. I show you how." Her practiced hands loop the sarong over, under, around, and through. She motions to Dannie. "Help please."

An awkwardly rooted tree in the garden of forbidden fruit, I stand motionless while Suzee transforms the vestment from shawl, to skirt, to dress. They twist and tuck. It tickles; I laugh.

"My turn." Dannie reaches into the samples of fabric. The brilliant emerald green she chooses matches the sass in her sparkling eyes. Edged with a ribbon of vivid violet and a web of gossamer white, it glistens like moonlight on water.

My attempt to help is thwarted by the velvety texture of Dannie's skin and the motion of her curvy hips as she seductively sways in rhythm to our ministrations.

"The finishing touch." Suzee draws forth an accordion of wrist bands from a basket. "And now I take your picture."

Dannie places her hand on the small of my back; sparks fly up and down my spine. I step closer and entwine my arm around her waist. "We shall go to the ball," she whispers in my ear.

Suzee clicks the digital image. "You change. I print out copies. You buy?"

Yes, we buy.

* * *

"Iced chai please," Dannie tells the waitress.

"Ditto." We sit across the table from each other under an awning at a café. The bags from *India & Company* are piled together on the extra chair. My mind and body are still reeling from the experience in the dressing room, and I find myself asking some ridiculous question about Lucy.

"I don't know Lucy. She and Marc are both new this year," she says. "Of course Jonas has been around forever and Sonja . . ."

"Doesn't like me," I cut her short. "I think maybe she's jealous. She seemed very upset the other day when I was talking to Julian."

Dannie starts to laugh. "She's not interested in Julian, or in any man for that matter. In fact, there was a time when she wanted something with me." Dannie leans across the table and touches my hand. "But she's not really my type."

My face registers relief, joy; fright. "Oh."

Dannie takes her hand away and picks up her chai. "Which was a bit of a problem," she continues, "when she thought we ought to be more than just business partners. She certainly has no reason to complain though, considering how successful I've helped make her career."

Dannie looks at me. "Anyway, enough about that. What are your plans when this most marvelous retreat comes to an end?"

I hadn't really thought much about it. I had another month's vacation before school started up again. "Maybe visit my mom and dad in Florida? Dad's in a shuffleboard tournament at the beginning of August."

"Sounds like a blast—not. No offense to your folks," she adds.

"The last two summers I've gone on trips with my daughter, but now that she's finished with college and has a real job . . ." my voice trails off.

"Mm," Dannie murmurs, swallowing her last mouthful of tea. "Well I'm sure you'll figure something out." She looks at her watch. "Let's go find John and Sue so we can put our bags in the van before we eat."

We don't go more than a block before we see them emerging from an antique toy shop. John is carrying a beat-up hobby horse over his shoulder.

"We're going to fix it up for John's little girl," Sue proudly informs us.

"Very domestic," Dannie points out, flashing me a knowing look.

Karin and Davy are already at the van, each with two large bundles of yarn. "What did you two buy?" Davy asks.

"Oh, just some trinkets and lingerie." Dannie winks and puts her arm around my shoulders.

"Sexy lingerie," I add encircling her waist with my own arm.

"Naughty girls," Davy giggles. "Good for you."

After we secure our purchases in the van, we walk to a restaurant that, according to the sign, serves the world's finest Italian cuisine. As the others chat about their afternoon adventures, I study Dannie's face. I love how it lights up when she laughs at Davy's impersonation of the little old lady at the yarn shop who reamed out the sales clerk for not having a match for a skein of yarn she'd bought ten years ago. I can understand why Sonja would be attracted to Dannie; so am I, but what did that mean? Hell, I'd hardly known what it was like to have a sexual encounter with my ex-husband, never mind Dannie, and anyway, why was I all of a sudden so obsessed with sex?

"Earth to Fern," Davy's voice breaks into my thoughts. "Where've you been, girl?"

"Wherever it was, it must have been good," Karin interjects. "You're absolutely glowing."

"I am?" I can feel my face flush red hot. At that very moment the waiter arrives with our food.

"Thank you," I say, relieved, as he places my food in front of me. *For coming to my rescue*, I say to myself.

Our conversation moves to the pops concert that evening. John and Sue go on and on about how they both love Cole Porter. Sue looks adoringly at John. "We have so much in common."

After dinner, which is acceptable but not even close to Julian's genius, we walk back to the van to retrieve our blankets and Karin's beach chair. By the time we reach the amphitheater on the village green, a small crowd has gathered. A collection of afghans, towels, and chairs are spread across the grass like a patchwork quilt.

Davy decides to take a stroll to seek out cute guys. Sue and John claim a blanket and behold each other like a couple of teenagers.

Karen sinks into her chair. "Those two remind me of when Jack and I were newlyweds,"

"Is something wrong, Fern?" Dannie asks. "You're very quiet."

"Lots to think about I guess."

"Well try not to strain your beautiful brain too much."

I turn away from Dannie's inquisitive expression.

"No worries," she says. "Just relax, listen to the music, and have a good time.'

We lean against each other, shoulder to shoulder, while the orchestra offers up tunes from *My Fair Lady* and a romantic medley of Cole Porter songs. Karin falls asleep; her intermittent snores mingle with the rhythmic percussion. John and Sue really do need to get a room, and we don't see Davy again until intermission.

Dannie stretches out on the blanket. "You still seem a bit tense." She flips on to her back. "Check out these stars."

Tentatively I lie down. Above our heads, the velvety night sky is illuminated with a million twinkling lights. I take a deep breath and move closer to Dannie. "Did you see that?" I say excitedly as a star flings itself through the universe.

The concert finale is the *1812 Overture*. As the round tones of the brass section hold us in the drama of the moment, Dannie takes hold of my hand. Our fingers intertwine, the music crescendos, and yes, there are fireworks.

*   *   *

The sultry water encircles my toes, caressing my feet, coaxing me away from the shallow edge and into the depth of its embrace. I step cautiously into the still pool, rippling the tranquil surface. Soundlessly I fold my naked form into the warm tropical water, allowing the steamy wetness to swirl over my breasts, my nipples, and in between my legs. When I try to move forward, something wraps itself around my ankles. With great force, I propel myself upward and out of the powerful grasp of the dream. I wake up soaked in sweat, my feet tangled in the sheets. I peel off my nightshirt and lie totally exposed. This was no hot flash.

Soul searching while soaping up in the shower, I know for sure that the tingling in my body is more than a mere hormonal imbalance, but do I dare acknowledge what it is? I pace rapidly around the room, wrapped in a towel, talking out loud. "You're a big girl, Fern. You can handle this. But what is *this*?" *This* is a long-ago, yet very familiar, feeling that I'd denied or ignored for years. "Damn you, Dannie. What have you done?"

Actually, no one had done anything. When the fireworks subsided, the crowd had erupted into a standing ovation. Davy had come bouncing over to introduce us to his new best friends, Max and Sam, and Sue and John insisted we must get back to the Water's Edge—they were tired. Yeah, right. Karen, who was now sufficiently rested, offered to drive. I'm not sure if I'm disappointed or relieved when, after kissing me on the cheek, Dannie wishes me a good sleep and whispers in my ear that she'll see me in the morning.

After my shower, I spill the contents of the bag from *India & Company* on to the bed. The sarong cushions the other two purchases, and I pick them up one at a time: my touristy souvenirs—a miniature white clapboard house with flower boxes on the windowsills and a swing on the porch, and a sack of red and pink gladiola bulbs. I remove the individual bulbs and arrange them in front of the house, imagining what they'd look like in full bloom. I unwind myself from the bath towel, slip a tank top over my head, and wrap the sarong around my waist; the soft material coddles my body in a feathery embrace. Sitting on the patio, I try to stay calm and patiently wait for Dannie. Even though I expect her arrival, I nearly jump out of my skin when she knocks on the door.

"Room service!"

"What's all this?" I ask when she sweeps into the room carrying a tray piled high with plastic covered bowls.

"Brunch, or at least what I could scrounge up in the kitchen." She puts the tray on the only available surface, my bed.

"You're brilliant," I laugh.

"And you look dashingly sweet in that getup."

"You like?" I spin around with a goofy grin on my face and nearly lose my balance. "Let's eat out on the patio."

Dannie mixes yogurt and fruit while I brew the coffee.

"Now, *this* is brilliant," she gestures to the lake. "I never thought I'd say this but I think I've lived in the city too long. My body really craves wide open spaces, and Central Park just doesn't cut it anymore."

"There's no substitute for the real thing," I agree, thinking once again about the sad little plants dying in my apartment.

"Amen to the real thing." An unfamiliar expression of vulnerability flashes across Dannie's face. She clears her throat. "Fern, about last night."

"Last night was wonderful," I blurt out. "I mean, the music, the stars." I pause.

Dannie smiles. "My sentiments exactly."

For a moment we say nothing but regard each other as if for the first time.

Reluctantly I break the silence. "What are your plans for the afternoon?"

"I have some phone calls to make." Dannie efficiently stacks our plates. "Business. What about you?"

"I guess I'll do some more weeding in the herb garden." I'm a little peeved that Dannie hadn't suggested we do something together. "Julian and I talked about expanding a few of the perennial beds." Perhaps time alone up to my elbows in dirt, time alone to think, is what just what I need.

"John said something about going out for pizza tonight."

"Sounds good," I say, suddenly finding her presence excruciating and wishing she would just go. "Thanks again for breakfast."

"See you later." She gives me a quick kiss me on the cheek and is gone.

CHAPTER 9

SEE YOU LATER? One minute I think she's about to jump my bones and the next she seems to vaporize into thin air. Does she want me or not? I ignore my own questions as I rough up the dirt around the base of the basil and oregano. I think instead about how strawberries would thrive in this kind of soil. I wonder where the nearest garden center is. We could always order them online, but then you're never sure how healthy they'll be or how soon they'll be delivered.

"Why am I stressing about this?" I say out loud. My stress has nothing to do with strawberries. The real question is do I want her? Do I want to share that kind of intimacy with another person again?

"Would you like some help?" Geraldine is standing over me.

"Help?" I leap to my feet.

"Sorry, I didn't mean to startle you."

"I can't figure this out." I hold up the trailing root I'd just yanked from the ground. "Is this an herb or a weed?"

"It looks like alecost," she says, squatting down with surprising agility. "I might be wrong but I think it was once used to brew ale. Makes a good tea too." She rubs one of the leaves between her fingers and touches her nose. "Don't be fooled by its agreeable minty scent, alecost is notoriously invasive. It can take over your entire garden in one season."

While Geraldine and I excavate the tenacious plant, we swap horticultural adventures. She speaks of the generations before her who cultivated acres and acres of crops; the abundant red tomatoes, purple eggplants, and golden squash. I share the evolution of my own gardening escapades—the bright pink azaleas, the delicate violet irises, the pale yellow roses that grew so profusely in my past life.

"Your garden sounds like a masterpiece." Geraldine gestures around her. "I've always thought that the earth made the perfect palate."

I give her a hug. "Thanks for your help."

She's right, I think as I shower and dress. In a way, my flower garden had become my magnum opus. In my journal I illustrate a bird's-eye view of the flowering bushes, ornamental trees, and beds of perennials that I remembered so well. With great affection, I admire the familiar scene and long to sip the magical potion that will allow me to step inside.

But there is no such potion. It's gone and there's no point in mourning what is past. I take a cleansing breath, turn to a clean page, and exchange my pencil for a rainbow of pastel crayons. Feverishly I ply the intense colors onto the paper.

"Mm," I sigh, "not quite there yet." Glancing at my watch, I suddenly realize that if I don't hurry I'll miss the pizza run.

*　　*　　*

The last to arrive, I end up sitting on the bench seat in the back of Jonas's hippie van, squished up against Pammy and Tom. Geraldine rides shotgun. Stuffed into John's minivan are Sue, of course, a couple of sorority sisters, and Sonja, who has surreptitiously wedged herself between Dannie and Fred.

To my dismay, Sonja attaches herself to Dannie all evening. I try not to sulk, and focus my attention instead on Fred as he entertains me with his theories on the epidemic of feline diabetes and the future of canine hip surgery. Did I mention he's a veterinarian? I gorge myself on pizza, and drown my sorrows in pitchers of beer as I watch Sonja brazenly flirt with Dannie.

*　　*　　*

Monday morning at breakfast, we are assigned to our new groups for the week. I'm thrilled to be with Geraldine and John. However, I'm tempted to scurry back to bed when I discover that our first class is silent meditation with Sonja. Geraldine convinces me to give it a try.

Since Sonja is already silent when we arrive, she hands each of us a 3-by-5-inch card with the meditation instructions printed on it. There's an enormous Buddha projected on one wall and sturdy cushions arranged in a circle on the floor. We are to sit cross legged with empty minds for fifteen minutes, and when we hear the bell ring, we are to follow Sonja in a meditative walk around the perimeter of the room. It's strongly suggested that we bow in reverence to the Buddha as we pass. After an hour, we'll be allowed a short break—still in silence—and then we'll convene outside on the lawn to repeat the practice.

From the very moment I sit my butt down on the cushion, my legs rebel, and after remaining tightly crossed for fifteen minutes they threaten to stiffen up permanently. To my surprise, I discover that the slow-paced walking is not only a respite for my legs, but therapeutic for my mind as well. I can't quite get myself to bow to the Buddha, and I nearly laugh out loud when we've moved outside and Sonja genuflects to an invisible Buddha somewhere out on the lake. It's more of a challenge for me to keep an empty mind while surrounded by nature's sounds and smells, but soon the warm sun thaws out my stiff muscles and the fresh air nourishes my lungs. Once I've mastered being silent, I think I may never speak again and at lunch, the dining room is so noisy that I carry my tray out to the terrace and eat by myself.

After lunch I peek into the kitchen.

"Do you have a moment?" I ask Julian.

He invites me in and hands me an apron. "I have plenty of time if you're willing to help with the dishes."

"What do you think about planting blueberries or strawberries in the kitchen garden?" I ask as I tie the apron around my waist. The idea had plagued my empty mind during meditation.

"I think it's a great idea," he says. "I'll just need to check with a few people first."

My mood is lighthearted, and for a moment, I even consider singing in the choir that Jonas is rehearsing this afternoon, but I'm not much of a singer and I'm anxious to explore another inspiration I'd had during meditation. I enter the art room with my leather journal in hand.

"You won't believe this." I show Marc the page filled with oil pastels. "Larger?" He grins from ear to ear and drags out a canvas the size of a small country from the supply closet. He also presents me with a supersize jug of white paint.

"The world's largest bottle of Wite-Out," he laughs.

"Amazing," Geraldine exclaims when she enters the art room and looks at the sweeping amounts of paint I've smeared across the massive canvas. Spectacular arrays of striking colors fan out from the center—a sunburst of blossoms.

"You inspired it," I remind her.

"Do you still need the white paint?" Marc asks as I carry my painting back to my room.

"No thanks."

*   *   *

"There you are!" Dannie practically grabs me when I enter the dining room for dinner that evening.

"Glad to see you too," I say, slightly taken aback.

"We need to talk," she says, adamantly. "Are you free to go canoeing later?"

"I guess." I wonder what's so urgent. I think back on how comfortable she looked last night with Sonja. I definitely don't like the mixed signals I'm getting.

By evening the temperature has dropped several degrees, so I dress in warm layers. There are clouds gathering in the sky and the dampness hangs in the air like a wet rag.

Dannie hands me a meditation pillow and a blanket. "Sit in the middle of the canoe," she says. "I want to be able to see your beautiful face." She kneels down on her own cushion and pushes off from the shore.

"I sincerely apologize for last night," she tells me, stowing her paddle. We float freely in the deeper water. "I couldn't seem to shake Sonja, but then I couldn't help but notice how enthralled you seemed to be with whatever Fred was talking about."

"Oh yes," I snort. "I was greatly enamored with his cryptic lecture on canine hip surgery."

"Oh. I thought . . . never mind."

"What's going on, Dannie?"

The boat teeter-totters as Dannie gingerly moves closer to me. She cups my face in her hands and we kiss.

"This is all new to me," I confess as we rest cradled in the bosom of our canoe. "I've only had one intimate relationship and that failed miserably. I'm not sure I know the right way to do this."

"No one knows the 'right way,'" she commiserates. "Shallow hook-ups have been my style in the past, but lately I've wondered what it would be like to have something more." She peers out into the darkness. "When I helped Harriet and Paul realize their dream of owning a bookshop, I was touched by the sensitivity they showed to each other. Married for more than forty years, they still held hands when they walked into my office. Their business will be successful because they already have a successful long-term partnership. I asked them what their secret was and they told me respect, lots of love, and four decades of practice."

"That's a long time," I say. What I don't say is that my own experience has warned me that longevity doesn't always guarantee success.

"Maybe I shouldn't tell you this," she continues, "but it was Sonja who persuaded me to attend this retreat. I thought she was concerned about me, but now I think she may have had ulterior motives."

KA-THUNK! The sound reverberates across the lake as our canoe collides with a rock.

"That's exactly how it felt when I first met you," Dannie laughs, giving me another kiss.

The canoe has drifted under the ledges and is hung up on the craggy rocks below.

"How would Harriet and Paul get out of this one?"

Well, it doesn't take us as long as forty years, but it does take us several frustrating moments of careful maneuvering before we finally extricate ourselves from the shallow waters. We are only halfway across the lake when the weighty clouds give way to rain. Not just a few drops, but a gully washer. Like a bucket of golf balls, the deluge roils the lake up over the sides of the canoe. "Next time we bring two paddles," I yell over the roaring torrent. When we reach the shore, we flip the canoe, stow the paddle, and dash up the trail. Cheers and applause greet us when we throw ourselves in through the dining room doors.

"Drenched to the skin, you poor dears," Karin coos. "Come over by the fire and get yourselves warm and dry."

"Didn't realize we had an audience," I say, shaking out my blanket and leaning the saturated pillow against the hearth.

"Live entertainment at your service." Dannie takes a bow. There's a bit of sarcasm in her voice, but she laughs along with everyone else.

All I want to do is take my soggy self up to my room, but the well-meaning crowd that surrounds us gives us little choice. They insist on draping dry blankets over our shoulders and offering us steamy hot mugs of cocoa. It isn't until everyone files into the music room to watch a movie that we finally get a moment to ourselves.

"Alone at last," Dannie says in a low voice.

We cuddle together on the couch and watch as the flickering flames burn the logs down to hot coals. I'm snuggled up against Dannie's warm body, nodding off to sleep, when the door of the dance studio slams open.

"How cozy." Sonja's voice cackles like the wicked witch of the West.

"Butt out," Dannie retorts.

I'm way too tired to get involved in their little spat, so I gather my things, say a hasty good night, and hustle back to my room.

CHAPTER 10

I HAUL MYSELF OUT of bed on Tuesday morning, my body still chilled to the bone from the night before. I stand at length beneath a scalding hot shower, hoping to wash clear the confusion in my mind. Choosing what to wear becomes a more difficult task than is necessary, but I finally settle on black stretch pants and a white T-shirt. My reflection in the mirror is as dreary as the day. I rest my eyes on the sarong draped innocently on the arm of the chair and I think, *what fun, what nonsense, what drama—what more? WHAT THE HELL?* I cast the dazzling fabric around my neck, fling one end heedlessly over one shoulder, and breeze out of the room.

Breakfast attendance is thin but lively. Davy, always up for an audience, is entertaining everyone with interior decorating anecdotes. "So I say to them," he flourishes his hand in the air, "linoleum is just so last century." He is rewarded with great gales of laughter.

"Cockeyed optimists." Ben frowns. "You all realize that this bloody precipitation is predicted to wash out the next two days?"

"Don't be such a wet blanket." Karin smirks. "We won't melt."

After breakfast we gather in the library for a writing class with Lucy. Votive candles illuminate an assortment of pens fanned out on the tables. The gentle sounds of classical music, something famous by J.S. Bach, emanate from a portable CD player. I hug my shawl closer to my body, a shield against the central air-conditioning and other pessimistic intruders.

"Take care that you select a writing implement that sits well in your hand," Lucy analogizes. "Like an artist might choose a paint brush."

Our assignment is to compose a haiku, a Japanese lyric poem. The formula: three simple lines; five syllables, seven syllables, five syllables. Geraldine and I share our poems with each other.

My first attempt:
> *Paddle in the dark*
> *Night of possibilities*
> *Rainsoaked to the skin*

Geraldine's:
> *Sweet nectar of life*
> *Flowering petals open*
> *Buzz on bumble bee*

"Lighten up," I remind myself.
> *Rainsoaked to the skin*
> *Kissed by the sun, the earth wakes*
> *Good morning Glories*

"Delightful." Geraldine pats me on the hand. "Just like you."

Our session ends with an exercise in deep breathing and loud sighs. Maybe it's because of Geraldine's enthusiasm for my haiku, maybe it's the infusion of oxygen into my brain, but I'm struck with a sudden inspiration and I excuse myself and dash back to my room.

On a clean palette I squeeze out alizarin crimson, ultramarine blue, hooker's green, and cadmium yellow. Along the edge of the giant flower painting, I brush in a multitude of purple and pink morning glories, weaving them through a lattice frame. I discard my brush and use my fingers to smear and blend in the colors. Setting the canvas on a chair, I sit on my bed and study my handiwork. I tuck myself into a fetal position on the bed, cocooning my body tightly in the sarong and close my eyes.

Electricity sizzles in the air. "I can save them all," I cry out as I frantically gather up bunches of blossoms. But every time I grasp them in my hands, they explode in my face, covering my body in a rainbow of petal confetti. *Bang!* My eyelids pop open to a brilliant flash of white light, and then total darkness. No sun, no electricity, no lights. I grope around the room until my eyes adjust to the evening sky. Is that the dinner gong? My empty belly rumbles in kind.

The glow from LED lamps on the tables cast eerie shadows across the dining room walls and windows.

Davy picks up a lantern and peers at my face. "What have you been up to, girlfriend? Is that war paint I see?"

"I guess I got a little carried away," I say, touching my forehead.

Dannie appears with a tray full of hot food. "Well, I think you look ravishing." She sits. "Good thing the kitchen is equipped with propane stoves or we'd all be chewing on celery and carrot sticks."

When I return to the table with my own food, I find Dannie sitting by herself. "Before you say anything," she begins, "I want you to know that Sonja and I straightened things out last night after you left. She claims that she wasn't upset about us but at herself. Apparently she'd tried to make a pass at one of the sorority sisters, and had been rejected. She's very sorry that she spoiled our moment."

"I guess it's good that you sorted things out with Sonja," I say, not really believing Sonja's pat excuse or the sincerity of her apology. "But I'm not sure I want to get in the middle of this thing with Sonja."

"This *thing*, as you call it, is *nothing*." Dannie enunciates her words then throws up her hands in exasperation. "Whatever." She collects her tray and moves to another table.

Whatever? I start to go after her but my legs are like lead weights. I'm no longer hungry and can only nibble at my soup. I help wash the dishes after dinner but I can't bring myself to join the crowd for a marshmallow roast around the fire.

At some point in the night, after I've gone to bed, the electricity kicks back on and my room is flooded with light. The last thing I see before turning off the lights and drifting back to sleep is the flower painting silently beckoning from across the room.

*   *   *

On Wednesday morning, the rain has subsided but it's still a dull, damp, gray day. I layer a navy blue hoodie over a long sleeve T-shirt, ignore the disaster my room has become, and haul myself down to the dining room.

The drumming session with Jonas goes a long way to lift my spirits, and I'm as thrilled as everyone else to be greeted by sunshine and blue sky when we break for lunch. Most of us migrate to the great outdoors with our ration of spinach calzones.

"Turned out to be a beautiful day," Dannie says, pulling up a chair. "Perfect for the hike with Marc later this afternoon." She touches my arm. "Look, I know you're pissed."

I try to look away but I can't.

"My fault," she continues. "I just wanted you to know that I talked to Lucy this morning—about us."

"Us?"

"I needed some perspective."

"Perspective might be helpful." I'm not sure whose perspective she's talking about.

"She offered us a session together." Dannie raises her eyebrows. "What do you think?"

Like marriage counseling? I speculate silently. "Maybe," is all I can say.

As it happens, I meet up with Lucy after lunch. She invites me to her room for a cup of tea.

Watching a flock of geese splash land into the lake, she prompts, "It must take courage to drop with such abandonment from that great height."

"They're not doing it alone," I point out.

"Support from others is critical if you're attempting an unfamiliar endeavor," she muses philosophically. "How is your garden project coming along?"

"Wonderful." I describe the purple morning glories and the trellis.

"Morning glories?"

I realize she's not asking about my flower painting but about Julian's garden. I correct my mistake; Lucy encourages me to say more about the painting.

"Do you feel comfortable showing it to me?" she asks.

I reply without hesitation. "I'll go and get it."

We contemplate the painting together.

"Some artist's title their work."

"It's a portrait of *My Heart's Desire*." I wipe my eyes. "Sorry. My eyes seem to leak with painful regularity these days."

She offers me a tissue. "Tears are usually a sign that something is truly important."

"Speaking of desires," I continue tentatively. "Can we talk about Dannie?"

When I finish my incoherent rambling about the unexpected, unconventional, unrelenting desires I'm having, she asks, "What does your gut tell you?"

"That it's terrific, tremendous—terrifying."

*   *   *

The heady scent of moist earth springs up from the lumps of spongy moss beneath our feet. Marc cautions us to try not to disturb the freshly sprouted mushrooms and the mud puddles pressed into moose tracks. Branches heavy with wet leaves shake themselves dry and shower our heads with cold, watery droplets.

The trail that surrounds the lake has been compromised by the heavy rains and is flooded in places, making our hike more of a challenge. When we reach the causeway, Dannie and I lag behind the rest of the group.

"I talked with Lucy," I say. "We talked about desires."

"So what's the verdict on desires?"

"They are terrific, tremendous, and terrifying."

"Ain't that the truth."

"Not exactly what I expected when I came on this retreat."

She nods. "Definitely the farthest thing from my mind. When I spoke with the good doctor, she inferred that it might have something to do with the intention of my heart, something that my mind isn't quite ready to be aware of, or some such psychological jargon." Dannie smiles at me. "She prescribed that we spend more time with each other, reminding me that we're both old enough to figure it out."

"I don't feel old enough. I feel like my middle-aged body has been injected with teenage hormones, and I'm having some kind of allergic reaction."

"That's the terrifying part," Dannie admits as she takes hold of my hand.

A tingling sensation rushes through my body. "This is the terrific part," I whisper, pulling her closer.

On our way back to the lodge, we cross paths with a doe and her two spotted fawns. The inquisitive fawns cautiously approach us, but their mom snorts and stamps out a warning. She flashes her white tail and the three of them leap gracefully off into the woods.

*　　*　　*

There's an alarming billow of smoke curling into the air as we approach the lodge. At first we think the place is on fire, but then the tangy aroma of barbeque sauce assaults our noses and we see that the only flames in sight are the ones lapping around the chicken wings and veggie burgers that Jonas and Julian are flipping on the gas grills.

A volleyball net has been set up on one side of the lawn, and on the other a familiar pattern of croquet wickets poke up from the ground.

After licking our sticky fingers clean, we play. Who would have guessed that Fred possessed an almost malicious competitive streak—viciously whacking his opponents' striped wooden balls into the trees—or that the sorority sisters are near professional volleyball players. We find out after they beat the pants off of us (not literally) that their college team won the national championships.

I'm sore all over and when Dannie walks me to my room, I refuse to let her in.

"Playing hard to get is not an attractive quality," she teases.

"I'm not," I confess. "Honestly. Even the muscles on my muscles hurt, and my room is an absolute catastrophe!"

"Another time, then." We kiss good night.

The room really is a disaster and I really do need to stand under a hot shower for the next light year, but I know my hesitancy to invite her in is more than that. After my shower, I can't get to sleep, and despite my sore limbs, I stay up half the night cleaning like a mad woman.

*   *   *

The next morning at breakfast, Marc gestures for me to follow him outside. "I'm hoping you will know what to do with all of this."

I gasp when I lay eyes on the blueberry bushes, raspberry canes, and flats of strawberry plants laid out on the lawn amid bags of compost, manure, and mulch. I think back to my conversation with Julian. "Everything I'd asked for," I murmur.

"Julian said you'd know what goes where, so I've taken the liberty of rounding up some volunteers to help get these beauties into the ground."

"And here we are!"

Fred, BJ, Dannie, RJ, and Geraldine process out of the dining room. Geraldine points to the others. "They can do all the heavy lifting, but I know how to handle one of these." She holds up a coil of green rubber hose.

At first I'm overwhelmed by the task, but once I map out a basic plan and we get to work, it's like having my own landscaping team. I appreciate their willingness to jump into muddy holes, wrestle blueberry bushes into place, fall victim to raspberry thorns, and crawl around on hands and knees setting down strawberry plants.

"I can almost taste the succulent berries," Fred exclaims while washing his hands off with the hose.

"You'll have to come back next year to do that," I tell him. "Unfortunately none of these plants will bear fruit until next season."

"No such thing as instant gratification when it comes to gardening," Geraldine agrees. "But just think of all the future retreat participants who will enjoy the harvest for years to come."

"All thanks to our most noble efforts." BJ bows dramatically.

Julian comes out of the kitchen to view our handiwork. "You are wonderful for arranging all of this!" I say. I throw my arms around him, smudging his gravy-splattered apron with my mud-encrusted shirt.

"Whoa, don't thank me." He pulls away, his cheeks flushed bright red. "I merely passed the word along."

"What do you mean?"

"It was Dannie who asked me to let her know if you needed anything."

"Dannie?" I remember the basket of gardening goodies. She must have been behind that as well? "But isn't there a board of directors who need to be consulted?"

"They're a pretty loose bunch," he laughs, "and since Jonas is the president, he merely makes a few phone calls and—presto!" Julian snaps his fingers.

*   *   *

After lunch, Jonas insists that everyone amble outside to admire the fruits of our labor. I start to explain how it's still a work in progress, but I'm immediately upstaged by BJ, who takes over as the garden guide and expounds on the great strength needed to lift the blueberry bushes. Fred acts like an expert horticulturist as he proudly describes how to comb out roots and train raspberries vines.

"Of course none of us would have known a raspberry cane from a pile of compost without our gardener in residence. Here's to you, Fern." Dannie cheers.

"Every gardener needs a benefactor," I'm quick to add, flashing Dannie a grateful look. "Without Dannie's generosity there wouldn't have been anything to plant."

"We do make a good team," Dannie agrees, putting her arm around me. As folks drift in various directions to enjoy their free time, she asks, "How about another canoe ride?"

*   *   *

"Playing in the dirt becomes you, Fern," she comments as we paddle out to the center of the lake.

"Some women pay big bucks to smear mud all over their bodies."

"You love it, don't you? Growing things, working with the soil."

"Yes, and I guess I miss it more than I realized."

Dannie is thoughtful for a moment. "Want to take a road trip with me this weekend?"

"A road trip?"

"I need to scope out some property," she explains, "and not only would I love to have your scintillating company on the long drive, I could also use a second opinion."

"All weekend?"

"We'll leave on Saturday morning and be back here by late Sunday afternoon. It'll give us a chance to spend more time together—alone."

"I'd love to go."

"Tremendous and terrific," she says, splashing a spray of water at me with her paddle.

"Hey, I can give as good as I get," I laugh, splashing back.

"I'm counting on it," she razzes. "We better put on some speed if we're going to make it back in time for music class."

I take that as a challenge and dig my paddle in deeper. "As Davy loves to say, 'You go, girl'!"

We race across the lake, howling wildly as we blast the canoe up on to the shore.

"That was great," I yell, stowing my paddle.

"Not over yet," Dannie dares, jogging to the path. I chase her up the trail and tackle her on to the soft grass when we reach the lawn, practically knocking down Sue and John.

"How old do you two think you are?"

CHAPTER 11

A BSOLUTELY NO ONE in our group has ever seen a tone chime before, never mind make music with one, but somehow Jonas teaches us how to manipulate the long metallic tubes, rung like hand bells, to play an old Shaker tune, "Simple Gifts," with a fair amount of success. We perform at dinner and receive praise for our accomplishment.

Dannie and I choose to eat our dessert, a triple chocolate torte, in my room while we prepare for our weekend trip. We search out maps and lodging on her laptop as we savor the rich treat.

"Julian's creations are almost as sexy as he is," I say, my mouth full of sweet cake.

"Oh, really?" She mimics the breathy voice of a sorority sister. "I think you are the one who is positively delicious." She kisses a stray dab of chocolate syrup on my lips. "Mm." She grins mischievously. "Got any lotion? My shoulders are starting to peel." Before I say a word, she strips off her shirt and her beautiful bare breasts spill out, round and lovely, nipples taut. I can't look away.

"Sorry."

"Oh, stop it, Fern. Go ahead and look. You can even touch if you'd like." She tugs on my shirt. "As long as I can return the favor."

Sometime in the predawn hours, she leaves my bed. I lie languishing in a pool of pleasure, hug my pillow close to my body, and breathe in her scent.

*   *   *

On my way to breakfast, I wander outside to water the garden. Jonas is coiling up an already spent hose.

"You'll need to give me instructions for watering, weeding, and pruning so I can take care of these babies after you leave," he says.

At first I think he's talking about this weekend, but then it occurs to me that after next week, the retreat will be over and I'll be leaving permanently.

"What's it like living here full time?" I ask.

"The Water's Edge is the only real home I've known. After dropping out of high school, I quite literally walked across the country with a few of my delinquent buddies. One by one, the others found jobs and settled down along the way." He scratches under his beard. "When I arrived here, I was alone, twenty pounds underweight, with calluses the size of corn husks on the bottoms of my feet." He grimaces at the memory. "Bet adopted me, tutored me for the GED, and generously paid my way through college. Now I'm practically in charge of the place. I must say that even though I enjoy meeting the folks who come for a visit, some of my favorite moments are when the lodge is empty and I am 'Lord of the Manor.'"

"I certainly understand why you love it here."

"Where's home for you?" he asks.

Good question. I explain about my tiny studio apartment and the job at the private school. He guffaws when I repeat my Dad's theory about hiding out.

"Some could say I'm hiding out by living here," Jonas counters, "but I know I have nothing to hide from. Do you?"

"There you are." Dannie trots over to us and greets me with a hug and a kiss. I know that I'm beaming.

"Nothing hidden there," Jonas says quietly as he walks away.

*   *   *

Lucy takes a group of us for a morning hike to the ledges. Once on the ridge, we're instructed to focus on a tree limb or a section of earth and attend closely to whatever we see. I scrutinize a string of ants hefting a dead bug, three times their size over the edge of a rock. Lucy is right: life's tasks can be made much easier when we're not alone.

At lunch some of us make plans to patronize a local pub on Friday night. I can't believe that it's the end of the second week.

Laundry and packing fill up most of the afternoon. Once again I fail in my feeble attempt to journal; instead, I wrap my body in my sarong, and soak up the last of the sun out on the patio.

*   *   *

Dannie heaves my bag into her trunk. "What have you got in here, rocks?"

The first appointment is scheduled for 11:00 a.m. in a town about a three-hour's drive from the Water's Edge. Dannie continues to be evasive about our destination so we chat amicably about the weather, politics, and family. We discover that we both prefer warm weather and we both voted for the same party in the last election; however, unlike my close-knit clan, Dannie's estranged relations are spread out all over the world.

We stop at Mabel's Mouthwatering Eatery for brunch. A quintessential greasy spoon, Mabel's offers the heavenly aroma of bacon and coffee on the other side of a funky screen door. We're both starving so we treat ourselves to the "Trucker's Special."

"No offense to Julian's fine cooking," Dannie says, her mouth full of spicy home fries, "but I really needed a junk food fix."

"Chocolate chip cookies to go?" I ask, flourishing two giant disks wrapped in plastic.

"I knew there was a reason why I brought you along."

We parallel park in front of a vacant shop. The realtor drives up behind us in her black Mercedes and meets us at the door with the key. She gives us each a manila folder containing the property particulars.

The space we enter is empty and spotless, but the air still holds a faint odor of roses and lilacs. A flower shop.

Bloom 'n' Buds was a viable business up until a few months ago when the owner decided to relocate to be closer to her grandchildren. The storage area in the back leads out to a warm green house and a parking area of crushed gravel. Dannie and I follow the realtor up a flight of stairs to the small apartment above the shop. Slightly larger than my studio, it has a single bedroom, a living area, and a galley kitchen.

"Well, what do you think?" Dannie asks me when we're outside again and the realtor is locking the door.

"I guess it all depends on what you have in mind?"

"My dear Fern, don't you get it?" Dannie waves her arm in a grand gesture. "I've decided to invest in floriculture, something for *you* to dabble in. A flower shop, a garden market, whatever your cute little green thumb desires."

She shakes hands with the realtor. "We still have several other properties to see, but we'll be in touch."

"Congratulations." Now the realtor is shaking my hand. "It sounds like the two of you have an exciting future ahead."

"Thank you, I guess."

*   *   *

"You have some explaining to do!" I accuse Dannie when we're on the road again.

"Don't be upset with me." Dannie pleads her case. "You have a gift for growing things, and I'm trying to be supportive."

But I'm a teacher, I think. Not a very happy one, no, but I wasn't at all sure that I was capable of running, or if I even wanted to run, a business.

"I just don't know," is all I can say.

"No quick decisions, Fern," Dannie says. "Just promise me you'll give the idea some thought and stay open to the possibilities."

And so I think about it. All during the long drive to our next appointment, I silently ponder the freedom of being my own boss, making a living doing something I love. I weigh it against the trepidation of actually doing it. I've been a teacher for the last twenty years, also something I love. Nevertheless I treat my imagination to a wander through Bloom 'n' Buds. I stock the shelves with exotic plants and cut flowers, multicolored ribbon, alabaster vases, and artistic arrangements. I consider the variety of seeds and cuttings I could experiment with in the greenhouse. The second floor apartment is very convenient—so what if my backyard is a parking lot.

"A penny for them," Dannie finally asks.

"They're worth more than a penny."

"Fair enough. We have two more places to visit today and two more tomorrow, so let's just wait and see."

To say that the second property we peruse needs some TLC would be morbidly inadequate, but according to Dannie it fit the basic criteria she'd used to narrow down possible venues—zoned for business with a greenhouse on the property.

"Totally lewd and creepy," I say when we've finally shaken free of the sleazy realtor who'd shown us the former funeral home, a soon-to-be-condemned building.

"I nearly died from the smell." She marks her file folder with a large red *X*.

The greenhouse had turned out to be nothing more than a lopsided atrium window tacked onto the back of the building like an afterthought.

Our final stop for the day is the Potpourri Plant Emporium. We meet the realtor, an energetic young man named Josh, at his office. He insists that we all go in his car, a decision we soon regret because his driving speed is topped only by the speed with which he ticks off the attributes of the thriving floral enterprise we're about to view. He asserts high admiration for Sophie and Sam, the current proprietors, who are now ready to retire and travel the globe. "Sophie is top notch," he gushes. "She knows everything about everyone of any importance."

We pull into the last available parking space in the mall-size parking lot. An enormous barn-style structure looms out in front of us like an elaborate set for the vintage TV show *Green Acres*. There are dozens of men dressed in black tie and tails wandering about.

"A bit overdressed for gardening," Dannie remarks as two women waltz past us, their sequined gowns hiked up above their ankles and their high heels clicking on the pavement.

Josh explains that Sam is a justice of the peace and that it's common to have at least one weekend wedding ceremony on the premises. "The gazebo in back is considered a wedding destination."

"So sorry, so sorry, so sorry!" A giant of a woman wearing yards and yards of violet chiffon rushes over to greet us. "The groom was late, the bride was later, and the flower girl was so excited that the poor thing wet her pants," she blathers, adjusting the billowing white plumes splaying out from her satiny headpiece. "Don't worry yourselves though because at any minute they'll be caravanning on to the reception at the country club, which the father of the bride can well afford, if you know what I mean. He made it big in . . ."

"We can come back another time," Dannie interjects. Josh clears his throat. I can see from the warning in his eyes that interrupting Sophie is a cardinal sin.

"Absolutely not! We'll convene in the barn in twenty minutes. That should be enough time for Josh to give you a tour." She makes a grand gesture with her hand and maneuvers herself back out into the stream of guests like a cruise liner picking up steam.

I'm speechless as Josh leads us down the cedar-mulched pathways that weave through a maze of exotic plantings, bringing us to a gazebo decorated in more white gauze and rose-petal garlands than a Vegas wedding chapel. The barn, which has never seen a lick of livestock, is chock full of a mélange of merchandise, ranging from pricy fine art to cheap souvenirs. We discover Sam, the justice of the peace, and the master gardener in one of the greenhouses tucked away in the rear. Wiry and thin, Sam is an exact opposite of his wife, and he accepts our high praise with a quiet grace.

We listen patiently for more than an hour as the animated Sophie details every aspect of their enterprise.

The asking price is exorbitant, and all I can do is watch with silent awe as Dannie fires forth a multitude of questions. In the end, we shake hands and exchange cards.

"A great piece of property," she reiterates when we say good-bye to Josh.

"Don't tell me we've just agreed to buy that place?" I stammer.

"Not at that price!"

CHAPTER 12

WE CHOOSE TO patronize the only Greek restaurant from a manifesto of local cuisine, a parting gift from Sophie.

I raise my glass of wine. "Here's to a woman who epitomizes the term *full figured*."

"To Sophie, the queen of the sugarplum fairies." Dannie clinks her glass into mine as she nudges my foot under the table. "But I think we've had more than enough business for today."

On the drive to the bed-and-breakfast, we sing along to the greatest hits of Carole King and Harry Chapin. In no real hurry, we take advantage of a scenic outlook on the side of the road and drink in the beauty of a pink and purple striped sky as the setting sun brings down the curtain on the day. "I wish I could paint like that."

*   *   *

Bob and Betty Goff, the elderly couple who own the bed-and-breakfast, have been married forever. They joke about their matching blue shirts and khaki trousers—unplanned, they assure us. "It just happens that way when you've been with someone so long." They even look alike, which I find a bit scary. When they graciously offer us a second room at half price so we can each have more privacy, we convince them that there's no need since we have a lot of girl talk to catch up on.

Dannie recaps their parting remark. "Nothing like an old-fashioned pajama party. Oh yeah—minus the pajamas."

"Shush," I whisper. "They might hear you."

She strips off her clothes. "Shower time."

We slide under the comfy cotton sheets on the four poster bed, our bodies still tingling from the steamy water and scented, foaming bubbles. Instead of the silent, speedy sex I vaguely remember with Ed, our lovemaking is slow and leisurely, full of playful stroking, as we murmur our desires to each other.

All night I spoon up against Dannie, our naked bodies in a continual caress, totally satisfied.

At breakfast we're treated to lavish portions of french toast stuffed with maple cream cheese and walnuts. Our hosts are so happy to hear that we've enjoyed our stay that they insist on packing us a bag lunch for the road.

*　　*　　*

The last two properties on the list are located in the town of Glendale. About five miles from the center of town, we pull into a pea stone driveway. Buffered from the road with a single row of white pine trees sits a red brick cottage. At first I think it must be someone's home, but then I notice the naked dress form poised motionless in the bay window.

The previous tenant had been slow in removing her belongings and the realtor is apologetic when she opens the front door. Scraps of fabric, wads of thread, and hundreds of common pins are scattered on the honey-colored floor like a mixed-media collage. The living room in a previous life, it had been converted into a sewing space for the "Unique Boutique." It's definitely zoned for business, but where is the greenhouse? It's obvious that Dannie isn't interested in looking any further at the property, because she's become engrossed in a conversation with the realtor about current market trends. While they chat I explore.

The craftsman-style wainscoting and solid wood trim is displayed throughout the house. The two bedrooms are spacious; the bath and kitchen have vintage fixtures but are in good condition. I ignore the dirty dishes and empty food containers cluttering the countertop—further evidence of the delinquent tenant—and open the back door. A blast of blistering heat shoots into the kitchen. Ah, the greenhouse, or rather the hothouse. The glass structure is fashioned from old doors and windows and sealed against the back side of the cottage—an ideal passive solar system in the winter, but almost unbearable at the moment. The two rows of varnished tables up against the walls are in mint condition, the cement floor is swept clean, and the glass panels are spotless. I slide back the bolt and open the outside door to release some of the heat. *This must have been farmland*, I think, looking out over the unkempt fields delineated by walls of indigenous stone.

"Very curious," I say out loud. Centered in the knee-high grass, tangle of wildflowers, and weeds—like a gem in a rag bag—is an immaculately cared-for flowerbed.

"Hotter than hell in here!" Dannie's voice startles me. I spin around and the door slams shut behind me. "Not quite what we had in mind," she clicks her tongue, "but the next place, a small turnkey florist in the center of town, sounds very interesting."

*   *   *

The Lazy Daisy is adorable. Sandwiched between what was once a Methodist church, now some kind of nondenominational meetinghouse, and the regional middle/high school, it resembles a restful comma in the middle of two tall exclamation points. The parking lots of both buildings have cars streaming from the exits, the conclusion of Sunday morning worship.

We duck into a donut shop across the street for a cup of coffee and wait until the congestion has sorted itself out, and the young couple, the current managers of the shop, have a chance to return home and escape from their Sunday duds.

Owned by an entrepreneur who has permanently moved to England, the Lazy Daisy is being operated by Caleb and Lydia Paige, barely out of high school, newlyweds who don't have two pennies to rub together nor a clue on how to run a business. Not much older than 'Ria. With a pang of guilt, I wonder if they'll end up on the street if we buy the place.

The pang only gets stronger when we meet them and I'm drawn to their genuine good-heartedness.

"Location, location, location," Dannie chimes out as we drive back to the Water's Edge. The two-day journey has taken us in a complete circle, and we're only a little more than an hour away.

She prattles on. "Of course we'd need to cultivate, pardon the pun, additional clientele. I mean it may be convenient, but it's not at all healthy for the church next door to provide almost half of their yearly income."

It's obvious that Dannie is intrigued by the Lazy Daisy. When we stop at a Chinese restaurant for dinner, she spouts off like a proverbial advertisement. I stuff moo shu pork into my egg and flour pancake and listen as she brainstorms—expansion, marketing, business loans. When she asks me what I think, my lame reply ranges somewhere between affection and bewilderment. "I can see the potential, but there's so much to consider."

"Poor Fern." She touches my cheek. "I forget that this is all new to you."

When we arrive back at the Water's Edge, she wants to go back to her room and crunch some numbers, but I need some fresh air to clear my head. We table business until later and take a short hike to the bog on the south side of the lake.

This is a huge mistake since both of us neglect to put on long pants, and we're immediately attacked by a swarm of mosquitoes. We hustle through the mossy bog while the tenacious bugs nip at our legs and faces.

"Charming," I mutter, slapping at my neck.

"Not." Dannie snorts. "I vote for a quick getaway."

"Second that."

In the dining room, we find Jonas and Professor Ben raiding the kitchen for burrito fixings. They offer to share their snack with us, but I'm ready for some alone time.

"Sleep on it," Dannie suggests.

Even though my head is relieved that we opt not to sleep on it together, my body longs for her touch. In reality, sleep is out of the question, so I brew a cup of tea and shuffle through the file folders from our weekend travels.

The defunct funeral home is relegated to the bottom of the pile, along with Sophie and Sam's emporium. I fan the other three out on the desk. The most realistic choice would be the Lazy Daisy or the former Bloom 'n' Buds. With colored pencils, I doodle a couple of drooping black-eyed susans on the front cover of the first, and on the second I sketch a bouquet of flawless red rosebuds in a vase of cut crystal.

I sort through the contents of the third folder and find a picture of the brick-front cottage. I recall the fields of wild flora growing behind the greenhouse. My pencil illustrations expand to a full palette of paint. I brush in stone walls corralling hoards of delicate white Queen Anne's lace, fiery gold jewel weed and rosepink bitterbloom. Embellishing the memory, I snake in a ribbon of bubbling water edged with wild geraniums, ground pine, and fiddleheads. The brook spills into a pond where water lilies unfurl on their gleaming green pads. Obsessed with my ruminations, I'm not satisfied until the entire folder, both front and back, is a panoramic vista of a riotous country landscape. When I'm finished, I gather up the sheaf of papers that have fallen on to the floor—the MLS listing, a detailed map of the area, and a copy of the local newspaper—and stack them into the open folder: the painted paradise.

$$* \quad * \quad *$$

On Monday morning, I get up early to water the blueberry bushes. Julian pokes his head out of the kitchen door. "Hey." I wave as I prop up a renegade raspberry cane. He disappears, returning a moment later with a book in his hand. It's an encyclopedia-size volume on herbs, savory recipes included. I thumb through the pages. "This is a great reference."

"Check out the photo illustrations, I won't even poison anyone by mistake," he chuckles.

He doesn't seem in any hurry to get back to the kitchen, so I tell him about the maple cream cheese french toast we'd sampled at the bed-and-breakfast.

"I know I have that recipe somewhere." He promises to put it on the breakfast menu later in the week.

"Did you have a good weekend?" I ask.

"I picked up my kids. Their mom and I are separated, and they'll be staying with me for the week. They're spending the day with their grandparents, but I'm sure you'll see them around. Well, I'd better get back to work."

During breakfast we're informed that Pammy and Tom have defected to a water ski resort, Flo and Jean have departed to search elsewhere for kiddie activities, and Marc has been called away on a family emergency.

Jonas hand me a lipstick-red envelope. "For you, Fern."

"A love letter?" Sonja asks tersely.

It's a card from Dannie. I know that my face flushes when I view the erotic picture on the front. Inside: "Decided to sleep in. Wish your sweet self was here. Meet me in my room after lunch?"

Our small groups have been suspended, at least until Marc returns, so everyone gathers in Sonja's room for a little light yoga. I concentrate on my breathing and disregard the antagonistic vibes that spark and crackle every time Sonja approaches me. Even though my mind is empty, my body is full of delicious anticipation.

*   *   *

Her room elicits an atmosphere of business more than a space of retreat. Stacks of papers and files hem in her computer on the desk like bookends. Multiple pages with pie charts and spread sheets cover most of the bed; these she scoops up and shoves into an expandable folder.

Our fervent embrace leads to the shedding of our clothes and a tumble into bed.

"Sweet Fern." She nuzzles my hair affectionately as we lay nestled amid her silky satin sheets—brought from home.

Sometime later I awake, alone in the bed. Dannie is fully dressed and at her desk, scanning papers and making notes. Her focus is on the business at hand and my attempts to distract her fail, so I get myself dressed and we contemplate the possibilities of each property.

She barely notices the distinctive doodles on the front covers of Lazy Daisy and Bloom 'n' Buds, and it isn't until we've unanimously decided to discard the freaky funeral home—too little to work with—and Sophie's place—too much—that I realize I'd neglected to bring my file for the brick cottage.

"I guess it's really a toss-up between Daisy and Bloom," I say, trying to be helpful.

"'Toss-up' is a bit flippant, don't you think?" She peers at me from above her reading glasses. Her face becomes instantly serious, her response stone cold, like she's addressing a corporate sponsor, not a tender lover. "The implication of this decision is contingent on whether you want to settle for taking over someone else's mess or starting from scratch."

She ticks off each option as if neither one is to her liking. Despite my nap, I suddenly feel weary. "Well, what do you think?" I finally ask.

"Perhaps my realtor can unearth some additional listings," she says, almost to herself.

"Are we going on the canoe expedition tonight?" I ask lightly, hoping to change the subject.

"Not this 'we,'" she retorts. "I've got a mountain of paperwork to sort through and several phone calls to make. This kind of proposition doesn't just happen by itself you know." Her tone sets me on edge and I decide I should leave before I go and put my foot in it again.

*   *   *

I'm unusually taciturn at dinner. Everyone else is merrily discussing their weekend adventures. When Karin asks me what Dannie and I did,

I mumble something about touring the adjacent towns. Sonja sidles up to our table and spouts off about how Dannie is eating in her room because she's *so* busy researching a new investment project. She throws me a scathing look—bitch.

"You are in some kind of funk, girl." Davy jostles my elbow as we flip over the canoes for our evening excursion on the lake.

"I don't want to talk about it."

"Be my bowman," Geraldine suggests, gently steering me in the direction of her canoe. She respects my reticence and we paddle silently as I try to concentrate on the soft night air and the star-filled sky. But even the gentle cooing of the mourning doves does little to dispel the uneasy suspicion that is growing in the center of my gut.

CHAPTER 13

O N TUESDAY MORNING, I see an unfamiliar form slung across the bench in the garden. A pile of laundry? No, a body; a live one I hope.

"Don't let me disturb you," I say gently. "I'm just going to water the strawberries." The body moans and rolls over, revealing the pimply face of a teenage boy. Both arms fling up to shield his eyes from the offending sunshine. I set the sprinkler in the strawberry patch and begin to pull up a few weeds around the raspberries. My finger catches on a thorn. "Shit!" I hear a snigger. I look up to see that the boy in black is now awake, a smirk plastered across his smart-aleck face.

"Need some help?" he asks.

"That'd be great," I say. "If we cover the ground with pine needles, it might keep these weeds in check." Before he can respond, I snatch up two large garbage bags from the kitchen landing and head toward the woods. He follows me. I'm not sure why, but I'm never sure why adolescents do what they do. When we get to the pine grove we stop abruptly. Trotting away from us is a red fox and her two young kits. She turns her head at our approach and hurriedly ushers her children into the safety of the underbrush.

"Cool." I can hear a trace of the little-boy wonder in his voice.

"Yes," I agree and begin loading up one of the bags with pine needles. Out of the corner of my eye, I see him pick up the other bag and start stuffing. When they are full, we sling them over our shoulders and carry them up the path. I know the bag must be heavy for him; it is for me.

"Santa friggin' Claus," he mutters.

I show him how to spread a thin layer of needles over the moist ground, densely packing them around the staked vines.

"Thanks," I say when we're finished. "My name's Fern." I extend my hand.

"Devin," he answers, frowning at the sticky sap on his own hands.

"A dab of peanut butter will clean that right off."

"I'll get some from Pop."

Pop? Ah, one of Julian's kids. I watch as he skulks away toward the kitchen.

*   *   *

I meet up with Devin again at breakfast, along with his younger sister, Tina. They're helping their dad serve.

"Did the peanut butter do the trick?" I ask as he lays a stack of banana pancakes on my plate.

"Yup."

I note the perplexed look on Julian's face. I simply smile and thank Devin for the pancakes.

I'm not at all surprised when Dannie doesn't appear at breakfast or at our Tuesday morning class. I've begun to realize how completely focused she can become, especially about business. A whisper of guilt tugs at me. I know that she's probably up in her room toiling away on the project. "Dannie's new project." Sonja's words ring out in my head like a gong. Is that what I am, a project?

"You're up next, Fern." Karin nudges my shoulder. It's my turn at the wheel. Allison, a local artisan, is substituting for Marc and teaching us how to use a potter's wheel.

My last experience with clay was almost twenty years ago, molding Christmas ornaments with 'Ria out of a flour and water concoction. It's a good thing we're all wearing industrial-size smocks, because my first attempt to manipulate the saturated blob of spinning clay results in a splattered mess.

Davy twitters affectionately, "Fern looks so cute all decorated with spots." He flicks one of the earthy dots off my cheek.

I try again, a little slower this time, and I succeed in forming a wobbly globe. I push a small hole into the center and voilà, it's a vase—sort of.

Our clay creations are carefully packed into a crate for transport to Allison's studio. They'll be fired up in her kiln and tomorrow we'll apply iridescent glazes. By the end of the week, we'll have stunning ceramic treasures to take home. *Stunning* may be a bit of an overstatement. With the exception of Sue, whose innate talent has fashioned a perfectly symmetrical bowl, most of us have only managed to produce lopsided earthenware.

"I think I'll stick to pinch pots," Geraldine exclaims good naturedly.

Dannie makes a belated appearance at lunch, just as I'm finishing one of Tina's frosted gingerbread cookies. She's flanked on both sides by Sonja and a couple of sorority sisters. They're all chattering away like a family of sparrows. I wave when she glances in my direction. I'm almost certain that I see her mouth the word *later*. I nod my head up and down like a bobble head doll.

"Want another cookie?" Karin asks, holding out the plate. "There's one left."

"No thanks. I think I've had enough."

Karin continues in a mournful voice. "I can't believe there are only four more days until we go home. Didn't we just get here?"

*   *   *

Back in my room, I wait. Wait for what? "Who am I, Cinder-friggin'-ella, waiting for my prince to breeze in?" I clear my work space, intending to do some sketching, and I come across the file folder for the brick-front cottage. After admiring my elaborate handiwork on the outside, I scan the contents.

The *Glendale Gazette* dated only a week ago has all the dramatic headlines of small-town life. There's a report from the public works department detailing future road construction, a notice that the library board has made the decision to expand its computer room, and a full-page article extolling how the middle/high school has collaborated with other schools across the country to develop yet another innovative teaching technique. How many times during my twenty years in education had I heard that song and dance? A great idea that usually fizzled out about the time the kids were required to take those god-awful standardized tests. I turn to the help-wanted advertisements and read down the list. "Well now," I say to the empty room. "What do you think of that?"

*   *   *

The note I tape to my door is an afterthought, and I nearly tear it down: *Went to the lake.* "She'll find me if she wants to," I say to myself.

Devin is once again lying in stately repose on the bench, his nose tucked into a computer game.

"I'm off for a canoe ride, want to come along?" The question is out of my mouth before I've given it any thought.

"What?" He's a thousand miles away.

"A canoe ride." I almost say *on the lake* but think better of it. "I wouldn't mind the company," I add, realizing that I really wouldn't mind the company.

"I don't know how to row," he stammers.

"No problem. You can paddle in the bow, I mean the front, and I'll do all the navigating from the stern, the back."

"I need to tell Pop." He disappears into the kitchen.

He sticks his head out the door. "Can Tina come too?"

"OK by me if it's OK by you."

We're a curious-looking trio lurching across the sparkling water. My straw hat flops in the breeze as I try to coordinate my smooth strokes with Devin's uneven water hoeing. He wipes the sweat on his face with his wrinkled Grateful Dead shirt and remains stone silent as he concentrates on his paddle. Tina is dressed in a designer short set and looks like she belongs on the cover of *Jr. Miss.* She's lounging in the middle of the canoe, trailing her hand through the water.

"Lily pads." She points to a floating carpet of green.

The heart-shaped leaves swish against the bottom of the canoe as we glide through. I show Devin how to hover the canoe by holding the paddle tight against the gunwale, so Tina can pluck out a white lily. I tell her she'll need to put it in water as soon as we get back, and that she shouldn't be surprised if it closes up during the night.

"Sure is hot out here," Devin complains.

I flick a spray of water on to his back with my paddle. "Oops."

"Hey!" he cries out, but I can tell he's not really upset.

A flock of geese fly over our heads in V formation.

"Why do they look like a check mark?" Tina asks.

"Optimum aerodynamics." I explain how the geese take turns leading the flock so the others can rest.

Devin turns to look at me. "What are you, a teacher or something?"

"As a matter of fact I am." We're in the middle of the lake and the sun is baking down on us. "You're right, it sure is hot out here." There's no mistaking the challenge in my voice.

Devin takes the bait and flips his paddle up, but instead of a trickle of water, he scoops up a bucketful and soaks both Tina and me. "Oops."

"Game on!" The three of us splash water at each other until we're all drenched. I finally caution them to steady the canoe before we flip over. We arrive at the beach dripping wet and slosh our way back to the lodge, where we are met by an astonished Julian.

"I take full responsibility," I apologize as we ring ourselves out.

Devin and Tina laugh. "Thanks, Fern," they say.

"I don't remember the last time I heard Devin laugh," Julian says. "You have great kids."

"Fern!" Dannie is hailing me from the dining room terrace.

"I guess I'd better go and get changed."

*   *   *

"Have fun?" Dannie asks when we're back in my room.

"Even more if you'd been with us." I pull on a dry cotton top and a clean pair of shorts.

"Well, I had business . . ." she begins to say but I cut her off.

"About that." I try to keep my voice under control as I trundle on. "I feel badly that you're spending so much time on our *project*." The word falters on my lips. "I really do appreciate your generous offer to set me up in business, but I was hoping that we could wait at least until the retreat is over before pursuing it any further?" I rush on. "We only have four more days to enjoy this beautiful place, and I really miss hiking, canoeing, and, you know, just being with you."

"Have you changed your mind about the flower shop?"

"Not exactly, but I do need more time to think it through." I choose my words carefully. "We are more than just a business project, aren't we?"

"This business project is for you. I'm doing all of this for you, Fern." She raises her voice. "But I guess you're really not all that interested."

Before I can object, she walks out the door.

*   *   *

"How's it going, Mom?" As soon as I hear my daughter's cheery voice, I begin to sob uncontrollably into the phone. I babble incoherently about screwing up every relationship I've ever had, and about the big mess I've made with Dannie.

"Chill, Mom," she blurts out when I pause to take a breath. "First of all, Dad was the one who screwed up, not you, and as far as this Dannie guy is concerned, you've known him for what, all of three seconds? Do I need to come down there and straighten him out?"

The absurdity of her question causes me to burst into hysterics from which I quickly recover, because I realize I'm probably frightening my poor child half to death. After a few shuddering breaths, I promise her that I really haven't lost my mind.

"I warned Gram and Gramps that this retreat might be too intense for you. My therapist even agreed that three weeks of heavy-duty catharsis could be just as powerful as detox."

"You're seeing a therapist?" Where had I been that I didn't know my little girl was in therapy? Hiding out in a tiny studio apartment at a convent, that's where.

"What exactly has been going on at the Water's Edge," 'Ria asks impatiently.

I convince her that it's been far from torture. I describe the lake, the hiking trails, the amazing wildlife . . .

"OK, Mom, I get it; you're having a life-changing experience. I only hope that you're preparing yourself to re-enter the real world."

"Maybe I won't re-enter." The authenticity of what I just said blows me away.

"Don't be ridiculous. You can't live at the Water's Edge indefinitely."

"Oh, I'm aware of that." I don't even try to explain Jonas's residential status. "But all this catharsis, as you call it, has motivated me to rethink what I've been doing with my life." I know I must sound like some kind of self-help guru, but the truth of what I'm saying wells up from my very soul like a newborn geyser.

"Just know that I love you, Mom," she says when we say good-bye. The empathy in my daughter's voice envelopes me like a cosmic hug.

If I don't go back to my real world, where do I go? Do I quit my job and open a flower shop with Dannie? Maybe now that's not even an option.

I grasp the miniature house ornament from the desk. I hold it in front of me like a magic talisman and pace the perimeter of the room until I'm nearly dizzy with confusion. I flop down on the bed and clutch the cottony sarong close to my body. Propped up against the opposite wall, bold with optimism and confidence, is the painting—*My Heart's Desire*. I open my journal and flip through the pictures I've sketched, the one-eyed bird, dead and buried beneath the rosemary; the moose calf, poised insecure and afraid on the shoreline. I fan out the file folders from the Lazy Daisy, the Bloom 'n' Buds, and the brick-front cottage; I even dare to dig the masks out from the desk draw. Surrounded by all I've created, I search for an answer.

The sun is low in the sky when the inkling of an idea dawns upon me. "Anyway," I say out loud. "It's a place to start."

"Fern?" Davy is at my door. "Are you feeling all right? We missed you at dinner. Geraldine and I brought you a salad and a piece of spinach and cheese quiche."

"There are fresh peaches for dessert," Geraldine adds. "We'll just leave it by the door in case you're busy or not up for company. We don't want to bother . . ."

I open the door before she finishes.

"You two are angels. Please come in."

Davy looks for a place to put the tray. "One angel, one fairy."

"Sorry about all this." I begin to stack up my art work.

Davy picks up the picture of the moose. "Girl, you sure can paint." He kisses me on the cheek. "Well, I'm off to meet Tony and discuss paint chips and fabric swatches. We're redecorating his condo next week."

"Can you stay for a moment?" I ask Geraldine "I need a second opinion."

"I think it's a great idea," she says after I've explained my plan. "And I think you shouldn't wait. Jonas has a fax machine. You can send it out first thing in the morning.

CHAPTER 14

I WAKE UP ON Wednesday with renewed energy. It's a morning of possibilities—of my own choosing. *Steady on, Fern*, I tell myself, *the position may already be filled*. Anxious to set my plan in motion, I run down to the kitchen and knock on the door.

"Any chance I can get a muffin to go?"

"Fresh from the oven." Julian holds the tray in his hot mitts and invites me to sit down.

"So where is Sir Devin?" I ask, scooting a stool next to Tina.

Tina swallows her mouthful of scrambled eggs. "Still in bed. He needs his beauty sleep so he can take me out in a canoe later."

I bite into my sweet, moist cake. Heavenly. "Don't forget to wear your life jackets." I wipe my mouth and breathe in the comfy baking aromas of the warm kitchen. "Thanks for the muffin."

The phone number I punch in actually connects me with a real, live person and our conversation is very encouraging. After several harrowing moments pushing buttons on Jonas's fax machine, I've accomplished my mission. I put in one final call to 'Ria. "The crisis is over," I record on my daughter's voice mail. "We'll talk when I get home. I love you too."

Jonas had assured me that I could sneak into class even if I was a little late. "I'll be boring everyone senseless with my master's thesis," he said. "Music through the ages." I arrive just in time to hear the familiar strains of "Hey Jude." Jonas finishes his presentation with an example of contemporary chance music by John Cage.

"I'll take the Beatles over John Cage any day," Fred comments when class is over and we're standing in the lunch line.

"That avant-garde stuff is a bit tough on the ears," Karin agrees.

Maybe it's the music, maybe it's the company, or maybe it's my optimism about my future prospects, but I find myself smiling with genuine happiness that doesn't even waver when I see Dannie eating lunch with Sonja.

Here goes nothing. I walk over to their table and set my tray down directly opposite them. "Hey, you two, how was your morning?"

"Great!" Sonja grins like a piranha. "I'm expanding my studio and so I've been spending night and day with my personal consultant." She drapes a possessive claw around Dannie's shoulders.

"Congratulations." My mouth is open, but it's John who speaks the felicitation. He and Sue are making themselves comfortable on my right.

"What are we celebrating?" Geraldine asks as she and Davy settle cozily on my left.

"Dannie, my dear, where have you been keeping yourself?" Karin drops herself down on the other side of Dannie, blatantly ignoring Sonja's exasperated expression.

Dannie looks at Karin, then at me, her face flickering from mild indifference to downright amusement.

I look gratefully around at my well-meaning advocates, shrug, and shovel a forkful of salad into my mouth.

With only three days remaining of our retreat, the dining room is a swirl with conversation as folks begin to discuss their future plans.

"It's been a great time," Karin spouts, "and I sure will miss Julian's culinary talents. "It's a shame that kidnapping is illegal."

"What about you, Fern?" Davy asks.

"Pardon?"

"What will you miss the most?"

To my dismay, my eyes stray in Dannie's direction; however, she is fastidiously stirring whipped cream into her Grape-Nuts pudding, oblivious to my presence.

*   *   *

Since canoeing on the lake and hiking in the woods had been my response to Davy's question, after lunch I hit the trail. The cool shade is a relief from the midday heat, and I languish along the well-worn pathway up to the ledges. The last two and a half weeks of daily exercise, fresh air, and sunshine have toned my muscles, tempered my lungs, and tanned my skin. Physically I am as agile and strong as a mountain lion; emotionally I am as clumsy and weak as a newborn kitten.

"Why not just tell her?" I say out loud.

The chipmunk, collecting seeds on a nearby rock, chirps in alarm and scampers back to the safety of his hole.

Tell her what? That I want us to be more than a one-night stand? Wasn't she the one who alluded to a long-term commitment? But she lives in New York City and I live, well, who knows where I'll be living. And what about Sonja? I clap my hand over my mouth to stifle a giggle. Directly in front of me, with the drawstring of his safari hat tied neatly beneath his chin, his crew socks pulled nearly up to his knees, is the good professor.

"Shush." Ben passes me his binoculars and points in the direction of a gnarly old oak tree. In the crook of the highest branch is a screech owl, sound asleep, its sienna feathered wings blanketed tightly around its body.

"So rare to see them during the daylight," I whisper.

"Lots of searching and careful attention," he says, "but it's worth it."

I leave him to study his discovery and continue on my way. When I reach the top of the ledges I'm once again awestruck by the incredible vista. I watch a lone turkey buzzard soar on the wind current, flying solo, unencumbered and free in the wide open space. Where is its mate? Does it even have a mate? I think of the wide open possibilities that await me when I leave the Water's Edge. I'll certainly miss this view. Yes, I'll miss the lake, the woods, the garden; I'll miss Davy's jovial antics, Lucy's peaceful countenance, Julian's phenomenal cooking, and I'll miss Dannie.

Stop it, I reprimand myself. Just enjoy these last few days at this amazing place. Stop acting like some love-sick teenager. Oh, yes, Devin and Tina—I'll miss them too.

* * *

Not long after I've returned to my room, the phone rings. It's the call I was hoping for.

"I look forward to meeting with you too. Good-bye."

I share my news with Geraldine. She's thrilled, and promises to cover for me while I'm gone. I'm glad she understands why I don't want anyone else to know. I'm not sure I understand it myself.

We spend the remainder of the afternoon applying colorful glazes to our ceramic creations. I bathe my clumsy excuse of a vase in a teal satin gloss. Allison guarantees a miraculous transformation after the second firing. "You'll hardly recognize your own work."

"It's practically a stranger to me now," Davy laughs, gesturing to his own clay sculpture.

* * *

"Game night tonight!" Jonas announces at dinner.

Sorry. That's the name of the game written on the slip of paper I draw from Jonas's top hat. It also informs me that I'm on team number two. We're playing board games, with the twist that every ten minutes we move on to a different game and take the place of another member of our team. It's even more complicated because the odd-number teams move clockwise and the even-number teams move counterclockwise. John, my team leader and a serious game player, huddles us together to plot out winning strategies.

"So sorry," BJ says to me as he knocks me back to my starting space. "Not."

"Switch!" Jonas calls out.

Karin chatters nonstop about her cribbage club as we bump each other on and off the Parcheesi board. "We all drink gin and tonics until we're soused," she boasts, "except for MaryAnn, our designated driver. She sucks down tomato juice laced with hot sauce. The woman has a stomach of steel."

During the game of Trouble, Sonja gets a phone call she "absolutely must take" and Julian sits in as her substitute. "How was the kids' canoe trip?" I ask him.

"You've inspired them," he tells me. "They packed a lunch and spent most of the day paddling about the lake. They wanted to know if you had any free time tomorrow so you could go with them."

"Tomorrow might be tricky." I pause. "Maybe after dinner?"

Even though I'm painfully aware of Dannie the entire night, we don't end up at the same game until the final round—Monopoly. The brilliant team member prior to me had purchased Park Place and Broadway and loaded them with hotels, so I sit back like a cutthroat landlord and bankrupt all the other players.

"A hell of a business woman," Dannie remarks as she watches me add up my millions.

Together we pack up the play money and plastic game pieces. "Got a minute?" I ask.

"Only a minute? Walk with me."

The dark sky is awash with stars and once again we watch as a pinpoint of light streaks across the sky.

Dannie moves closer. "All we need now is old Tchaikovsky's overture."

I miss you is what I want to say; instead, what comes out of my mouth explodes into the stillness like canon fire. "I take it you and Sonja are back together again."

Dannie steps away from me, her arms folded across her chest.

"Sorry, that was totally uncalled for." I try to backtrack. "I know I'm a disappointment to you because I'm so tentative about our business proposition, but . . ."

"Stop apologizing, for god's sake. You're just being honest. I like that about you. There are a great many things I like about you, and they have nothing to do with any kind of business proposition. I should be the one to apologize. I made the mistake of riding to your rescue on my entrepreneurial white horse."

"You think I need to be rescued?"

"Well, you were always moaning about your job. I thought I could help."

"My job? Yes, well, I'm working on that."

"Oh?"

I'm not ready to tell her so I evade her questioning eyes and take her hand. "You're a talented and successful business woman, but I'm not looking for a business partner."

Her face softens. "I get it," she teases. "You're only after my body."

"No, well, yes, I mean . . ."

"You don't want my body?"

"Yes, but I want us to be more."

Dannie pulls her hand away. "We've had a great time together here at the Water's Edge," she says, "but in two days I'll be going back to my work in the city, and you'll be going back to your job, your daughter . . ."

"And we won't ever see each other again?"

"I can't answer that." She links her arm in mine. "What I can say is that I want to spend as much of the next two days with you as possible."

"I guess I can live with that. Shall we begin tomorrow with an early morning canoe?"

"Why wait until tomorrow?" She winks. "I may need a wakeup call."

"OK," I laugh. "I'll give you a wakeup call—up close and personal."

*   *   *

Neither one of us wake up until the gong sounds off its own wakeup call.

"Damn thing conjures up scenes from *The King and I*," Dannie grumbles. "Every time I hear it I expect to see Yul Brynner waltz into the room."

"Shall we dance?" I bow.

"Who'll lead?"

"We can take turns."

We drift over to the window. It's a perfect summer day, bright blue sky, sun on the water, clear, fresh air.

"I'm still up for that morning canoe," I say. "Early or not. Can you play hooky this morning or do you have business?"

"Don't even say the word!" She jostles me back on to the bed.

It's another hour before we're finally dressed and ready to leave. We score some muffins and juice for a floating breakfast and a slice of bread for the ducks. Tina and Devin make me promise to go for a hike around the lake with them. Devin wants to see more cool critters.

"Dawn or dusk is the best time," I tell them. Devin screws up his face. "A night hike it is."

After we've fed ourselves and the ducks, Dannie and I explore some of the tributaries that feed into the lake. "I need to get back pretty soon," I say, glancing at my watch.

"You have a hot date or something?"

"Something like that. Actually, I have an appointment this afternoon."

"An appointment? Sounds a bit mysterious."

"That's me." I smile, lifting my paddle and spraying her with water. "A woman of mystery."

CHAPTER 15

CHARGED UP WITH nervous energy, I'm showered, dressed, and on the road in record time. The air conditioner is cranked up to maximum and I pray that my deodorant lives up to its claim to keep my white cotton blouse super dry. My legs feel confined in the long pants clinging to my thighs, and a part of me wants to turn around, shed my grown-up clothes, and retreat into the woods. I fidget with the wampum shell around my neck—a good-luck token from Geraldine—and drive on, retracing the very same route that Dannie and I traversed four days ago.

Welcome to Glendale. Even though this is only my second journey down Main Street, I'm impressed by the sense of familiarity that washes over me as I pass the Lazy Daisy. On the marquee at the stone church is Sunday's sermon title: "Satan Is in the Heat of the Moment." In contrast, the donut shop across the street is inviting everyone to "indulge in a frozen latte." I make a left turn into the parking lot of the Jenkins Regional School. Behind the school, there is an athletic field and an outdoor swimming pool. I stand by my car for a moment and drink in the ambiance of children squealing and splashing as they cool themselves off in the heat of the day. The normality of the scene hits home and I feel like I've been sequestered on some foreign planet for about a hundred years.

Like many schools built in the early twentieth century, the original structure has been annexed over time with several updated wings. I smile as I climb the wide granite steps and use the *Boys'* entrance. *Girls'* is carved into a similar stone above the door on the opposite end of the building. Regardless of clean carpets, fresh paint, and contemporary light fixtures, the aroma of chalkboards, floor wax, and mimeograph ink still leaks out from the saturated walls and greets me like an old friend. I breathe in with gratitude and ask a girl with a ring in her nose for directions to the principal's office. Why there are so many kids milling about?

"Summer session," the perceptive young man sitting at the reception desk explains. According to the plaque on his desk, his name is Jon Smith and he's the administrative assistant. "May I help you?"

"Fern DeGiulio. I have an appointment with Dr. Jenkins."

He scrolls down the schedule on his computer screen. "Yes, Dr. Jenkins and Dr. Rosa are expecting you."

Instead of being barricaded behind an authoritative oak desk, Dr. Timothy Jenkins is seated in a comfortable leather arm chair at a marble top round table. He rises immediately when I enter. Stout in stature and built like a linebacker, his face displays a diversity of nuances. There are well-worn dimples in his cheeks and creases in his face that suggest jovial outbursts, but in his bright blue eyes there's a glint of steel that I imagine can discern the naked truth in any situation. In contrast, Dr. Marilyn Rosa is without a doubt the most beautiful woman I've ever seen. Nearly a head taller than Dr. Jenkins, she draws herself out of her chair with the grace and poise of a woman secure in who she is. Her bronze body is clothed in a bold, flowery print. Her Jamaican accent is as luxurious as the silk scarf encircling her hair.

Dr. Jenkins and Dr. Rosa have been the co-principals at Jenkins for the last ten years. They've been a happily married couple for the past twenty.

"Ms. DeGiulio, how wonderful to make your acquaintance." Dr. Rosa flashes a lovely smile and enfolds my hand in hers. It's been weeks since anyone has used my surname.

"We are indeed impressed by your resume." Dr. Jenkins's hand shake is firm and his eyes never leave mine. "I've spoken to both the principal at the junior high school and the headmaster at Saint Barnabas. Apparently they miss you greatly at the junior high and wanted me to pass along the message that the garden still grows." He raises his eyebrows in question. There is amusement in his voice as he continues. "However, even though the headmaster at Saint Barnabas gave you high marks as a teacher, he warned me about a grievance filed against you by a custodian—an incident involving compost in the classroom?"

"Container gardens," I start to clarify, but Dr. Jenkins flicks his hand.

"Never mind," he chuckles. "Saint Barnabas is a fine school, but I believe when it comes to educational innovation it operates in a previous century. Someday you can tell me the whole story. What really intrigues us is this student organization you initiated, the Grub Club?"

As we talk about the club and share anecdotes from our years of scholarly adventures, I recognize a mutual affection in their voices and I know that I am in good company.

"How did you hear about Jenkins?" Dr. Rosa asks at the end of the interview.

I explain that I'm attending a creative arts retreat at the Water's Edge, and I'd come across Glendale's local newspaper.

Dr. Rosa smiles. "So you're also an artist."

"I'm only an amateur."

"One who does something purely for the love of it," she defines, nodding her head in affirmation.

They offer me a full-time position teaching the earth sciences. I accept.

They escort me through the halls. "Are you familiar with this area?" Dr. Jenkins opens the door to a well-equipped science room.

I try not to drool. I mention that a friend of mine and I had been exploring nearby towns for business possibilities. "We looked at the Lazy Daisy and a place called the Unique Boutique."

Dr. Jenkins laughs. "We know the place well."

I assume that he is talking about the Lazy Daisy because of its proximity to the school, but no; he begins to describe in detail the brick cottage—the Unique Boutique. It turns out that the house belonged to his late Uncle Joe and was part of the original family homestead. Joseph and his brother, William Jenkins, were the venerable founders of the Jenkins School.

"Uncle Joe passed on a few years ago, but Uncle Willie still lives next door," Dr. Jenkins continues. "The rest of the farm land was donated to the Nature Conservancy. I think Willie secretly hopes that Marilyn and I will move into Joe's house—keep it in the family—but we're happy where we are.

Our meeting ends with the promise to exchange e-mails when I return home from the Water's Edge.

Exhausted but exhilarated when I'm on the road again, I find I just can't help myself. As if drawn in by an invisible magnet, I turn into the driveway of the brick cottage. I don't really mean to get out of the car, just take a quick peek, but before I know it, I find myself wandering around to the back of the house, once again admiring the tidy greenhouse. I squat down to examine the recently turned soil. The pungent smell of marigolds beckons in welcome. All I need now is my straw hat. My foot disturbs one of the rocks lining the edge of the flower bed. Not an ordinary rock, but an agate the size of a golf ball. I rub the dirt from the glossy ebony and ivory striations and slip the smooth stone into my pocket. I gaze back at the house. The greenhouse glass fractures the late afternoon sun, enchanting the back wall with prism slivers of dancing light.

"Home." The word slips out quite naturally as I turn to leave. "Just wish I had someone to share it with."

"What you need is a cat," the friendly voice calls out from behind me. Not a cat, but the wet, sloppy tongue of dog gently laps at my hand.

Surprised but somehow not alarmed, I pat the head of the black Labrador now flapping his tail at my side. "A dog advising me to get a cat?" I say. "How very open minded of you."

The elderly gentleman belonging to the dog approaches me, walking stick in one hand, cap in the other, and a calico feline weaving back and forth between his legs. "A dog or a cat will prevent folks from thinking that you're soft in the head when you talk to yourself," he says.

"Well it looks like you've got one of each."

"Eliot here is one of the most attentive listeners in the cosmos." Hearing his name, the dog bounds back to his master's side.

"And who is this?" I ask as the cat rubs affectionately against my calf.

"May I present Ivy League—Ivy to her friends, and clearly she already considers you a friend."

"Hello, Ivy." She regards me for a moment, blinks her eyes, scampers over to the greenhouse, and disappears through a cleverly concealed door flap.

The truth dawns on me. "This is her home," I say, "and you must be Uncle Willie."

"At your service, young lady." He bows. "And you must be psychic or something?"

"Fern. Fern DeGiulio. And I'm actually not clairvoyant; I've just come from an interview with your nephew."

"Well I'm glad he had the good sense to hire you," Willie says after I tell him about my new job. We discuss the joys of teaching and the possibility of me buying the cottage until Eliot begins to nudge Willie's walking stick.

"Eliot's stomach is his clock. It must be time for kibble." Willie fits his cap back on his head. "Good-bye for now, neighbor."

I watch the two of them stroll away. Neighbor? He sounded so sure. Why not?

*   *   *

I return to the Water's Edge in time to snag a piece of Julian's gorgonzola and mushroom pizza before Tina and Devin whisk me away for our evening hike. They've invited Dannie to join us.

"You must be very, very quiet," Devin advises his sister. With the stealth and agility of a Navy SEAL, he leads the way to the bog. We climb aboard a large boulder and try to stay as still as possible. The minutes click by, the mosquitoes buzz about our heads, and our necks ache from cranking them around whenever we hear the slightest sound. Our patience is soon rewarded. Two does, escorted by a young buck, lead four spotted fawns down to the bog for a drink. They linger for only a moment and then disappear into the trees. We strain our eyes in the approaching dusk and observe a pair of screech owls feeding their offspring. Even Tina watches intently when papa owl brings home supper, still alive and kicking. The grand finale is actually a wee bit scary. I'm not the only one to stifle a gasp when a lone juvenile bear trundles down the path just beyond the bog.

"Oh my god," Devin hisses as the black furry bottom vanishes into the brush. "Did you see that?"

"Shush," Tina reprimands.

When we arrive back at the lodge, Julian treats us to ice cream sundaes. Devin can hardly contain himself as he recounts our wilderness adventures.

"You're absolutely amazing, Fern," Dannie tells me after we've said good-night to the kids and are on our way to my room. "That bear freaked me out, but you were so calm."

"Honestly?" I admit, "I was petrified! I'm not sure what I would have done if I'd been alone—thanks for being there."

"I wouldn't have missed Devin's reaction for the world, and that Tina is one unflappable chick."

We settle ourselves on the patio with blankets and pillows and drink in the beauty of the night.

"OK, Fern, time to spill the beans."

"What?"

"This afternoon? The appointment? Your face is a mass of emotion and I don't know you well enough to read it."

So I tell her. I tell her everything.

"I had an inkling something was up when we looked at that house. So you've decided to move to Glendale?"

"Yes." I sound so definite. "I'm sorry that I copped out of the flower business, I know that working with you would have been a blast."

"Don't be ridiculous. I'd have to be blind not to see that your passion is gardening outdoors, not cooped up in some shop. And watching you with Devin and Tina; there's no question that being with kids and being a teacher is your calling." She kisses my nose. "An incredibly sexy teacher, I might add."

Somewhere out on the lake, a loon calls out to its mate. When there's no answer, I'm suddenly seized by an overwhelming sense of loneliness. *A chance to restart my life*, I think, remembering 'Ria's admonition prior to the retreat. A new job, a home of my own . . . and Dannie. What about Dannie? I snuggle closer to her. "Stay with me," I whisper.

"I'm not going anywhere."

"I don't just mean tonight. I mean . . ."

She puts her finger on my lips. "Don't fret, Fern. Dwell in this marvelous moment with me and let tomorrow be tomorrow."

I shake off my melancholy and touch Dannie's cheek. "So beautiful."

"And you."

CHAPTER 16

I N THE DINING room at breakfast the next morning, we push the tables end to end so that we can sit as one big, happy family. It's our final day together and regardless of who has gotten on whose nerves during the last three weeks, all is forgiven. Even Sonja is remarkably cordial when Dannie and I make our appearance.

Davy waves us over to a couple of empty seats. "Great to see the two of you together."

Karin is already slicing into a cheesy omelet. "Julian is making crepes for tomorrow's brunch," she spouts happily. "I called my husband and told him to be sure to come early when he picks me up so he can try one."

Professor Ben is beaming. "Two redtails and finally—a bald eagle! And thanks to John's expert guidance, I was able to capture their flight with my telephoto lens." We all admire the minimovie displayed on the tiny screen of his digital video camera.

"Shall we tell them, John?" Sue has one hand snaked through his arm and the other hand hidden behind her back. "We're engaged!"

All four sorority sisters gather around to behold the spectacular rock that now adorns the ring finger of Sue's left hand. RJ and BJ enthusiastically shake John's hand.

When I share the news about my new job, there is a spontaneous toast to my success. Geraldine insists that I keep the wampum. "Continued good luck," she says.

"Well, look who's back." Fred starts a round of applause as Marc pulls up a chair.

"What's on the schedule for this morning, boss?" Tony asks. Before Marc can answer, Jonas sounds the gong to get our attention.

"Good morning, everyone," his deep voice greets us, "Happy Mardi Gras!"

It turns out that our final day at the Water's Edge is going to be one hell of a wild party.

*　　*　　*

In preparation for this hedonistic celebration, Jonas assigns us various tasks. Geraldine, Lucy, and Tony assist Julian in the kitchen with the hot and spicy Cajun cuisine. Fred and Dannie put their heads together and mix up an assortment of delectable drinks, while Sonja, BJ, and a couple of the sorority sisters are in charge of the decorations. The rest of us, under Marc's artistic eye, are up to our elbows in glitter, sequins and feathers, creating ornately outlandish masquerade masks.

The pre-party begins when Jonas pipes New Orleans jazz through the sound system, and Dannie and Fred start encouraging us to test their alcoholic concoctions. We are all well on our way to intoxication when we adjourn to our rooms for a bit of personal primping.

It is hot and humid and we've been warned that we may get wet, so I dress simply in a black bathing suit and twist the sarong around my waist.

"Choose your disguise," Sonja says, pointing to the masks and handing out strands of green, gold, and purple beads.

"How do I look?" I ask Dannie when I've covered my face with the sequined plumage.

"If I hadn't already sampled too many drinks, I'd say we both looked ridiculous." She swings her beads Mae West style around her neck.

"We are in good company," I laugh as King Jonas struts forward in a rhinestone top hat and velvet cape.

He taps his golden scepter twice. "I am Comus, the Greek god of revelry. Follow me at your peril."

Karin and Fred toot a fanfare on their recorders, Tony and Ben crash a couple of oversized pan covers together, and we all clamor and clatter out to the veranda.

"It's a good thing that Devin and Tina are with their grandparents today," I say to Dannie as two sorority sisters flounce past us in finery that borders on the obscene. We rabble-rouse our way across the lawn where Jonas leads us to an inflatable swimming pool full of, you guessed it, water balloons!

Jonas raises his king-size chalice. "Before we begin the festivities, I propose a toast to this merry band of misfits." He takes a sip, nods his approval, gulps a generous mouthful, and bids us all to partake.

I'm not sure who starts it, probably the good professor, but someone tosses a water balloon into the crowd. Like the removal of the proverbial finger from the dike, it becomes an open invitation to fire off the liquid ammunition at will. Explosions both great and small drench even the most agile among us. I don't know who starts it, again I blame Ben, but a sorority sister loses her bathing suit top, then Davy gets pantsed. Before you know it, we're all gallivanting around with our unmentionables partially or totally exposed.

When our stockpile of balloons is depleted, we peel off our saturated masks and sodden feathers, refill our goblets with more nectar of the gods, and lunge about on the lawn like dizzy toddlers.

Dannie flops down beside me on my towel. "If I have any more to drink I'll be comatose," she slurs.

"It doesn't help that we haven't had anything to eat since breakfast." I plant a kiss on her naked belly. "Maybe if we make ourselves more presentable, someone will take pity on us and feed us." We gather up our soggy belongings and stagger up to our rooms.

*　　*　　*

Dressed in just about the last clean outfit I own, I arrive back in the dining room in time to help Geraldine set the tables. Julian's outdone himself: eggs Sardou, shrimp remoulade, a zesty bean and rice dish that zips the spice meter off the charts. For dessert, a flaming Bananas Foster.

"Time to crown the queen," Lucy announces when we've consumed the last bite of sweet, hot banana. She reaches into Jonas's top hat and pulls out a piece of paper. "Long live Queen Fern!" Everyone cheers in approval, and the dancing begins.

Dannie bows low. "Your wish is my command." And she whisks me out to the dance floor.

*   *   *

I drag myself out of bed by 8:00 a.m., reluctant to leave a peacefully sleeping Dannie but determined to treat myself to one final canoe ride on the lake.

Quietly I draw my paddle in and out of the still waters, hoping not to disturb any animals that may have wandered out to the embankment for their morning ablution. Carefully I make my way around the point to the mouth of one of the inlets. The moose calf stands alone on the opposite shoreline. I watch as she wades into the water, confidently going deeper until only her head is visible.

"Good swimming," I say softly as she turns away from me and moves out across the expansive lake. I maneuver my canoe toward the causeway and consider picking a water lily but know it will only wilt before I get home. The reality of leaving the Water's Edge and returning home begins to sink in. So much has changed. I have changed. I rest my paddle on my lap and think about last night. How lovely. How could Dannie and I not see each other again? The canoe bumps up against a rock and I realize that I've floated under the ledges. My thoughts shift to how good life will be working at Jenkins, living in the brick cottage; playing in the greenhouse, digging in my new gardens. I feather the canoe out of the rocky maze and slice through the water until I reach the middle of the lake. A strong breeze kicks up at my back. I paddle hard, picking up speed; I whip my paddle over my head and into the air. Like a wooden sail, it catches a gust of wind that propels the canoe into the shallows and up onto the beach.

*   *   *

Before I return to my room, I enjoy one last stroll in the garden. Jonas has assured me that he will do his best to care for the fledgling plants. "You can always come for a visit," he says.

Tina and Devin greet me from the kitchen door. "Dad says we should say good-bye now." Tina gives me a hug.

"I'll miss you, guys."

"Us too." Devin shakes my hand.

They are excited about their upcoming trip to Disney World with their mom and her new beau.

"Send me a postcard."

"We'll e-card you," they promise.

There's a note on my desk from Dannie: *See you at brunch.*

I shower and pack, and after several trips to the parking lot, manage to squeeze most of my things into the car—paints, books, clothes, journal, masks, clay vase, canvases; everything but the moose painting.

Marc has set up a gallery in the fireplace room for us to show something we've done during the retreat. Courageously I prop *Testing the Waters* on an easel. I walk around the room scanning the art that is on display, the culmination of our three weeks together.

Sue and John have completely refurbished the hobby horse for his daughter. Sitting proudly on its freshly painted saddle is a teddy bear wearing a pink knitted sweater, Karin's handiwork. Davy's sculpture is rather phallic in appearance, but I suppose it could be a tree. There is a framed copy of Geraldine's bumblebee haiku written out in beautiful calligraphy, and Tony has chosen to display his ceramic bowl, avant-garde enough for a museum of modern art.

Missing from the exhibit is an offering from RJ or BJ They had to take an early flight home. Most amusing is the collage Fred and Ben had created.

"Damn handy with a glue gun," Ben preens. He is standing behind me as I survey a collage of memorabilia from the retreat. "Thank god Fred can draw stick figures," Ben says. On a large canvas, like a life-size page from a comic book, they've created their own interpretations of some of our more momentous escapades at the Water's Edge. My favorite is the tangle of circle heads, lined bodies, and remnants of shredded water balloons—the Mardi-Gras aftermath.

Quite surprising is Dannie's papier-mâché mask propped on a picture stand. With its swirls of blue and gold it could be a replica of Van Gogh's *Starry Night*.

Most astonishing is the series of exquisite nude sketches done by one of the sorority sisters, and I'm nearly moved to tears when I see the pen and ink bald eagle that Geraldine presents to Professor Ben. Who are these extraordinarily accomplished people that I've shared the last three weeks with?

*   *   *

After brunch, a smorgasbord of Julian's most delectable creations, it's time to say our good-byes.

Our final farewells are as diverse as our individual personalities. There are those who need to linger, indulging in lengthy good-byes, and there are those who need brevity, bordering on the indifferent—time to move on.

Dannie prefers abbreviated departures, and my need for words is less significant than I anticipate.

"Thank you," I say simply, giving her a prolonged hug.

"Sweet, sweet Fern." She kisses me. "Have a safe journey. I'll be in touch."

PART TWO

The Return

CHAPTER 1

" SAND, SAND EVERYWHERE, between my toes and in my hair." The nonsensical rhyme 'Ria chanted as a little girl while we modeled castles on the beach dances playfully in my head.

"Where should I put this extra bag of sand?"

"Under the table next to the peat moss," I answer Devin's question. It's Saturday morning and the two of us have labored since breakfast stocking the greenhouse. We've finally finished layering insulating rock particles over the propagation tables. "Thanks again for all your help."

"No problem, Fern. I mean Ms. DeGiulio."

"Is Tina at ballet this morning?"

"Tap class."

"Tap and ballet? Very talented."

Devin plugs his ears with his fingertips. "Very noisy." He straps on his helmet and jumps on his bike. "Later."

"I'll see you at the game. Be safe." I watch him pedal down the road, bobbing and weaving around loose pavement and potholes. Every maternal bone in my body worries about the five miles he'll cycle back to his mom's house. I remind myself that he's a very capable fourteen-year-old and in less than two years he'll be driving a car—yikes. I'll never forget how my stomach churned the first time 'Ria got behind the wheel.

"Can't protect them forever," I assert aloud. Ivy, luxuriating in a patch of sun between a stack of flower pots, responds with a bored yawn. I refill my water bottle, step out the back door of the greenhouse, and sit at the wrought-iron table under the apple trees. Ivy pops out from her cat door, rubs affectionately against my legs, and propels her ample body into my lap. An autumn breeze riffles her fur and catches at the loose locks that have escaped from my hair clip. I push a stray strand behind my ear and take stock of the three-sided glass structure attached to the back wall of my house. My house, my greenhouse, my apple trees; I love how that sounds.

Once I'd made up my mind, the actual purchase of the property had been less daunting than I'd anticipated. The divorce settlement had provided enough for a down payment, and when the bank manager discovered I'd be teaching at Jenkins, where his daughter was an honor student, the mortgage was "No problem."

'Ria's disappointment that she hadn't had the chance to house hunt with me was placated when I asked her to help me move. The seven-hour drive from Saint Barnabas to Glendale was a chance for us to do some catching up.

As the miles flew by, I listened to 'Ria chat enthusiastically about her new job, her new friends, and her new beaus. "One guy was nice and one was a real jerk."

When she inquires about Dannie, I mumble some nebulous comment about deciding to be "just friends." "I'm sure there are plenty of nice guys in Glendale," she says.

I just nod silently.

"It's perfect for you, Mom," she exclaims when we drive beyond the pine trees that border the entrance to the brick cottage.

I'm relieved to see a vacant bay window—devoid of the naked dress form. The realtor had assured me that all traces of the Unique Boutique would be totally eradicated.

"Restored once again to a lovely home," she pronounces when she meets us at the door for the final walk-through. The rooms are more spacious than I remember; the varnished maple floors gleam in the sunlight. I skim my fingers along the dust-free mantle on the fireplace, previously occluded by shelves of fabric and thread. The kitchen is spotless, there's a candy-red teakettle on the vintage gas stove—a gift from the realtor—and the Hotpoint refrigerator hums quietly in the corner like an old friend.

"Retro is in," 'Ria swoons when she pulls on the knobbed faucets and a stream of water splashes into the porcelain sink.

"Funky," she decrees when she sees the claw-footed tub with its pole shower and wrap around curtain.

"Dull," she declares when I point out the freshly painted cream-colored walls. "This will liven things up." She props *My Heart's Desire* on the mantle. She's right; the brilliant hues of tangerine and lime give the room a bright focus. "And we'll hang *Testing the Waters* in your bedroom," she says. I'd had both paintings framed as a congratulatory gift to myself after I'd handed the headmaster at Saint Barnabas my resignation.

'Ria frowns at the futon I've been using as a bed. "What you need now is some new furniture," she says. She convinces me to purchase a queen-size bed for my room and a sleep sofa for the living area. We delegate the futon to the second bedroom—my office. "A comfy place where you can read when you're not correcting papers at your desk."

She predicts a Thanksgiving family reunion. "Gram and Gramps can have your room and I'll crash on the sofa bed. And until then," she scratches Ivy behind the ears, "at least I don't have to worry about you being alone."

*   *   *

"I wonder if we'll ever see her again," I whisper now to Ivy, the thought of being alone and the thought of Dannie merging together. Ivy vibrates her body beneath my hand and stretches out a paw.

The week following the retreat I had called Dannie and left a "just want to say hello" message on her answering machine, and then again a month later I'd recorded my new address and phone number, just in case. When I didn't hear from her, I swallowed my disappointment and wrote off our time together as merely a summer fling. And so at the end of August, I'm totally unprepared, even a little incensed, when she arrives unannounced.

She'd admired the house, stamped her approval on the surrounding acreage, and we'd both partaken in the pleasures of my new bed. In less than twenty-four hours, she boomerangs back to the city. "I'll return," she assures me.

"When?"

"Soon."

"Call next time," I say, but she'd already started her car and I'm not sure she even heard me.

Physically I know that I've never been more intimate with anyone; emotionally I'm not sure I want to navigate her volatile tendencies. Coming, then going; staying, then not staying. The apple-tree branch above my head sheds an empathetic leaf onto the glass tabletop. I rub Ivy's belly. "Thankfully you are a far less complicated housemate," I say. She trills in agreement. "Speaking of housemates." I glance at my watch. "I expect Eliot and Willie will be along shortly."

Less than a week after I'd moved in, Willie had sent me a hand-written invitation to come to his home for tea. Over mugs of iced chamomile nectar, he had solemnly requested permission to continue his daily constitutionals with Eliot on the trails along the back side of my five acres of field and forest.

"Only if Ivy and I can join you occasionally," I'd said.

"Did you hear that, Eliot? Two beautiful ladies to accompany us."

Willie talked affectionately about the land that used to be a working farm—the family homestead.

"Perhaps you can restore old Joe's patch of tillage," he said after I told him about my love of gardening. When I left, he handed me a leather-bound satchel, his brother's horticultural journal. "When we retired from education, Joe reclaimed his farming heritage. Vegetables, flowers, fruit trees; if he planted it, it would grow."

Now, looking out over the meadows of overgrown tussocks, I can barely see the skeletal outline of plotted earth. However, just above the tall grassy weeds, waving like a feathery flag, I see Eliot's tail.

Ivy jumps from my lap and flits off to intercept the bounding retriever. His master follows at a more leisurely pace, but even at the age of ninety-five his gait is steady, and I suspect that the hand-carved stick he carries is more for show than for aid. He's wearing a bow tie and matching suspenders. My students would call him a sharp old dude.

"Deep in thought she is, Eliot." He removes his brown tweed cap from his snow white hair and sits down in the opposite chair. "How goes it at Jenkins? I was visiting Tim and I saw your notice about the Grub Club. Any takers?"

"Five so far, thanks to Devin. Our official meeting is next week. By the way, I invited Devin to help us prune the apple trees on Saturday. He agreed only if you supervised."

"That young man is a hot ticket."

"Are you still up for going to his soccer game this afternoon?"

"Eliot and I will be ready with cleats on."

"I'll pick you up around 1:45 p.m."

"Sounds good." He gives a short whistle and Eliot tears himself away from whatever he'd been investigating.

As I watch them disappear from view, I think back to my first day at Jenkins. It seemed like déjà vu when I'd stepped out into the hallway at the end of second period, and who saunters by? None other than Devin, with his dark curls and black T-shirt. I am pleased to see him but at the same time a bit bewildered. With the end of the retreat I'd imagined that the experience and the people I'd encountered would remain encapsulated at the Water's Edge. At times, the memory of my midsummer adventure had all the earmarks of a fanciful dream. In real life, Devin and Tina live in Glendale with their mom, and visit their dad on weekends and school vacations, so it's perfectly natural for Devin to be at Jenkins. However, the resemblance of my colleagues at Jenkins to the characters at the Water's Edge is slightly disorienting. My foray into the teacher's lounge for that premiere lunch is even a bit freakish.

"Indubitably charmed, I'm sure." George Bard, English teacher, channels the spirit of Professor Ben when I'm introduced. Although she's far more serious and dowdy, Priscilla Badger, the librarian, reminds me of Karen at first. Later I discover I couldn't have been more wrong about her.

"Finding everything you need?" I'd already met Evan Tobins, the chair of the science department. He's a Rastafarian with shoulder-length dreadlocks and a dead ringer for Jonas in his younger days.

My first instinct when I meet Peter Syner, the flamboyant art teacher, is to contact Davy, until I find out he's been living with his college sweetheart, Melody, forever. My heart nearly stops when someone in the corridor calls out to Dannie. Not Dannie, but Manny, a senior, the president of the student council.

"What's gotten under your skin?" Bea MacNamara asks. She's the wood-shop teacher and the sanest one in the room.

"Oh, nothing," I say, fanning my flushed face. "I hope I can remember everyone's name."

"Don't worry. With the exception of a few bad apples we're a fairly friendly bunch." Stepping back into my role as a teacher in a public school is not the problem. The students, the routine, even the switch from chalkboards to whiteboards is a welcome transition. Outwardly I'm a seasoned teacher who knows her stuff, but inwardly I'm a jilted lover who doesn't know squat.

To say the retreat rocked my socks is an understatement. Exploring wildlife along woodland trails, creating visual art under Marc's supervision, even participating in Jonas's musical challenges had been somewhat expected; falling in love had not. Falling in love with a woman, a woman I'd known for only three weeks. So many times in my life I'd wondered *what if*? My commitment to my marriage and my devotion to 'Ria had always trumped any of these forbidden desires, but now—had I missed my only chance?

*   *   *

Eliot's head hangs out the car window, ears and tongue flapping madly. Willie is describing to me what Jenkins looked like in the 1930s as we pull into the school parking lot.

"All we needed back then was an open space to toss a ball around in."

The well-appointed athletic complex now situated behind the school is equipped with a soccer field, a basketball court, a baseball diamond, and a four-lane running track. Willie and I are greeted by both teachers and students as we find seats on the bottom row of bleachers. Eliot does his prescribed three turn-arounds and settles himself at Willie's feet. He thumps his tail in greeting when Julian and Tina sit down beside us.

"How's ballet?" I ask Tina.

"I love it." She twirls around and chirps excitedly about the pink, gauzy costume she'll be wearing in her upcoming recital. I compliment her on the french braid in her hair.

"Dad did it," she squeals. "Do you believe it?" I look at Julian in surprise.

"What, you think the only talent I have is cooking?"

We cheer loudly as the teams get into position. Devin immediately takes possession of the ball as soon as the referee blows the starting whistle. He passes it deftly down the field. The teams are well matched and at halftime the score is still tied zero to zero. Devin attains hero status when he scores the one and only goal to win the game.

After a congratulatory meal of burgers, fries, and ice cream sundaes, I deliver an exhausted Willie and Eliot safely to their doorstep. When I arrive home, Ivy is waiting impatiently at her empty dish. The phone rings just as I fork the tuna into her bowl. It's Dannie. She wants to know if I have plans for the Columbus Day weekend.

"I long for your delicious company," she flirts over the phone.

"I miss you too." I tell her that my only agenda on Saturday is to prune apple trees and correct lab reports.

"Ah, the thankless job of a dedicated teacher. Do you think you can find some time to tutor me?"

"Absolutely." I have a sudden desire to pull her right through the phone. "Dannie, I've really missed you," I repeat.

"It has been too long," she agrees. I'm almost certain I hear a similar urgency in her voice. "I may have some interesting news to share."

"Can't wait." I want her to tell me more, but I know she won't. Dannie loves to create suspense.

"I'll leave the city on Saturday morning and arrive sometime after lunch."

After I promise to cook her a romantic, candlelit dinner and she promises to bring something decadent for dessert, we say a reluctant *bien noir*.

Only one week from tonight, I think when I get into bed. Pleasant dreams invade my sleep and I wake in the morning with a smile on my face.

I should get busy outlining my lecture on photosynthesis but my usual ritual on Sundays is to curl up on the couch in my sweatpants and ease slowly into the day. I flip through several cookbooks in search of a recipe for next Saturday. Nothing inspires me, but the well-worn pages crammed with magazine clippings remind me of Joe's garden journal. I pad out to the greenhouse and scoot up onto one of the high-back stools. The pub table and stools had been a treasure I'd found at a yard sale the same day I'd unpacked the last box of books and tools, and hung a pair of new garden gloves next to my straw hat.

Carefully I open Joe's journal. The smell of the faded leather mingles with a faint smell of lemon. The source of the fragrance is revealed when I thumb through the pages and find several sprigs of lemon thyme pressed between them. Ivy leaps up on to the table and rubs her chin ecstatically along the binding. She flings her body down in rapture among the pile of her master's notes and papers. A moment passes and I sense the presence of something larger than either one of us. I leave Ivy with whatever sentient spirit the journal has conjured up and walk the perimeter of the greenhouse. Lucy's question about what I wanted to take back after my divorce careens into my mind. My answer: everything! I spin around in the center of my glass-encased garden, fling my arms wide to the walls and then back again into a self-embrace, and whoop for joy.

CHAPTER 2

T HE HALL BUZZER signals the commencement of another Monday morning, and it is with some amusement that I survey the eclectic assemblage slumped in the chairs of my homeroom class. I try not to smile as the starry-eyed lovers who'd been doing some last-minute smooching in the hall scurry over to their seats.

"Good morning." I welcome my lethargic charges with the weekly announcement that articles for the school newspaper are due on Friday. There is an audible groan when I tell them that the entire student body is expected to convene in the courtyard after final period for trash patrol, and I add, "Don't forget that fund-raising candy is still available at the main office."

"I hate selling candy," I hear someone mumble as they trundle off to first period.

"Boiling points!" I only hope that my eighth-grade general science class is sufficiently awake enough to manage the experiment without burning the place down. I had spent most of my career trying to grasp the idiosyncrasies of the adolescent brain. One minute they are totally into it, the next they are rolling their eyes, morphing without warning from being your best friend to acting like ornery children. My apathy to the teenage condition became more sympathetic the year I embarked on that marvelous journey called menopause. I began to commiserate with every hormonal mood swing and body mutation. "I can relate," I told them, knowing that they really didn't believe me.

On my way to the cafeteria, I stop in the faculty lounge for a cup of coffee. It's only Monday, but my colleagues are already preoccupied with their plans for the long weekend. Evan and his family are packing up for their final camping trip of the season, and Peter is taking Melody to the Cape for a romantic getaway. What would they say if I shared my own romantic hopes for the weekend?

Priscilla rears her brown-nosing head from behind the coffee pot. "I, for one, will be showing some school spirit by joining Dr. Jenkins in watching the Columbus Day parade," she says. No one seems to take any notice of her.

Jenny, a first-year algebra teacher, interjects, "Fern, Bea wants to see you after school." She shakes her head at me. "You're in trouble now."

I put my finger to my lips. "We're working on a top-secret project," I tell her. "Very hush-hush. How was your algebra relay?"

"They never knew math could be, like, *fun*."

"Were you the one responsible for that god-awful smell in the science wing this morning?" George accuses. I can never quite tell whether he is teasing or not.

So I apologize to serious George, and explain how one of the students let their milk boil down to a burnt crisp. "Did I hear a rumor that your AP class wants to perform a heavy-metal version of *Macbeth*—the musical?" I ask him.

He laughs, but Priscilla clicks her tongue in disgust. "Sacrilege!"

For the most part, I enjoy sparring with my coworkers. We all ignore Priscilla, who feels it's her duty to amend every discussion with a sanctimonious final word.

*　　*　　*

Bea pokes her curly red head and busty overall-clad body into my room. "All done for the day?" she asks. I'm washing up the last of the test tubes and beakers. "Ah, the mad scientist at work." She whips out her tape measure. "Is this the window?"

I'd asked Bea's woodworking class to design and build a plant table for my room. Whether it's divine intervention or Dr. Jenkins's influence, the corner of my room has a south-facing window, and when I'd requested permission to set up a propagation area, I was given not only an enthusiastic green light but a generous budget for supplies.

Bea slides her pencil above her ear. "Seth wants to know when you can come over for dinner again. He said that his buddy Jeff had a great time the other night."

"I can't imagine why. I make a lousy bridge partner."

"We did skunk the two of you, didn't we."

Jeff was yet another eligible bachelor that Bea and Seth had invited to even up the number whenever they had me over to their house. I change the subject. "Has Seth finished the proposal for his next book?"

"He's meeting with his publisher as we speak. So are you going away this weekend?"

"I have a friend coming for a visit."

"Why don't you both join us for dinner on Sunday night—we'd love to meet him or her?"

"Her name's Dannie." I pause. "Can I let you know?"

"No problem." She glances at her pad. "Well, I guess I have all the measurements that I need. When can you could come to my class and explain the reason for the slat design?"

"I have a free period on Thursday."

*　　*　　*

My own preoccupation with Dannie's weekend arrival mirrors my students' inability to focus on schoolwork, and the week crawls forward. Several teachers try to secure the students' attendance by scheduling exams on Friday, but I slate my exams for earlier in the week. I've learned from experience that families with travel plans don't change them for a test that can be made up. Instead, on Friday I plan a lab experiment that I hope will intrigue the kids enough to show up. My motives are purely selfish because lab experiments are fun and make-up tests are a pain in the ass.

I arrive at school with a container of worms and several tubs of dirt.

Dr. Rosa peeks in during my final class. There are ten kids gathered around a table in the center of the room; their intense concentration is interrupted by an occasional cheer. "What's going on in here?" she asks.

"Will someone please explain to Dr. Rosa what we are doing?"

"It's a worm race. Look, mine's nearly buried," Chrystal says.

"Don't forget to record the time, soil density, and moisture level," I remind the young lady with the double nose piercing.

Two guys with matching arm tattoos ask, "Can we do this again next week?"

"What will happen to them over the weekend?" Brad worries.

"Never fear," I assure them. "Their next gig is in my garden."

"That had to be a first," Dr. Rosa remarks as the kids gather up their things and meander out of the room. They continue to argue about who had the fastest worm.

"Not fair," one of them whines, "Wiggles was in hard-packed clay. He didn't have a chance."

"Shi—I mean stuff happens," someone else says.

Dr. Rosa lifts a container. "I'll get this one." She insists on carrying it out to my car.

"Thanks," I say, closing the hatch. "Enjoy your weekend."

"We will be going north to do some leaf peeping, but we'll be back for the parade on Monday. What about you?"

"I'll be pruning apple trees."

"Good old Uncle Willie. Don't let him work you too hard."

On my way home, I stock up on groceries and stop at the Lazy Daisy to buy a dozen roses. Caleb Paige greets me like an old friend. When I ask where Lydia is, he tells me that she has taken a job as a teacher's aide at the preschool in the church next door.

"We needed the money," he explains. "I'm not much of a business man." He gestures to the "for sale" sign still propped in the window.

"Keep the change," I tell him as he wraps my bouquet in paper.

After unpacking my car and assigning the worms to a patch of soil, I strip my bed and clean the house.

Maybe Dannie will stay a bit longer this time, I think, biting into a tomato and cheese sandwich as I try to correct the mound of exams cluttering up my desk. I consider Bea's dinner invitation. How would I introduce Dannie? My friend, my date, my lover? What if I don't want to share Dannie with anyone else? We have so little time together as it is, and besides, it would be far less complicated if we just stayed home all weekend. Dannie's presence could change everything. My thoughts turn hyperbolic and I imagine scenarios of wild reactions, starting with Bea and Seth and splaying throughout the school, the community, the world.

"Stop it!" I scold myself. Ivy, who is acting as a living paperweight on the small pile of graded papers, regards me through one lazy green eye. She tips her head over and offers up her chin for a rub.

*   *   *

"Steady as she goes," Uncle Willie says, bracing the ladder for Devin. We have successfully pruned three of my four apple trees. Devin had clipped, I had bundled, and Willie had instructed us about fruit buds, growth buds, leaders, laterals, and spurs. "Next season you'll have magnificent blossoms followed by more Cortland apples than you'll know what to do with."

"Apple pie, apple crisp, apple sauce," I begin to chant.

Devin chimes in. "Candy apples, apple turnovers."

"And cinnamon apple strudel." Willie pokes his cane at a gaping hole in the fourth tree.

"But not from this one I'm afraid. Rotted clear through. It will have to come down."

I protest. "But we'll be evicting a woodpecker family."

"You can always plant another," he begins, but then he notices my frown and concedes, "OK, just trim away everything but the trunk."

After heaping the branches and boughs into the wood bin—good kindling for the winter—Devin jumps on his bike and pedals toward the front of the house. I hear the roar of an engine, the blast of a horn, and the sound of Devin's cry.

"Awesome!"

A Mini Cooper, florescent yellow with jet black racing stripes, is squatting in my driveway. The face of the woman behind the wheel is hidden behind enormous sunglasses, but I recognize the mass of gray curls. Dannie!

"Traffic was a bitch!" She unfolds her lovely body out of the car leaving the door wide open. "Be my guest," she gestures to the dumbfounded Devin. "Zero to sixty in eight seconds."

"Cool, wait till I tell Dad." He doesn't pry himself out of the front seat until Dannie promises to take him for a ride while she's here. "When you get your license I may even let you take her for a spin."

I glance at my watch. "Meanwhile, don't you have a soccer game to play?"

"Great to see you again, Dannie." He waves, his eyes still pinned to the car.

Willie pats the hood. "Nothing like a new set of wheels to get the blood flowing."

"Daniella Stevens, my neighbor, Dr. William Jenkins."

"Uncle Willie to my friends," he corrects. "Quite a vehicle you've got there. How does she handle?"

"Like a dream, and please, call me Dannie."

A curious Eliot circles the car and sniffs the tires.

Dannie clears her throat. "Don't even think about lifting your leg," she warns. Eliot sidles over and leans up against her leg. She pats his head. "I suppose you want a ride too." He thumps his tail and gazes up at her with adoring eyes.

"He's certainly taken a shine to you," Willie remarks. Eliot bounds back to his master.

"Fickle aren't we now?" Dannie laughs.

"Time for us to head along home," Willie says, retrieving his walking stick.

"Want a lift?" Dannie spreads out a towel in the back seat for Eliot and gallantly opens the door for Willie.

"Top-notch friends you have." Willie salutes and they zoom away.

A dry leaf falls out of my hair and I realize how grungy I am. I dash into the house, rinse off with a quick shower, and throw on some clean clothes. In less than fifteen minutes, Ivy and I are waiting out on the front steps. Just when I'm convinced that Willie has hijacked Dannie's car, she peels back into the driveway.

"Jump in."

"Aren't you tired of driving?" I ask, descending into the soft leathery seat and inhaling that new-car smell.

"Just need to put the top up." She presses a button; there's a whirring sound and the canvas accordion unfurls above our heads. She leans over and kisses me. "Sorry it took so long, but I just couldn't resist finding a stretch of road where I could open her up and give the old man a thrill."

We bring her bags into the bedroom. She pulls me onto the bed. "And speaking of thrills . . ."

*   *   *

Dannie scoops up the last of her shrimp and pasta salad. "I could get used to this; great sex, beautiful flowers, romantic candlelight, and a delicious dinner."

I flutter my hand, "Oh, I offer this to all my guests."

"Do you now?" Dannie raises her eyebrows. "Are you saying I have competition? Perhaps I need to stick around for a while, keep tabs on my lovely Fern."

We load the dishwasher and walk out into the greenhouse. I show off the well-stocked shelves and the pots of annuals I've brought in for the winter. As we walk through the back field and into the woods, I tell her about Bea's dinner invitation.

"Sounds like fun."

The rich aroma of all things decaying drifts around us as we stroll along the path. The trees are dressed in their autumn wardrobe: orange, red, and gold. They wave their branches gently in the breeze as the squirrels scramble up and down barky trunks collecting their winter hoards. We reach the spring-fed pond and step onto the plank platform that juts out into the middle; I squat down to watch a couple of sunfish swim beneath the surface.

"Next month my earth science class will come out here for a field trip," I say. "I never dreamed I'd be able to introduce a unit on ecosystems in my very own backyard."

"Location is everything," Dannie agrees, sitting down beside me. We peer over the edge at our reflection.

"Don't we look like a couple of middle-aged beauties?"

"Young middle-aged." Dannie is quiet for a moment. I realize that with all my endless chatter, Dannie has yet to give me her news. We listen to the peepers begin their song and watch the sun sink down into the trees. "I've been seeing someone," she begins.

CHAPTER 3

I 'M ALMOST ANNOYED at how relieved I am when she explains that the "someone" is a life coach.

"It was either that or a psychiatrist," she says. "And I detest head shrinks. I went to one after I came out, my parents said they would disown me if I didn't, and he told me that the reason I didn't like men was because of some repressed childhood trauma. I told him I did not conveniently decide to become a lesbian just because some kid at the playground called me a tomboy, and then I told him to go screw himself. I'm sure he was greatly relieved when I canceled my second appointment."

"What did your parents say?"

"They agreed with him and disowned me just the same. I realized at the tender age of seventeen that I would need to figure things out for myself."

"You seem to have done a pretty good job of it. I've always thought you had it all together."

"I did, at least I thought I did, until I came home from the Water's Edge. Two weeks after the retreat I couldn't eat or sleep. The thought of launching a new project gave me a head-splitting migraine, and instead of giving me an adrenaline rush, the hustle and bustle of the city totally sapped my energy. Even the sweet smell of a New York wiener—my favorite food in the entire world—brought on waves of nausea."

"Why didn't you just call me?"

"Because you are part of the problem."

I don't know what to say, so I listen.

In July Dannie had driven away from the Water's Edge with no intention of calling me. I gulp down my protest. She pushed the retreat to the back of her mind and poured her creative energies into Sonja's expansion proposal. It wasn't long before Sonja tried to manipulate the relationship again and they had a major blowup. "She stepped in it big time when she badmouthed you."

"Me? What did she say?"

Dannie picks up an acorn and tosses it into the water. "She said, no, actually she screeched, that I had lost my mercurial edge. She accused me of being impotent, and she suggested that I go play house with the earth mother bitch."

"Earth mother bitch?" I start to laugh hysterically. "I'm sorry," I say wiping my eyes.

"And so I slapped her," Dannie continues. "She threatened to press charges, I wrote her a check for an obscene amount of money and called Lucy."

Lucy had referred her to a colleague, previously a Wall Street mogul, now a licensed life coach. After a battery of tests, the Myers-Briggs kind—no needles, no blood or urine samples—they determined that what her professional life needed was a new venture, preferably one away from the city, and what her personal life needed was a face-to-face encounter—with me.

"Luckily I'd saved the message with your new address. I did think about calling first, but I didn't know what to say."

"But your visit in August was so short and you left so abruptly, like you couldn't wait to get away from my face."

"Your face isn't the problem," she leans closer, kissing my cheek and sliding her hand along the curve of my hip. "Being with you all cozy and domestic-like in your homey digs scared the shit out of me."

"So what changed to make you come back?" I strain to see her expression in the gathering darkness.

"That's what we need to talk about." Her words spill out of her mouth in a jumble. "I did something rather impulsive and I realize now that maybe I should have checked with you first. I'm not accustomed to running my decisions by someone else, but the flower shop idea turned into such a fiasco," her voice falters. "Maybe it's too late and I've already botched things up again."

I place my finger on her lips. "Just tell me."

She's silent for a moment. "Well." She peers into the inky woods. "Since now I can't even see your face, I'd rather explain back at the house." Her voice is tentative. "And I sure hope you know your way out of here, because this time I didn't bring a flashlight."

"I got this one." I smile, remembering our first encounter at the Water's Edge. I slip my arm around her, and lead her up the path.

Ivy scoots past us when we enter the kitchen. "How about some of that decadent dessert you brought?" I put the kettle on to boil water for tea and Dannie rummages through the cupboards for plates.

"Quite an interesting variety of dishware you have," she comments when we've made ourselves comfortable on the couch.

"Ed got the Royal Worcester."

"Well then, madame." Dannie adopts a sexy French accent. "Dessert this evening will be enjoyed on a fine selection of blue glass and L.L.Bean Blueberry ware."

"Mm," I swoon, my mouth full of sweet, creamy bites. "My compliments to the chef."

"Any appreciation you wish to show the chef must go through me."

"Then you shall be greatly rewarded." I kiss her chocolaty lips. "So you think that the domestic life is a little too tame for you?"

"I think that maybe I shouldn't judge it until I've given it a try."

Our luscious repast carries on well after our plates have been licked clean.

*   *   *

This is the good life, I think, as the heavenly aroma of smoked bacon and scrambled eggs wafts into the greenhouse. I'm watering the trays of begonia and fuchsia cuttings and Dannie is cooking breakfast. Ivy darts back and forth between us like a yo-yo. Her fascination with my watering can is as much of a temptation as the bits of bacon Dannie is dropping into her dish.

The air is cool but the sun is strong and we decide to eat our morning brunch outside under the neatly pruned apple trees. My straw hat shades my eyes and Dannie has angled her green fedora to block out the bright light. We share our outdoor café with four goldfinches dressed in lemony-yellow plumage. They peck greedily at a sock full of thistle. A lone chipmunk sprints under our feet, his mouth full of sunflower seeds. Good thing Ivy is in the house taking a nap.

"Now that we're sufficiently awake," I say, sipping my coffee. "It's time to 'fess up."

"What?"

"What is this impulsive thing that you've done?"

"I bought the Lazy Daisy."

"You bought the Lazy Daisy," I parrot her words back to her. "But I already . . ."

"Not for you, silly," she interrupts, "for me. I sign the papers on Tuesday morning. I hope you don't mind if I stay with you another night."

I'm so blown away I don't answer.

"Fern? If not I can always find a room in town."

"No, I mean, yes, of course you can stay with me."

"Thanks." She gives me a funny look. "You had me worried there for a second."

My head spins with questions as she spells out the details: purchase agreements, closing costs, inventory lists. What does she know about the floral business? Will she live in the apartment above the shop? What will happen to Lydia and Caleb?

"Are you all right?" she asks.

"I guess I'm just having trouble wrapping my mind around all of this. What about Lydia and Caleb?" I know I sound defensive. "Caleb has single-handedly been trying to keep the Lazy Daisy afloat."

"Yes, I know that, and I hope he will stay on, as long as he understands that I won't be just a silent partner. I want to get my hands dirty." She rubs her palms together, her eyes sparkling with efflorescence. "Implement new marketing ideas, grow the product." She laughs.

Her joy is contagious. I lift my coffee mug. "To the Lazy Daisy and your future as a flower tycoon. And," I add, "you can stay with me as long as you want to."

*　　*　　*

I clean up the breakfast dishes, and Dannie fills the bathtub with hot, soapy water. It's midafternoon before we are socially presentable and ready to make our way out into the real world.

We spin down Main Street like a couple of Hollywood divas, the Cooper's convertible top down, the wind whipping through our hair. Our plan to make a quick pass by the Lazy Daisy on our way to Bea and Seth's house is thwarted by some kind of revival at the church. We end up crawling along the pavement behind long lines of traffic. There are mobs of people crossing the street, carrying tote bags and ten-pound Bibles. When we finally reach the flower shop, we are disappointed to see the blinds drawn and the Sorry, We Are Closed sign prominently displayed. I hear Dannie mumble something about missing the entrepreneurial opportunity of a lifetime. Did she actually say "beatitude bouquets and gospel gardenias"?

We wave to Priscilla Badger. She waves back with uncertain recognition. Several people eyeball Dannie's car with envy, especially the cluster of teens loitering on the front steps of the school.

When we stop at the flashing yellow light across from the library—open, despite it being Sunday—there is more mumbling from Dannie. They're having a sidewalk sale, selling used books and raffle tickets. After we wait for a couple of young mothers pushing a double—, and yes, a triple-seated stroller, to cross the street, a very impatient Dannie revs the engine and accelerates to a speed that pushes my stomach into my throat.

The Cooper eats up the miles, and the congestion gives way to houses sprawled spaciously out on rolling hills. Thanks to the Land Preservation

Act, any new construction requires at least a five-acre parcel. Bea and Seth had purchased two such plots seven years ago to build their log cabin and raise free-range chickens. The two of them greet us as we step onto their wraparound porch. They've been snapping beans.

"Probably the last mess of the season," Bea mourns in response to our excitement over the mound of crispy, green produce.

"Don't forget the ten quarts we have in the freezer." Seth, in his overalls and flannel shirt, and Bea, with her head scarf and denim apron, are a walking advertisement for *Yankee* magazine. They are both about the same height, but where Seth's rippling muscles are clearly visible within his lean frame, Bea's strength is softened by her voluptuous curves.

She gestures to Dannie's golden chariot. "I'll show you my 'coop' if you show me yours." I listen as they revere the heated leather seats, the convertible top, and the shiny new engine under the hood. There is mutual admiration when we check out Bea's chicken coop.

Bea takes a basket from a peg on the wall. "I see that we have a couple of overachievers today." She extracts several brown eggs from the straw roosts.

We enter the house through the back door and Bea sets the eggs on the center island in the kitchen. Despite its rustic exterior, the house is more than adequately equipped with creature comforts: state-of-the-art kitchen appliances, a wall-mounted HDTV, and, I notice, no less than three computers in Seth's work space. The living room stretches the full length of the house, and the fieldstone fireplace has a chimney that climbs up through an unfinished loft to the vaulted ceiling. Most of the furniture and custom wall units are either Bea originals or inherited antiques.

Dannie and I arrange place settings on the trestle table at one end of the living room while Bea and Seth finish preparing dinner in the kitchen. The menu: green beans and blue cheese, rice pilaf with almond slices, and a baked flounder.

"Smells divine," Dannie calls out. "Almost as divine as you," she whispers in my ear as we lay down forks and napkins.

"Later," I answer, bumping up against her and nearly upsetting the water glasses.

"Chow's ready!" Bea bustles out of the kitchen carrying a steaming platter in each hand. Seth is close behind her with the buttery flounder, and a bottle of white wine.

"So how did you two meet?" Bea asks.

"One dark and starry night," Dannie intones, "I found Fern wandering aimlessly in an enchanted wilderness."

"Was she under some kind of spell?" Seth asks.

Dannie clinks her glass. "Lady Liquor had rendered her delirious."

"I was only slightly inebriated," I protest.

Bea laughs. "This is getting interesting."

While we eat our meal, Dannie and I take turns narrating choice anecdotes from our stay at the Water's Edge.

*   *   *

"Why didn't you tell us about Dannie?" Bea asks me after dinner when the two of us are at the sink. She's washing. I'm drying. Seth and Dannie are outside putting up the top on the car and procuring logs for a fire.

"Dannie and I are . . ." I begin. This is the moment of truth. This is the first time I will declare my romantic relationship with Dannie outside the protective bubble of the Water's Edge. My dish towel falls to the floor.

"My god, Fern, you look like you're going to be sick." Bea pushes a chair behind me. I sit. She hands me a glass of water.

Seth and Dannie erupt through the back door, their arms laden with split wood. "And the bear was gargantuan," Dannie's voice peels out. "I'm shaking in my boots, and there's brave little Fern, all calm and cool like it's no big deal."

"Fern you didn't tell us that you . . ." Seth stops. "What's wrong?"

"Just a little light-headed I think," Bea offers.

"No more wine for you." Dannie puts down her bundle and rubs my shoulders.

Bea gathers up the discarded firewood. "We'll give you a few minutes. Seth, come and help me with the fire." They disappear into the living room.

"Are you sure you're all right?" Dannie's voice is full of concern. "Is it the fish?"

"No." I start to feel silly. "Bea was just asking about us . . ."

"Ah, I see. Not to worry." She helps me out of the chair and puts her arm around me; I cringe just slightly, immediately ashamed. "Trust me," she says.

Bea is kneeling at the hearth igniting a bed of tinder, and Seth is dishing out slices of tart. Dannie and I sit down together on the love seat and watch the flames lick at the twigs; they flare brightly as the seasoned logs catch and burn. An embarrassing vacuum envelops the clinking of forks against china as we pick at our chocolate cake.

Dannie inhales anxiously. "Will someone please offer the elephant in the room a piece of tart?"

The tension in the room dissolves into a cascade of chatter.

Bea is all apologetic. "And to think I was constantly racking my brain to find suitable guys for you to meet—how insensitive."

"My fault," I say, flicking my fork in the air. "I should have said something sooner. It's just all so new."

Dannie flings up her hands. "I'm the one you should blame. Love 'em and leave 'em, that's me. After rocking Fern's world, I flee like the proverbial roadrunner."

"But you're here now." To my dismay, I start to cry.

Bea dabs at her eyes.

"Hold everything." Seth snatches up a box of tissues. "Let's not turn on the waterfalls just yet. Seems to me that we all want the same thing. Bea and I care for Fern, and we want her to be happy."

"Well, I care for her too," Dannie counters. "And I hope I do make her happy."

"Stop," I cut in. "Fern is right here and she is, I mean, I am quite happy. I'm practically drowning in happiness." I hug both Bea and Seth. I kiss Dannie full on the mouth.

CHAPTER 4

I GRATE THE CHEDDAR cheese into the omelet. How utterly exquisite, waking up all warm and cozy in someone's embrace—an embrace that equals the fervor of my own.

"Good morning, sweet Fern." She brushes her lips against my neck. The cheese oozes out from between the folded eggs. "How about I make us some toast?"

"Oh, yes." I lean back into her. "'Cause if you keep this up, I'll scorch these eggs for sure."

After breakfast we go for a walk around the pond. The woods are damp with the morning dew, the air moist with the promise of rain to come. Clusters of mushrooms cover fallen logs and decorate the edge of the trail, crimson parasols shielding spots of dusty soil. Deer tracks indent the spongy ground, and I tell Dannie about the young doe I'd seen shortly after I'd moved in.

"She probably thought I was crazy. I told her how beautiful she was and asked her to walk with me. She swiveled her ears, stomped her hoof, and bounded away. Maybe I am 'Earth Mother.'"

"Earth mother, yes, bitch, no."

"Do you think I'm daft?"

"I think maybe you spend too much time alone in the woods."

"But being in the woods energizes me. The invigorating smell of pine, the organic alterations of the seasons, the hustle and bustle of creatures going about their tasks; nature has always been my adrenaline boost."

Dannie looks at me. "Perhaps I need to spend more time in the wild."

"Wouldn't you eventually miss the city?"

"I don't know."

Reluctantly, we leave the cover of the forest and step back out into the clearing. We are immediately intercepted by Willie and Eliot. Dannie and I are still holding hands.

Willie regards us for a moment, and then he smiles. "Glad to see you're both out enjoying the best part of the day." He points to the gathering rain clouds. Eliot zips over to Dannie and drops a soggy tennis ball at her feet.

"It's been a long time since I've thrown one of these." She wings the ball out across the field. Eliot tears off in hot pursuit.

"That's some arm you have, young lady," Willie laughs. "Eliot could use a good workout. I sure do hope that the rain holds off. Columbus Day is a big deal around here. Tim and Marilyn are picking me up in less than an hour. They're having a gathering at their house so folks can watch the parade from their front porch. Knowing Marilyn, there'll be enough food to feed a small country. You two should stop by."

"Uninvited?" I ask, looking at Dannie.

"I just invited you."

"Thanks," Dannie says, "but unfortunately I have a business meeting to prepare for."

*   *   *

"Of course you should go," Dannie says. "They're your bosses. I'll get some work done while you're out schmoozing with the academics, and when you come home, we'll have the whole evening to be together."

I'm conscious of a twinge of jealousy when I leave. Dannie and Ivy look so comfortable on the couch, even though they are surrounded by file folders. A part of me would really like Dannie to be accompanying me, but I'm not sure I can handle more than one coming-out per weekend.

The party is in full swing when I arrive. Dr. Jenkins and Dr. Rosa—"Please, call us Tim and Marilyn"—are delighted to see me. "Willie said you might be joining us. Too bad your friend had to work—another time, perhaps." They introduce me to some of their esteemed guests: the members of the school committee and a few town officials, all of whom are balancing plates groaning with a disparate combination of American burgers and Jamaican delicacies.

The unpublished dress code for the men seems to be tan khaki pants and navy polo shirts. Most of the women are conservatively dressed in black slacks and silk blouses. Dr. Rosa—Marilyn—travels among them like a bird of paradise, her dress, a startling shade of vermilion.

Self-consciously I adjust my pink cotton sweater over my brushed-corduroy jeans. I tap the wampum necklace that Geraldine gave me.

Apparently my reputation has preceded me, because the school superintendent praises me for initiating the Grub Club.

"So good to have young people interested in something besides Facebook," he says. "I understand that they are sprucing up the school grounds too. Do you think they might be interested in representing Jenkins with a float in the Memorial Day parade next May? Our theme is Save the Planet. Perhaps they could create a float that promotes the new eco-friendly stance the town of Glendale has adopted?"

"I'm sure the club would love to participate. I'll ask them at the next meeting."

Priscilla, who has been standing right behind me the whole time, chimes in. "We could devote the entire month of May to environmental awareness." She starts to proffer advice about poster-board displays and student assemblies.

What a suck-up I think, marveling at her appearance. She must not have received the wardrobe memo. The elastic bands on her knee-high stockings are clearly visible beneath a skirt that's not quite long enough. The matching velvet jacket straining to hold in her ample bosom is a musty shade of ochre, and the hairspray she's shellacked on her hair is failing miserably.

"The band!" Dr. Jenkins announces. To my dismay, Priscilla scoots her chair next to mine as we take our places behind the porch railing. Thankfully the snare drums roll out a deafening cadence preventing her from further exhortation.

We cheer as the marching band and color guard high step to a John Philip Sousa march. We wave as the Pumpkin Seed preschoolers, costumed as adorable barnyard animals, ride by in a horse-drawn hay wagon. My cell phone rings just as Tina's dance troupe twirls past us and the parade is officially over.

"Thought I'd give you an excuse to leave," Dannie quips in my ear. "You can pretend I'm some kind of emergency that needs your immediate attention. Actually, I do require your attention, but nothing you want to advertise to the public."

My laugh is louder than I intend.

"Who's that?" Priscilla noses in.

"Just a pesky telephone marketer," I reply, my voice dead serious. "Sir, I'm sure your product is very useful but I never buy anything I'm not familiar with."

"Get your pretty little ass home and I'll show you familiar!" Dannie's voice is so piercing I'm sure Priscilla can hear, but thankfully the appearance of the mayor has distracted her. I seek out the good doctors, express my appreciative farewell, offer Willie a ride home, and make my exit.

"It must be my advanced age," Willie observes as he directs me to a shortcut away from the gridlock of traffic, "but I'm becoming less tolerant of the politicking that goes on at these social events. Now back when Joe and I ran the show . . ." he chortles. "I sound like an ornery old codger. It was probably exactly the same."

He thanks me for the ride and issues a standing invitation to Dannie and me to come for a visit any time. I wait until he unlocks his door, catch a glimpse of Eliot's furry tail wagging his welcome, and travel the short distance to my own driveway. I park the hatchback alongside the Mini Cooper.

"I'm back." The house is empty. I find Dannie and Ivy in the greenhouse chasing a cricket. Actually, Ivy is the one in pursuit of the tiny creature; Dannie is trying to facilitate the cricket's escape.

"Sadistic beast." She kisses me. "Not you, your cat. How was the parade? See any clowns?"

"None in the street, but there was one at the party." I distract Ivy with a bowl of kibble, while Dannie scoops up the poor cricket and sets it outside.

I tell her about the superintendent's request and Priscilla's meddlesome intrusion.

"Sounds like you've met Glendale's finest—both the official and the officious."

Because of the mounds of food I'd consumed earlier, we decide to make a salad for a light supper.

"How delightfully domestic," Dannie says as we slice tomatoes and wash romaine lettuce.

"Yes," I agree, "someone to come home to, eat dinner with—go to bed with." I look out the window. The sky splits open and glows an electric blue. A low rumble sends Ivy slinking off to her undisclosed safe place. *Splat*, *split*, *splat*, large drops of rain spatter in irregular rhythms against the glass panes of the greenhouse. Another thunderous crack, louder and closer this time. The lights flicker then go out.

*　　*　　*

When I leave for school the following morning, Dannie's just barely awake. I ask her if she will drive back to the city following the closing. She mumbles something about possible complications.

I don't have time to consider what those complications might be as I'm thrust into the chaos at school. Following a long weekend, the kids are sidetracked with chatter about parties and parades, and it takes all of my concentration to get them settled down and focused on a review of the material for midterm exams.

My intention to call Dannie at lunchtime is hindered by an insistent Priscilla. It appears that she has galvanized the entire staff in support of the grand ecological production slated for May.

"I'll assign my fifth-period English class to write poems for the earth," George promises.

"The science department can put together an exhibition about arctic glacial melting," Evan offers.

"How can the math people get involved?" Jenny wants to know.

The brainstorming only escalates when Dr. Jenkins makes an appearance. The next thing I know, lunch is over and I've been elected to write a formal proposal to present at the next teachers' conference day.

"Damnation," I mutter when the bell rings and my last period class waltzes out the door.

The driveway is devoid of one yellow car. The note tacked under a refrigerator magnet reads:

Closing went without a hitch. I'll be back on Friday. May need to stay with you a bit longer. Call me, D.

I throw my bag on the couch and call her at once. *Beep*—her answering machine. "This message is for the sexy new proprietor of the Lazy Daisy. A room is available for you at my humble abode with the understanding that it is double occupancy only. Please call to confirm your reservations."

It's no surprise that she doesn't call back, but I have more than enough on my plate to keep me occupied. On Wednesday, after I dazzle her class with my discourse on plant propagation, Bea takes me aside. "Heard Priscilla's roped you into another one of her insane schemes."

"Schemes?"

"She's been broadcasting to the world about her 'save the planet' convention."

"I guess the original idea to feature the Grub Club on a float for the Memorial Day parade has hemorrhaged out of control."

Bea lowers her voice. "Be careful, Fern. Priscilla is famous for dreaming up massive ideas only to rope a gullible newbie into doing the immense amount of work needed to bring it to fruition. And guess who takes all the credit?"

"Well, Evan and Jenny said they'd help, and George seems excited about it too."

"You can definitely count on Evan, and probably on Jenny, but George is excited because he has a crush on you and he'll do anything to get into someone's panties."

"Guess we know that isn't going to work."

Bea remains skeptical. "George is probably harmless, but Priscilla has her own agenda."

*   *   *

By Friday afternoon, I have a mind-numbing headache, a flexi-file overflowing with midterms to correct, and no blooming idea when Dannie will be arriving or how long she might be staying. My hope for a lengthy visit motivates me to clear off the desk in the spare room to make space for Dannie to wield her entrepreneurial prowess. It is no hardship for me to do my school work in the greenhouse.

Sipping a creamy mug of hot chai, I make a valiant attempt to create a dent in the midterms. After struggling through a mere five, I find myself wandering up and down the greenhouse tables, adding water to dry soil, pinching off dead heads—procrastination at its best. Reluctantly, I return to the stack of papers. *Click, click, clicking* my red pen, I agonize over Tracy Simmon's exam. I know that she can do so much better, but she has an unbearable life at home. Some afternoons she stays in my classroom long after school is over, offering to erase the board or help set up experiments. Any excuse to avoid going home. Mostly she's starved for someone safe to listen to her vent without judgment. I'm aware of how privileged I am that she's comfortable talking with me, and I guard that trust with my life. I hope Tracy will accept my invitation to join the Grub Club. She seemed especially interested when I told her that Devin was the president.

I manage to finagle partial credit here and there on her exam and bring her grade up to a C minus. Halfway into the next test, I hear the sound of wheels crunching up the gravel in the driveway. I throw down my pen. Ivy, who has been snoozing on the corrected stack of papers, raises her head. "She's here." I sprint out the front door.

A flash of yellow speeds into view followed by . . . a U-Haul truck?

CHAPTER 5

A S IT TURNS out, clearing off my desk was a superfluous gesture at best. Dannie has provided a desk of her own. In addition to the antique rolltop, she's brought a leather recliner, two sets of mahogany bookshelves, and a pair of wrought iron floor lamps. I stand clear as three brawny men promenade through the front door hauling crate after crate. I watch as they surround the couch with a mountain of boxes. I wince when they drag a rack of clothes with reticent casters across my pristine floor.

"Where do you want the tree?"

"Tree?"

"English holly," Dannie clarifies. "Through the kitchen and out to the greenhouse."

When their truck is empty, I offer the sweat-drenched men bottles of water for their trip back to the city and direct them to the nearest burger joint.

Dannie fills a decanter of wine from the copious selection of bottles now crowding the kitchen table. "That was exhausting."

I survey the living room. "So I take it you'll be staying for a while?"

"For as long as you'll put up with me." She rests her head on my shoulder. "What do you think of *Yellow Lotus*?"

I consider the water flower with its delicate petals and potent fragrance. "Not quite as bright a yellow as the Mini Cooper. Why?"

"I'm contemplating a name change."

"For you or the car?"

"My car? No, no, the Lazy Daisy. It needs a new image. Brilliant idea about the car though."

I shake my head. "You've lost me."

"The Lazy Daisy is wilting," she explains. "No new clients since Caleb took over. The kid is smart and eager to learn, but he lacks business savvy." She slaps her knee. "I've got it! We'll paint the shop to match my car and I'll get vanity plates—YLOTUS. Free advertising!"

"Isn't the lotus also a yoga position?"

"Fabulous! An angle for the enlightened crowd. Holistically balanced flower arrangements." Danny is over the top with enthusiasm.

An inquisitive *meow* announces Ivy's reappearance. She'd beat a hasty retreat when *those men* so rudely invaded her territory. She hesitates when she sees the disarray of alien furniture and cardboard boxes.

I click my tongue reassuringly. "It's OK, Ivy." Carefully, she tiptoes her way around the unfamiliar objects. She trills and chirps, sniffs and rubs, and then she leaps gracefully to the top of the leather recliner, arranging her furry body into a sphinxlike pose, her paws tucked neatly under her chest. She gazes down at us and blinks her eyes.

Dannie genuflects with her hand. "I guess Her Royal Highness approves."

*   *   *

The golden carpet of curling leaves crackles beneath my feet. I disturb a pair of chipmunks chasing each other into a burrow. A barrage of chattering ensues as one little guy is unapologetically dispatched from the mouth of the hole. He scampers away to find his own winter nest. Cohabitation is a challenge for any species

During the past three years, I'd once again slipped quite comfortably into solitary living, possessive of my time to do whatever I wanted to, whenever I wanted to do it. Unlike my black-and-white life at Saint Barnabas, I was learning to dabble with an exciting new palette of colors, colors of my own choosing. The sporadic sharing of space and time that Dannie and I had engaged in so far had been shaky at best, and now I wonder how long it will be before one or both of us begins to feel claustrophobic in my four-room cottage.

The chipmunk pokes his head up out of his hole. "And furthermore," I ask him, "can two women actually survive any kind of relationship in a house with only one bathroom?" He chirps in alarm and disappears.

Dannie is still asleep when I return from my walk, so I slice up a pint of strawberries, sprinkle a handful over a dish of yogurt, and pad out to the greenhouse to correct a few more exams.

Doing my school work in the greenhouse is both a delight and a distraction. The combination of warm sunshine on soil and herbs is a calming aroma therapy; however, it's too easy for me to become sidetracked. Like now, when I regard the holly tree that the movers abandoned in the middle of the floor. I jab my finger into the soil; it needs water, but how much? Searching for my book on trees, I come across Joe's journal. On the first page there is a drawing of the original design for the greenhouse and a receipt for the propane heater that was dead and gone long before I arrived. "Probably double the price to replace it," I say out loud.

Dannie appears in the doorway wearing a rather revealing kimono. "It's not me you want to replace I hope."

"Not on your life."

*   *   *

The rainbow of fabric billows out with a deafening roar. I cling to the basket with a Herculean grip and a blast of power propels me straight up. The ground drops away at a tremendous speed and my stomach double flips into my throat.

The childhood memory of riding in a hot air balloon at the county fair is an apt analogy of what life is like riding shotgun in Dannie's company—every moment reaching new heights, some exhilarating, others intimidating.

Since Dannie tends to operate on a more nocturnal schedule, two women sharing one bathroom becomes a nonissue. I leave for school almost two hours before Dannie even gets out of bed, and I return home long before she gets back from the Yellow Lotus. Since neither one of us is passionate about cooking, our meals are quick and easy. *Pasta for Dummies* is our bible, and our library of takeout menus is encyclopedic.

Our first joint task is a whirlwind of domicile improvement. We decide to give the interior wall a much needed face-lift.

Neutral colors are passé, so we paint the bedroom walls a sensual sunset salsa. We decorate the den a deep shade of periwinkle, we choose a sour-apple green for the living room, and a blazing sunflower yellow for the kitchen. For fun we wallpaper the bathroom with a novelty print from a renovator's supply catalog. Naked cherubs dance about the room engaging in provocative frivolity. When we are finished, every room in the house radiates hospitable vitality—I love it.

The freshly painted canary kitchen walls become the inspiration for the outside trim of the newly christened Yellow Lotus. The artistic logo of a bowl-shaped leaf containing one delicate yellow flower is skillfully rendered by yours truly, and reproduced multiple times on letterhead, tissue wrap, and eco-friendly tote bags. In preparation for the grand reopening, Dannie sends Caleb and Lydia to a flower show in Boston. Lydia is more interested in shopping, but Caleb returns with copious notes and innovative ideas. It is his genius that suggests we procure a candy company to mold fine dark chocolate lotus flowers. The sweet confection will be offered to anyone who visits the shop on Saturday, October 31—All Hallows Even.

*   *   *

I tug on my white gloves, adjust my black-and-white striped shirt, and peruse my creamy white face in the mirror. Dannie dances into the bathroom wearing a peasant blouse and long flowing skirt. Bangles and bobbles dangle from her arms and ears; a head scarf is secured at the back of her neck.

"Rings on my fingers and bells on my toes," she chants. "Too much cleavage, you think?" She thrusts her chest forward. I gaze up at her and mime a sorrowful expression, zipping my lips with pinched fingers.

"You are a fresh little fellow. So sad. This wanton gypsy may just have to scoop you up and carry you back to her caravan." She flings her shawl flamboyantly around her shoulders. I cover my mouth in feigned alarm.

It's barely dusk when we arrive at the Yellow Lotus, but the street lights are beaming down on sidewalks crawling with bizarre figures. There are Biblical celebrities on their way to the church, and goblins and ghosts roaming the streets waiting to enter Jenkins for the Halloween dance. It's a bit of a shock to see Frankenstein helping Jesus heft a cross up the church steps, and equally puzzling to watch a sorceress with pointy hat assist a young angel with her halo. The church is throwing a party for the under-twelve crowd—bobbing for apples and donuts on a string. At nine o'clock, the older kids will gather in the school gymnasium for a ghoulish celebration.

Up and down Main Street businesses are open, offering free candy for the trick-or—treaters and sidewalk sales for their parents. Caleb, decked out in formal butler attire, is kissing his lovely Lydia, also the Biblical Lydia, a wealthy seller of purple cloth. She's on her way to the church, of course.

"Showtime," Dannie announces, adjusting Caleb's tie and affixing a red carnation into the brim of my hat. She ushers us both outside to our posts in front of the shop.

"Hey, Ms. Deguilio!"

I wave to a couple of students, dressed as Salome and John the Baptist. Salome is carrying John's head on a silver tray. I guess they could be going to either party.

I hear John's muffled voice from his protruding neck. "She can't talk, stupid, she's a mime."

I give them each a carnation from my pail, and Caleb bows low, offering them his tray of chocolates.

"How are we doing?" I ask Dannie an hour later when I go back inside the shop to replenish my flowers. She's been schmoozing with potential customers.

"Business is booming! I've already booked two Christmas weddings and have taken at least a dozen orders for Thanksgiving arrangements."

"That's great. Will I see you later at the dance?"

"I'll be there as soon as we close up."

At 8:45 p.m., I leave my pail of flowers with Caleb and walk over to the school. Bea and I have volunteered to be chaperones.

"Dynamite costume," she says. "Better than this old thing." She's dressed in a graduation cap and gown. "I almost didn't come at all. I didn't feel well this morning, but I'm fine now." She points to the far corner of the room. "I bet you can't guess who that hobo is."

Even in his disheveled state, the man in the tattered clothes looks remarkably well groomed. The smudges of dirt on his face are suspiciously symmetrical, and his leather shoes are immaculate.

I grin. "Pete Syner," I say. The self proclaimed metrosexual teacher of visual arts was trying to pull off the persona of a homeless bum. "Not very convincing is he."

During the last dance of the evening, Dannie appears at my side. I'm watching Moses wrestle a cardboard tablet scripted with the Ten Commandments away from a Teenage Mutant Ninja Turtle. A flirtatious witch comes to his aid with her broomstick.

"Now that's something you don't see every day," I say.

Dannie's not paying attention. "Something happened at the Lotus." She screws up her face.

"Good or bad?"

"Well . . ." We're interrupted by Devin and Tracy. They need help folding up tables and chairs. "I'll fill you in later."

It's another hour before we are home and changed. "So what happened?"

"We'd just closed the shop and I was on a stepladder putting away a new shipment of vases. Caleb had locked the front door and was loosening his tie and unbuttoning his shirt. I must have lost my balance because the next thing I knew I'd fallen right into his arms. It was rather comical at first. With his half naked chest against my barely concealed bosom we could have been posing for the cover of a cheap romance novel. And then I guess I got a little carried away. I didn't know that Lydia was going to walk through the back door." Her voice trails off.

"For god's sake, what did you do?"

"I pretended to swoon and I said something like, 'You're my hero, you great big hunk of man.' That's when Lydia walked in."

"I'm sure she knew that you were just joking around."

"Maybe, if it weren't for the kiss."

"Caleb kissed you?"

"No, I kissed Caleb. And before you go ballistic, it was an innocent peck on the cheek. A thank-you kiss. After all if I'd landed on the floor, I might have broken something."

"Vases can be replaced." I'm not sure I like the thought of Dannie kissing Caleb, no matter how innocent.

Dannie gave me an incredulous look. "I meant me. I meant I could have been broken, but maybe you don't care about that, and don't tell me you're mad because I kissed Caleb. The poor kid was so embarrassed his face turned five hundred shades of red. Lydia's histrionics made it even worse."

"What did she say?"

"'They warned me about you,' she said. Then she ran up the stairs and slammed the door. Caleb couldn't get away from me fast enough."

We were both quiet for a moment.

"Oh my god," Dannie shrieks. Ivy has materialized out of nowhere with a limp, gray critter dangling from her mouth. She lays it at our feet. A peace offering.

"I do care," I say, after I'd regained my composure, we'd praised Ivy for her good work, and judiciously disposed of the dead mouse. "I'm very glad that you didn't hurt yourself. But next time I think it would be better if you thank Caleb with a handshake."

*   *   *

During the next three weeks, the pace of life races on in tandem with the rapid success at the Yellow Lotus. Dannie has to work late just about every night. When I don't have crazy amounts of school work to do, I bring dinner to the Lotus and help out. Despite Caleb's assurance that he'd smoothed things over with Lydia, he goes out of his way to keep his distance from Dannie, making the atmosphere a bit strained. As for Lydia, she is downright frigid to both Dannie and me.

*　　*　　*

The Friday before Thanksgiving turns out to be a perfect day for the art and science field trip into the woods behind my house. After I review the basic science behind autumn's seasonal transformation, Pete equips the students with paper and pastel crayons so they can render artistic images of the scenic view.

"Can we see the inside of the greenhouse?" the kids plead when it's time to board the bus. I acquiesce, and my ego is promptly flattered as they admire my indoor garden, even though I realize that some of their interest is a procrastination tactic: anything to delay going back to school. Pete and I promise them another field trip in the spring.

On our way back to Jenkins, we pass the Yellow Lotus. Dannie is in the window adding hints of Christmas to the Thanksgiving display.

It had been my idea to drape the red and green fabric around the cornucopia, and scatter a few pine branches here and there. Never too early to remind folks about the upcoming holidays.

One of the more unexpected perks in our relationship is that we share a similar philosophy and passion about our work. We both agree, whether in business or teaching, it's all about good marketing: wrap it up in eye-catching paper and they will buy it. We really enjoy swapping creative ideas to use at our respective jobs.

"That's Ms. DeGiulio's girlfriend," I hear someone say.

"Cool," is the collective response.

Partners, lovers, best friends. Yes, it is cool. But how in the world will my family react to Dannie? Mom and Dad are flying up from Florida next Tuesday, and 'Ria is due to arrive sometime late Wednesday night for the infamous Thanksgiving reunion.

CHAPTER 6

"YOU HAVEN'T TOLD them yet, have you?"

It's the day before Thanksgiving. My half day of classes is over and I'm helping Dannie with last-minute deliveries. We're loading floral arrangements into my car, and yes, she's partially right, I haven't told them. "I have a friend staying with me for a while," is what I told Mom and Dad when I picked them up at the airport. What I told 'Ria had been more specific—sort of. "Dannie will be with us for Thanksgiving," I'd said. She'd sounded a little disappointed that it wouldn't be just the family, so I didn't elaborate.

Dannie closed the hatch. "Your mom thanked me again for sharing my room with you so they could stay in your bedroom—our bedroom. I didn't correct her, but I don't like to lie."

"I'll talk to them tonight," I promise. I had wanted to wait until 'Ria's arrival: one announcement, one disaster, one recovery—I hoped.

Traffic is horrific. After fulfilling my delivery obligations, I stop at the market—not the place to be the day before the great feast when last-minute shopping is at epic proportions, but Mom had called me in a panic. She needed one more pound of butter and two cups of whipping cream for the pies. I know I'm late, but I stand patiently in line with my two paltry items. The mob behind me threatens to riot as the lady ahead of me methodically counts out exact change.

I rush into the kitchen. "Dinner's nearly on the table," Mom says, relieving me of the grocery bag. "Go get washed up." Age is irrelevant when Mom is in charge.

"Dannie said not to wait," I call out on my way to the bathroom. "Said she'd grab a deli sandwich later."

My mom lives to cook. The counter is already laden with two mouthwatering pies, a butternut-squash casserole, and a mammoth pan of extra stuffing. The turkey has been washed and rubbed with herbs and is in the oven, bedded down under its foil tent for a night of slow roasting. For dinner she's put together a pork and rice stir-fry—nothing fancy.

"'Ria called while you were out," Dad says. "She couldn't leave work early because of some report she had to finish. She's a hard worker, that one." He smiles at me. "Just like her mom."

During dinner I try several times to talk about my feelings for Dannie, but Mom dominates the conversation with the cooking and eating schedule for tomorrow. I skillfully dance around what I really should be telling them by describing Bea and Seth's chicken coop and updating them on the Grub Club.

After dessert Dad and I go for a walk. Strolling around the perimeter of the fields, Dad admires the rugged stone walls marking the property. "A map of the past," he says. At seventy-seven he's still remarkably fit and trim. Mom carries some extra weight—all that good cooking—but she also operates at a high energy level. They are both thrilled about my new job at Jenkins.

"A piece of the puzzle," he says, picking up a stray rock and fitting it back into the wall. "It sounds like you've made some good friends and are finding your niche in the community."

"Yes, Dad, I'm no longer in seclusion."

"Your mother and I still worry about you being alone."

"I have Dannie."

"Great gal," he agrees as we enter the greenhouse. "She certainly keeps things lively, but she'll be going back to New York. I'm sure in a town this size you will eventually meet someone special."

"I already have," I say, but Ivy has caught his attention and he doesn't hear me.

I smooth out the sheets on the pull out couch for 'Ria. OK, I concede, so I didn't tell them. Just not the right time.

'Ria won't be arriving until close to midnight, so Mom and Dad decide to go to bed. "We'll catch up with her in the morning." I wish them a good sleep, and assure Mom that I'll get up early and help her debone the turkey. An hour later Dannie drags herself into the house.

"My final stop," she sighs wearily. She arranges the ceramic pot of cut chrysanthemums on the table and collapses into a chair.

I rub her shoulders and nuzzle her neck. "You must be wiped out."

"It's worth it. Happy customers mean a happy business." She pulls me onto her lap. "And the best part is coming home to you. I take it Mom and Pops have gone to bed. How about a soak in the tub?"

"I'd love to, but 'Ria will be here soon."

Dannie yawns, "I'd wait with you, but I'm done in. Don't wake me till the fat turkey sings." She kisses me good night and shuffles off to the bathroom.

I doze in the recliner until I hear 'Ria at the door.

"Sorry I'm so late." She throws her bags on the floor and gives me a hug. "I could smell Gram's pies as soon as I got out of the car."

She looks exhausted. "Have you eaten?" I ask. "Can I make you some tea?"

"No thanks, Mom. I just want to brush my teeth and hit the sack."

*   *   *

Somewhere around eight o'clock I sense more than hear my mother's presence in the kitchen. I kiss my snoring beauty, creep past my sleeping daughter, and join Mom for a cup of coffee.

"Dad's out for a walk with that cat of yours," she says. "I think it was love at first sight. When we leave, I suggest you check his suitcase for a calico stowaway."

I inhale deeply. The crispy, brown bird is cooling in its salty juices on top of the stove, and the cherry pie is emanating sweetness from inside the oven. "Mom, if there's a heaven, I believe it smells like your Thanksgiving dinner."

She admires the chrysanthemums on the table. "Dannie's handiwork?"

"Probably Caleb's. He cuts the flowers and Dannie crunches the numbers."

"Dad and I really like her. You two make good housemates."

"She's more than my housemate," I begin. My confession is cut short when Dad and Ivy breeze into the kitchen. Ivy leaps up into the sink, taps the faucet with her paw, and looks at Dad.

"I checked out the hook-ups for your new propane heater," he says, setting the water at a trickle. "It seems fairly easy to install."

Mom shushes him. "What about Dannie?" she asks.

'Ria rushes into the room. "Dannie is a woman!"

"Well of course she's a woman." Dad looks at Mom, suddenly bewildered. "Unless she's one of those transvestments."

"A trans what?" Dannie explodes through the door. "I most certainly am not!" She draws me to her and kisses me on the nose. "Sweet cakes, I love you greatly, but now is the time to come clean."

I scan the faces of my family. Betrayal, confusion, relief? "Dannie and I are, well, we're more than housemates, more than just friends; we're seeing each other. We are . . ."

"Yes, yes," Mom breaks in, embracing me and then Dannie. "We understand. How wonderful."

"What?" The single question is voiced by everyone in the room.

"I think we all need some coffee," Mom continues. She gives Dad a pat on the cheek. "Clear the table, dear, so we can sit down. Fern, make us a fresh pot will you? And we need another chair. I think there's one in the bedroom."

"I know where it is," Dannie offers.

"Of course you do."

Dannie's exit initiates a chain of hesitant action. In slow motion, Dad transfers the pies from the table to the counter, Mom drops warm blueberry muffins onto a plate, and I measure out spoonful after spoonful of coffee grounds into the pot. Dannie returns, sets the chair down at the table, and stands beside me.

"'Ria? Are you all right?" She isn't. She's staring at me, microscopically scrutinizing my face, my body, Dannie's hand touching mine. The look of contempt in her eyes withers me to my soul.

"How could you!" She's out the door before I can reach her.

I finally catch up with her out by the far stone wall. Her back is to me, her shoulders heave up and down from both physical and emotional exertion.

"Use your words," I say. The well-worn maternal phrase slips from my mouth, but 'Ria's not four-years-old anymore. She's not just a child pissed off because she didn't get her own way. And so the angry words she uses cut into me like a scalpel.

"So when did you decide you were a lesbian? Is that why Dad left? How can Gram think that it's wonderful?" She pumps her fist hard against her chest. "And why am I the last to know that my mother is a dyke?" She spits out the word *dyke* like a vulgar expletive.

I want to slap her. I want to hold her. I want to tell her I can make it all better. "I wanted to explain," I say feebly, not sure if she's really listening. I decide not to remind her that it was her father who'd had the affair. "Meeting Dannie at the retreat was just as much of a surprise to me. The important thing is that it doesn't change my love for you. Weren't you the one who encouraged me to meet new people, date again?" I know the last assertion is a bit unfair, but maybe it's time to step out of the mother-daughter role and return to being two grown adults. "You didn't have a problem with your gay friends at school."

"My friends, yes," she stammers. "My mom? No. No!"

"Can we at least go back to the house?"

"I'm not sure I can stay."

My heart sinks.

"But I will." She holds up her hand. "Only because of Gram and Gramps."

*   *   *

"Give her time," Mom advises me when we're cleaning up after the most uncomfortable meal I've ever eaten. Somehow we'd managed to work our way through the meal, although none of us had eaten very much. "More leftovers for later," my mom says gently. Dannie's hiding out at her desk, Dad and 'Ria have gone for a drive.

"What about you and Dad?" I ask. "I mean, you seem almost sanguine about the whole thing."

"Your father adores you more than life itself, and Fern, I'm your mother. I not only carried you in my womb, but I watched you grow up. When you were seven-years-old you asked me why Cinderella couldn't marry Sleeping Beauty. You never seemed to be interested in proms or dating, and when you spent all your time with Vicki I was fairly certain. But when you married Ed, I assumed that I'd been wrong."

"I guess I wasn't brave enough to be that different from everyone else. All my friends were making wedding plans, having babies. I really wanted children, and back then to have children it was preferable to have a husband." I shake my head. I have absolutely no regrets; after all I have 'Ria. But then I met Dannie."

"And all hell broke loose." Dannie comes into the kitchen to refill her coffee mug. She looks thoughtfully at me. "I can leave if you need me to."

"No, avoidance is not helpful. That much I've learned." I look at Mom. "I love my daughter, but this is my life, and Dannie is a part of my life. We'll work it out."

On Friday morning, Dannie goes to the Lotus even though I know she had planned to take the day off, Dad and I install the propane heater, and Mom and 'Ria make turkey soup. In Dannie's absence, 'Ria thaws slightly.

"Just like last year," she says when we play cards after lunch. She acts as if nothing has happened, and the possessive way she claims me as her bridge partner makes me wonder if her reaction to my relationship with Dannie is more about jealousy than about gender.

It is late afternoon before Dannie calls. "I'm at Willie's, and he and Eliot want me to stay for supper," Dannie says over the phone.

Her return home coincides with Bea and Seth's arrival. "We're pregnant!" they announce. "Due at the end of May." We break out another pie in celebration.

"Well we've certainly worn this day down to a stump," Dad says, yawning and eyeing my mother. "We'll need to leave fairly early tomorrow." They had plans to visit with some friends in the area through Sunday morning.

"I'm right behind you," Mom says.

Dannie sighs regrettably. "I have to work again tomorrow, but perhaps the three of us could go out for dinner?"

I look at 'Ria. She shrugs.

* * *

"We have the whole day to ourselves." 'Ria and I are still in our pajamas, perched on the bar stools in the greenhouse. "Shall we go on some adventure or sit here and veg out?" It's a magnificent day, with just enough of a chill in the air to crave a snuggly sweater or velvety fleece jacket.

'Ria is thoughtful for a moment. "How far are we from the Water's Edge?"

Her question catches me completely off guard. "About an hour's drive. What did you have in mind?"

"I'm not sure," she hesitates. "I don't suppose people who are not on retreat can just drop by for a visit."

"I know how to find out." I call Jonas.

"Absolutely!" His excitement erupts out of the phone. "Come on ahead, stay for lunch?"

I'm unprepared for the sense of nostalgia that sweeps over me when we pull into the parking lot. I smile at 'Ria's confusion over the austere exterior. "Ugly, isn't it," I say, then take pleasure in her wonderment when we cross over the threshold.

"Welcome, welcome." Jonas envelops both of us in a gargantuan hug. He turns on the charm. "As beautiful as your mom."

Everything is polished clean and ready for the conference of environmental activists due to arrive the following afternoon. I envy them. Perhaps this one-day retreat with my daughter at this extraordinary place will help us sort some things out.

We walk out on to the back terrace, and 'Ria murmurs her approval at the view. Jonas shows her the herb garden, "Your mom's handiwork. Julian and I have followed your instructions to the letter," he assures me. "Notice the new atrium window in the kitchen for the potted herbs, and yours truly covered the strawberry plants with a thick blanket of leaves."

Lunch is a delicious veggie and cheese calzone, a Julian original, reheated to perfection by Jonas, after which 'Ria and I enjoy a leisurely paddle around the lake. Wildlife is easier to spot through the naked trees, and because it's rutting season, the deer—having only one thing on their minds—are oblivious to our presence. We are treated to the sight of a full-grown buck chasing a doe over the causeway.

Tentatively I tell 'Ria about some of the moments Dannie and I spent together at the Water's Edge, moments when I first began to realize that there was a deeper attraction.

"So unexpected," I say.

"That's one way to put it."

I search her face. "I can only imagine how difficult this is for you."

"I do love you, Mom," is all she says.

*   *   *

Our visit to the Water's Edge becomes a tiny patch of common ground.

"Jonas is a trip, isn't he?" Dannie says after the waiter has taken our order.

"I thought he was the perfect gentleman." 'Ria's tone has a bite of contradiction to it.

Dannie doesn't take the bait. "He is indeed."

I wonder who will explode first. "So how were things at the Lotus?"

"We've been hired to work the wedding from hell." Dannie warms to her narrative. "What started as a simple request for bridal bouquets and an altar arrangement has now blossomed, sorry, into a nightmare of complicated demands." She salts her speech with hoity-toity inflection. "Now they are insisting that each bridesmaid be able to personally select their favorite flowers so that each of the eight, yes, I said eight, bouquets is absolutely unique. Of course the boutonnieres for the respective groomsmen have to match their partners' bouquet exactly. To further complicate matters, the groom's mother is allergic to carnations, the best man can't be within two feet of a rose, and the bride hates baby's breath."

"Sounds like a job for Sophia, the queen of the sugarplum fairies," I say. I tell 'Ria the saga of Sophia and Sam and the infamous Plant Emporium.

Dannie interjects, "I thought your mother would pee her pants when I suggested a counter offer to their enormous asking price."

'Ria laughs in spite of herself.

Just when I think we may have made some progress, the check arrives and both Dannie and 'Ria reach for it. Thankfully Dannie backs off. I realize the importance of the gesture on both their parts and flash them each a grateful smile.

*   *   *

"We survived." Mom and Dad had just called to say their flight was on time and they were safely home, and 'Ria had actually grasped Dannie's hand in a somewhat civil handshake on her way out the door. I feel as though I've spent the entire weekend bailing out the *Titanic* with a thimble. "Are you OK?"

Dannie had been unusually quiet since the family exodus. "Honestly? I don't know."

CHAPTER 7

"**M**EDDLING SON OF a bitch!"

Ten days before Christmas and the air is filled with holiday cheer. With two weddings on Saturday, Dannie is working 24-7 and her stress level is off the charts.

"Which bride changed her mind this time?" I ask.

"Not the bride." She slams her leather case on the kitchen table. "It's the damn pastor!"

"You mean the priest?" Since the venue for both weddings is the Episcopal chapel, I assume she's referring to Father John, a nice enough man, but at least five hundred years old and deaf as a post.

"The ignorant twit." She viciously jams a corkscrew into the top of a bottle of cabernet. The cork releases with a violent bang. Knowing that the storm will pass, I try to stay calm and retrieve two glasses from the dish drainer. What has triggered Dannie's explosion this time? After nearly two months of living with her, I've come to realize that along with her intensity for life comes a volatility that can shift the seemingly insignificant incident into a monumental event.

"Just think," I say, "by Saturday night, both weddings will be nothing more than someone else's memories."

"The weddings are the least of our problems." She swirls her wine into a tsunami. "It's Pastor Chad."

"What has Mad-Chad done this time?" Mad-Chad was our nickname for the pastor at the nondenominational church next door to the Lotus. He'd earned the pet name after he'd stopped in for a "hello, neighbor" visit when Dannie first bought the place. He'd offered her a tract explaining how Jesus saves. She thanked him for his patronage—after all, at that point he was their biggest customer—and then she informed him that she did not need his coupon for salvation. She thought she was being clever. He had not appreciated her wit.

'This is no joking matter,' he had said, his bushy eyebrows bristling up like an angry porcupine. He'd slapped the pamphlet onto the counter and stormed out of the shop.

"He can believe anything he wants to," Dannie continues, "but he should mind his own damn business." She drops her glass down on the counter. It wobbles precariously, falls to the floor, and shatters. The burgundy liquid splashes off the floor and stains the front of the cupboard. "Waste of good wine," she moans.

I open the back door. "I think we need some fresh air," I say. The air is bitter cold and we can see our breath as we walk toward the pond. From the clear, wintry sky, the full moon casts beams of light and shadow through the leafless tree branches and onto the path. The pond has a thin layer of ice, and I flip a pebble onto the fragile surface. It skitters into the middle then drops out of sight. "Tell me exactly what happened."

Her voice climbs in agitation as she speaks. "He saunters into the Lotus all puffed up and full of himself."

"'Marriage is an institution sanctified by God!' he says. I agree with him. I'm too tired for a confrontation. 'Would you like to buy some roses for your wife?' I ask, thinking maybe they'd had a fight or something. He flings his Bible on the display case. I see a hairline fracture begin to form in the glass. That's when he launches into his tirade. 'Marriage is an institution sanctified by God,' he repeats. 'Young men are too easily tempted by attractive, mature women.' He gets right up into my face. 'Especially when they are in close proximity to each other.'"

I gasp out loud, "My god, he thinks you're having an affair with Caleb?"

"Can you believe it?" Dannie's laugh is not a pleasant sound. "Apparently Lydia had gone to the Right Reverend, full-of-horseshit pastor with her paranoid suspicions. He counseled her to leave her job at the preschool—some crap about how women should be a constant presence in the home so that their husbands wouldn't stray. He also offered to pay for a hotel room so that they could be free of this 'den of iniquity'!"

"What century does he live in?"

"He's been against us since we changed the name from Daisy to Lotus. He cautioned Caleb that if he found out we were into any 'New Age nonsense' he would close his church account and instruct his parishioners to boycott the shop."

"Are you worried?"

"About the business, no. His is not the only church in town, and none of the others seem to share his sordid opinion of the Lotus, but Glendale is a small town and he could make things rather ugly."

*   *   *

Treacherous sleet and rain make the first wedding on Saturday morning a meteorological challenge. We look like the Three Stooges as we slip and slide up the walk balancing six gigantic arrangements of gardenias on our shoulders. We just barely manage to attach the sprays of orchids to the end of each and every pew and pin the roll of virginal white carpet into place before the bride and her entourage flock into the foyer. Since they are caught up in the task of shaking out their soggy feathers and repairing rain damage, I'm given the task of sorting out the tangle of bouquets and boutonnieres. Like a gaggle of geese, the ladies fuss and fume, fumble and complain until the strains of *Pachelbel's Canon* float forth from the string quartet. The protracted procession begins when six flower girls skip merrily down the aisle flinging rose pedals all over creation. The groom and best man are waiting at the altar, their eyes glazed over either from too many glasses of celebrative bubbly or too many allergy pills. Less than thirty minutes later, the organ recesses the happy couple out the door. But the torture isn't over. It resumes when the entire wedding party and their relatives trample back into the sanctuary for the staged photographs, which end up taking twice as long as the actual ceremony.

"I do believe there is such a thing as karma," Caleb says when the sun comes out just as they load themselves into their limousines.

In contrast, the second wedding resembles Shakespeare's *A Midsummer Night's Dream*. The bride and her single attendant are costumed in milky-white eyelet shifts with silvery fringed shawls draped over their shoulders. Daisy-chain wreaths halo their thick, wavy tresses.

"And who is this handsome young man?" I ask. Devin, looking awkward and uncomfortable in a wrinkled tie and ill-fitting jacket, is escorting the lovely Tracy, second cousin to the bride. She looks particularly lovely in a strapless, tea-length dress.

I pin the boutonniere on the father of the bride's lapel, make a final adjustment to the daisy hair clusters, and take a seat next to Dannie at the back of the sanctuary. A classical guitarist picks out Beethoven's *Ode to Joy*.

"They look so cute together," I whisper in Dannie's ear, gesturing at Devin and Tracy.

"Young love," she whispers back, taking my hand.

Overflowing with happiness, the newlyweds invite everyone, including us, to the potluck reception at their home. Dannie and Caleb receive a plethora of compliments for the floral arrangements.

"Valentine's Day is just around the corner," Dannie cheerfully reminds everyone. "Tell your friends."

As much as we all appreciate their kind invitation, Caleb needs to go home to his wife, and Dannie and I are a bit weary of the whole matrimony thing.

"Chinese takeout for dinner?" I ask.

"How about Thai."

"In Glendale?"

"No, the Big Apple. *Taste of Thai* has the best pad thai in the world. Let's blow this burb."

Dannie is dead serious. She convinces me to play hooky on Monday to spend a long weekend in her neck of the woods. "We all deserve a personal day now and then," she says. Ivy looks on disapprovingly as we heap several dishes full of kibble and leave the sink full of water.

* * *

New York City at anytime is a singular experience. New York City at Christmastime is magical. When I ask her how she procured a room at the most popular hotel during the peak season of the year, she merely shrugs. "I know people." Two orders of the most delicious pad thai I've ever tasted are delivered to our room shortly after our arrival.

The bird's-eye view from our window is spectacular. Above and below us, white lights sparkle and flash a continuous pulse of energy into the night sky.

Dannie encircles me with her arms. "Shooting stars seem to be our signature."

I turn into her warm body, the sweet aroma of rose petals in her shirt pocket tickles my nose.

There is no longer any hesitation in our lovemaking. We stoke our pleasures to the final drop. Dannie quietly clears her throat.

"What is it?" I ask. When she remains silent I prop myself up on my elbow so I can see her beautiful hazel eyes. They are wet with tears.

"You'll think that I'm soft in the head," she starts.

"Never." I cradle her soft parts closer to mine. "What has you so upset?"

"It's this thing with Mad-Chad. Maybe I shouldn't be spending so much time at the Lotus with Caleb. My flirtatious nature has gotten me into trouble before."

"It takes two to flirt," I remind her, brushing away her tears. "And Caleb is devoted to Lydia."

"But he's so young and impressionable."

"Now you sound like an old woman." I look her straight in the eyes. "Caleb is a grown man, and so is Mad—Chad. Perhaps it's time for the two of us to be more demonstrative in public."

"Are you ready for that?"

She doesn't need to elaborate. I'm aware that the chosen few in Glendale who know about us have accepted our relationship without question. However, when we're in town, at the shop, or in the school we certainly don't behave like lovers, and I'm not so naïve as to think that there aren't people who wouldn't decide to make things uncomfortable for both of us.

* * *

I dangle my feet over the side of the bed. It's hardly dawn, but the disturbing dream had startled me out of a sound sleep. The sudden storm in my nightmare had capsized our canoe, and we were frantically treading water, scanning the horizon for the shoreline. No sandy beach in sight, only a pile of rocks with one scraggly tree clinging to the jagged edge. I grab hold of a low branch and climb up on to the rocks. I fling my other arm out to give Dannie a hand up. She's just out of reach. "Swim closer," I call to her. "I don't think I can," the frightened voice calls back—not Dannie's voice. To my horror I see that the woman struggling in the water isn't Dannie—it's me.

Breathing deeply to cleanse the dream from my mind, I wrap my naked body around Dannie. She tucks my hand between her breasts and I feel her steady heartbeat against my fingertips.

* * *

Breakfast is fresh mangos, scrambled eggs, and buttermilk pancakes—in bed, of course. Then we take to the New York streets like a couple of felines in heat, prowling the stores on Fifth Avenue until our credit cards chafe in alarm.

I satisfy everyone on my Christmas list in record time. A feathery mohair sweater for 'Ria, a thousand-piece puzzle from the Metropolitan Museum of Art for Mom, a coffee-table book of geological wonders for Dad, and the ubiquitous sweatshirts, mugs, and coasters for neighbors and friends. After lunch we go our separate ways to make secret purchases for that someone special. Our final destination is Dannie's condo, where we'll be having dinner with Cath and Camdon Randolph, the friends who are subletting her place while their house in Mont Clare is undergoing renovations.

The elevator from the parking garage shoots us straight up to the penthouse! So this is Dannie's other life. I try not to be intimidated as we enter the massive double doors. Vaulted ceilings, skylights, and sleek, modern decor sprawl extravagantly throughout the capacious, open floor plan.

"So you're the one who has captured our Daniella's heart." The Randolph's have known Dannie for more than twenty years. Camdon is a former colleague and Cath teaches at a high school in the Bronx.

Our lively conversation ping-pongs back and forth between Wall Street woes and the frustrations of the educational system. Cath and Camdon are intrigued with the progress at the Yellow Lotus.

"All of Dannie's other projects have been here in the city," Cath says. "Now that we see the two of you together, we understand why she chose to stray so far into the wilderness."

It's late when we make our descent in the elevator. "Why would you choose to leave all of this, settle down with a country bumpkin like me, work your butt off at a flower/sweatshop where you are forced to put up with a judgmental preacher and a school full of teenage hooligans?"

Her words are light but in her expression I sense a deeper truth. "Perhaps I've become undeniably smitten." She looks away as soon as she's said it.

I wonder at my own tender response. "As have I." Is this love? I cannot bring myself to ask the question out loud.

*   *   *

We return home early Monday evening to find a distraught Ivy pacing beside her empty bowls. "Don't look so pathetic," I say. "I've seen how quickly you dispatch a mouse—you will never starve."

The remainder of the school week is a smorgasbord of final labs, unit tests, and holiday festivities. I receive no fewer than ten coffee mugs, all spouting words of academic drivel, and an insane number of red and green frosted cookies.

On the day before Christmas, after the multitudes of poinsettias have been artfully arranged on sacred altars up and down Main Street, Dannie invites me to attend an office party at the Lotus. It is an office party for four. Besides Dannie and me, she's invited Caleb and a very reluctant Lydia.

"I have an announcement to make," Dannie says. "I'm closing the Lotus."

CHAPTER 8

"I'M DREAMING OF *a white Christmas*," Dannie croons at the top of her lungs. It is Christmas morning and we are in the greenhouse watching big, fat, lazy flakes float like lacy bits of cotton candy onto the warm glass. The watery white crystals melt quickly, blurring our view of the wintry wonderland outside. Like children we draw crazy designs and love messages on the foggy windows.

By midafternoon the snow has coated the ground with more than six inches of powdery fluff. Dannie, Ivy, and I are curled up on the couch, hemmed in by an abundance of wrapping paper, boxes, and bows, evidence of our gift exchange.

"That's one mellowed-out cat," Dannie says. Ivy is snoring contentedly, her new catnip toy tucked under her chin, a shredded ribbon draped roguishly over one ear. "Santa certainly knew what she wanted."

"I'd say all around that Santa was a genius." I admire the exquisite gold watch by Cartier encircling my wrist.

"She definitely has great taste." Dannie tugs at the lapis earrings dangling from her ears. The lights on our Christmas tree blink in rhythm with Manheim Steamroller's *Jingle Bell Rock*. We had foregone the traditional evergreen sacrifice and commandeered the English holly from the greenhouse to serve as our Yule arborvitae.

Dannie stretches her arms over her head. "Closing the Lotus was the right thing to do. A week off will do us all good."

"I thought Caleb and Lydia were going to pass out when you gave them the gift certificate for a week's vacation at the Harbor Light Inn on the Cape."

"I have to admit that my motives were far from pure. It was partially a peace offering and partially a bribe, but I think Lydia got the message."

After Dannie had announced her plan to close the shop for a week she had drawn me into a full embrace and said to Lydia, "I do not now, nor will I ever covet your husband, capiche?"

*   *   *

The next morning, there were another four inches of snow on the ground. I toss Dannie her gloves and hat. "Shall we play in the snow?" We clear off the cars, shovel the driveway, and stomp on over to Uncle Willie's. Eliot bounds out to meet us, burrowing his nose in the deep drifts and chomping snowballs in his mouth.

"How about a snow angel?" I ask when we've finished digging out Willie's walkway. We sweep the snow with our arms and legs to make angelic figures while Eliot charges excitedly around in circles.

"Time for you younguns to come in and have some hot chocolate," Willie calls out. He's standing in the doorway, proudly wearing his *I love New York* sweatshirt.

"Damn fine Christmas," Dannie proclaims later, after we've Skyped with Mom and Dad. They loved the puzzle and the book, but they were over the moon about the Caribbean cruise Dannie and I had pooled our resources to give them.

Only one thing marred my holiday spirit. I had called 'Ria just after we'd returned from the city and invited her to come for Christmas and stay for a few days. "I wished you'd called earlier, Mom." Her voice sounded so far away. "I've already made plans." The doubt that she really had any plans still niggled at the back of my mind, and I wondered if she had even opened the gift card for the spa treatments we'd sent her. I look over at Dannie. She's building a tepee of kindling over rolls of newspaper. We are roasting marshmallows to make s'mores. Living with Dannie, sharing the holidays with her, sharing every day with her, makes me really happy. Someday 'Ria will understand.

"Thank you."

"For what?"

"I know this may sound sappy, but thank you for being in my life. I love you."

I wait for a cheeky response, but instead she says, "And I love you."

*   *   *

Dannie is away at a conference for the whole day. It's a bitter twenty degrees outside, but with the solar gain and the propane heater the greenhouse is a tropical paradise. "Nothing like a little heliotherapy," I say to Ivy as she settles herself among the blooming Christmas cactus and gloxinia. Soon I will plant my carrots and seed potatoes. Plans for the spring vegetable garden Dannie and I sketched are safely tucked away in a flower pot at the end of the table.

I set up my easel and unearth the untouched canvas and unopened tubes of acrylic paint I'd ambitiously purchased following the retreat. I stare at the vacant three-foot square. Selecting a wide nylon brush, I layer the lower half of the canvas with shades of smoky blue and hunter green. Above the horizon I splash on a pale yellow wash with a tiny hint of red; apricot streaks radiating from a white ball of fire. Sunrise or sunset? *Red at night sailor's delight, red in the morn sailors take warn,"* I rhyme. On my palate I smudge ample amounts of alizarin crimson into prussian blue and onto my brush, and push up a majestic magenta mountain range into the rising sun.

I clean my brush and step back from my work. My thoughts ascend to that pinnacle moment when Dannie and I declared our love for each other. I think back to the previous evening.

"Burnt to a crisp with extra chocolate, nice and gooey, just how I like it." Dannie was licking the remains of the charred s'more off her fingers.

I was still carefully turning my marshmallow over the hot coals, every inch a golden brown. "We are so very different," I'd said.

"And your point being . . . ?"

"How long before you become bored with me and my sedate lifestyle?"

"Perhaps you will be the first to become irritated with me and my bullshit. Love is a risky business."

"It can change everything."

"Of course it can. Love is dynamic and exciting. Now bring your exiting and dynamic body over here and we'll explore more important matters."

Dawn: The beginning of a new day is the title of my finished painting. Perhaps the rising sun is tinged a darker shade of red than is necessary. "*Sailors take warn.*" But for the moment, I will choose to ignore the warning and stand on the mountaintop with my arms wide open.

*　　*　　*

New Year's Eve is a blast! We are at Seth and Bea's house, munching our way through cheesy super nachos and sticky caramel popcorn while we wait for the ball to drop.

"Do you miss being live in Times Square?" Thomas asks Dannie. Thomas is Seth's younger brother from California. He's working on a master's degree in green energy, and he's the life of the party. We've spent the evening playing charades and making paper chains.

When the midnight hour approaches, Thomas informs us that since he's the only one with no significant other at the moment, he expects a kiss from everyone in the room. We oblige by showering his face with sloppy, wet kisses. "Not quite what I had in mind," he laughs.

"To us." Dannie clinks my glass. I soak in her expression of love, acknowledge my own heart's desire, and give up a silent moment of gratitude.

"To extreme happiness." Bea pats her baby belly and raises her glass of sparkling cider.

"Send some over this way," Thomas pleads.

When we get ready to leave, Seth does an impression of Mae West with his paper chain. "Perhaps we should wear these to the Jenkins's open house tomorrow, uh, I mean tonight."

"Maybe that's all we should wear," Dannie banters back.

"And give Priscilla the vapors?" Bea hands us our coats.

"Now that might be entertaining." Seth opens the door and the midnight air blasts into our faces. "But here's to a New Year's resolution of kinder thoughts."

"You're too good." Dannie waves as we get into the car.

*   *   *

At four o'clock that afternoon, we meander up the stone walk leading to the Jenkins's home. In contrast to the flags and patriotic banners from the Columbus Day celebration, our pathway is lit by votive candles in elegant glass lanterns. Pine garland laced with red bows and white lights is looped around the porch banister.

Dannie takes my breath away in her brocade jacket, a lush forest green with flecks of gold, her slivery-white hair swept up in a comb behind her head, the earrings I gave her suspended from her lovely earlobes like jeweled ornaments.

"Ravishing," she had murmured earlier when I'd slipped the sheer indigo shell over my black lace camisole. She helped me fasten the dainty strand of freshwater pearls around my neck, and whistled softly when I slid on a short skirt, black stockings, and heels.

We're welcomed at the door by Uncle Willie, looking extremely smart in a vermilion tartan vest. At his side is a freshly groomed, well-behaved Eliot wearing a matching neck bandana.

Dannie needs no introduction. Almost everyone in town has patronized the Yellow Lotus. They congratulate her on the shop's success. Teachers that had had Caleb as a former student remark on the dramatic change in him.

The air is dense with an amalgamation of smells. The tantalizing aroma of Julian's delicious catering wafts above a diverse odor of perfumes, aftershave lotions, and deodorants.

"So glad you two could be with us," Marilyn greets us. She points us in the direction of the living room. "Tim is around here somewhere. Please eat and enjoy."

We stroll through the beautifully decorated rooms, our mouths watering as we encounter table after table saturated with delectable treats. Bea and Seth are standing beside a marble fireplace, Yule log blazing, sucking up jumbo shrimp and sipping eggnog.

"Haven't seen you in a while," Seth jokes as we exchange hugs and kisses.

"Where's Thomas?" I ask.

"He has been absconded by Jenny and friends," Bea explains.

"They sure know how to throw a party," Dannie says, swallowing her third crab cake. "The place is crawling with dignitaries. Isn't that the president of Glendale's First National Bank talking to Tim?"

"Tim and Marilyn are well connected," I agree. "Try a mini quiche." I drop one on her plate beside the cucumber slices smothered in creamy dip, and ask Bea how she's feeling.

"No more morning sickness, thank god." She pats her distended belly. "However, I've succumbed to my first pair of maternity pants."

"I know what you mean," Mary, Evan's even more pregnant wife commiserates. "I'll be glad when I have my waist back again. This will be our fourth, and last."

Mary compliments Dannie on the window display at the Lotus. "When things get crazy at our house, which is most of the time, I daydream about sinking into that bed of roses."

"Fern designs our window dressings." Dannie puts her arm around me. "She's the artist, and my inspiration."

"How wonderful you all look!" Priscilla flounces over. In her fire-engine red dress with fuzzy white collar, and cuffs and black belt straining around her waist, all that's missing is the *ho, ho, ho.*

None of us like Priscilla. One can never tell if she's friend or foe. "So how long have the two of you been together?" Evan asks Dannie, trying to deflect Priscilla's presence.

"Together?" The question is barely a whisper, but the inference behind Priscilla's observation prickles the hair on the back of my neck. "You two live together?" She regards us over the rims of her granny glasses.

Like a beneficent angel, Marilyn descends upon our group and announces that the buffet dinner is being served in the dining room. "And Dannie, my dear," she says, "we can't thank you enough for recommending Julian. He has created a feast for the gods."

"Julian has certainly outdone himself," I say as we approach the feast of plated food laid out on the gargantuan oak table. Platters and tureens are burgeoning with yummy delicacies.

"So that's Priscilla the prude," Dannie elbows me as I ladle hollandaise sauce over my roasted asparagus spears.

"Shush." I look around, but for the moment Priscilla seems to have faded into the crowd.

"A spinster I suppose."

"No, she's married to the guy spooning artichokes onto his plate. He's the town clerk."

"So you know the chef?" Priscilla suddenly materializes beside us.

"He's a personal friend," Dannie brags. "Chef Julian's culinary talent far exceeds any of the upscale caterers I've engaged in the city."

I hardly recognize Dannie's voice it's so heavily peppered with snobbery. She further impresses upon Priscilla elaborate descriptions of the many dinner parties she's hosted at her penthouse suite, dropping famous names like a fireworks finale. Priscilla keeps right up with her, with an impressive list of celebrities she was personally responsible for during the filming of a movie right here in Glendale several years ago. Just when I'm not sure my nerves can take much more from either one of them, George distracts Priscilla with a question about a first-edition Dickens he rescued from a flea market. I sigh in relief when we finally settle at a table with Seth, Bea, Pete, and his fiancée, Melody. She's flashing a large, sparkling rock on the ring finger of her left hand.

"And then he went down on one knee and popped the question. So romantic," Melody swoons.

"And a fine romantic answer I received," Pete razzes her. "'Are you kidding?' she asks." He explains that they had been living together for almost five years with no urgent desire to step into the ranks of matrimony.

"I thought maybe you were just tired of sleeping in separate bedrooms when we visited my parents," Melody clarifies.

"Whether legally binding or not," Seth pipes up, sending a full bottle of wine around the table, "living with someone certainly has its perks." He grins mischievously. "Like having someone to share those unpleasant tasks with—cleaning the toilet, taking out the trash."

"I do believe some of us do more than our share," Bea jests.

Melody giggles. "I know exactly what you mean. Pete usually claims a sudden urge to correct papers every time the dog has an accident. I think there should be a prenuptial household chores agreement."

"You people are having way too much fun over here," Thomas says as he bestows a huge tray of desserts on the table. "I come bringing gifts and playmates." Behind him are Jenny, Lauren, and Dominic.

I introduce Dannie to Jenny and friends.

"Sounds like a Friday night situation comedy," she says, digging into a double fudge brownie and refilling her wine glass.

"George coined the name when the three of us moved in together"

"Ah, coed living," Dannie says, winking at me. "I guess this town isn't as provincial as I thought it was."

"Don't be too sure," Dominic corrects. "There are some who take great offense at our alternative lifestyle. For me it's simply a case of economics. Believe me, I have no designs on these women or any others. Now that Julian, on the other hand, too bad he wouldn't be interested."

"Shush." Lauren glances around, her eyes bright, her cheeks pink. "You never know who might be listening."

I can't tell if she's serious or just drunk. The wine has been flowing rather freely.

"My theory is," Dannie starts, her words slurring slightly, "that if someone is uptight about sex, it's because they just aren't getting enough of it."

"Here, here," Dominic raises his glass. "To more sex!"

The conversation takes a turn toward the rather raunchy, and I realize that besides me and the two women-with-child, most of the group is most definitely inebriated.

"Look out," Dannie warns none too softly. "The matron of the North Pole commeth, along with her Poindexter elf."

"Have you met my husband, Herbert?" Priscilla looks around expectantly.

"Herbert," Dannie says. She is most definitely drunk. "Is the wife getting enough, or what?"

Dominic clears his throat, "Well, I'd say it's time for us to be moving on." I hear muffled titters as Jenny and Lauren scrape up the last of their desserts, refill their glasses, and push away from the table.

"Well, I never," Priscilla sniffs. "A bad influence and a disgrace."

"Coffee anyone?" It's Tim Jenkins. He places the coffee pot directly in front of Dannie. "Priscilla, Hebert, I've been looking all over for you. Do you have a moment? I received a letter from the Landry's attorney. The estate has finally been settled and he wants to arrange a meeting with you to discuss the bequest for the library."

Priscilla nearly levitates off the floor. "Yes." She bats her eyes. "Excuse me everyone, but one must sometimes answer to a higher calling."

"Who died and made you moral compass of the world?" Dannie asks. I don't know if Priscilla heard Dannie's question or just choose to ignore it.

"Ow!" Dannie glares in my direction.

"Sorry. Didn't know that was your leg." I'm livid, but somehow I manage to control myself long enough to say our good-byes.

I swipe the keys from Dannie's hand. "I'll drive."

CHAPTER 9

T HE MORNING SUNLIGHT reflects off the row of Bunsen burners, spotlighting the recently polished lab tables. I sigh. The lemony-scented waxed floors will soon be scarred by hundreds of scuff marks. I enjoy one last moment of blessed quietness before the hoards of teenagers trample their sweaty bodies and nervous energy into the second semester of the school year. Some will return with a genuine resolve to start the new year off right; others will not be so motivated and will just manage to keep their heads above water until June.

I tap the sharp point of my pencil on the edge of my neat and tidy desk. Dannie and I definitely started our new year off with a bang.

The tiffs we'd survived on the retreat seemed like minor skirmishes compared to the major league blow up that had played out after the Jenkins's party. I confess I'm a first-class wuss when it comes to conflict. No practice at it. My folks' isolated spats always ended with Mom giving the final word and Dad going along with it, and confrontation with Ed was nonexistent because we were rarely in the same room long enough. During our counseling sessions, Ed and I were told that in order to experience passion in the bedroom we had to display passion in other aspects of our lives—arguments included. That being the case, Dannie and I could look forward to a tempestuous time together—if we stayed together.

"What the hell was that for?" By the time we'd returned home that night, Dannie had sobered up sufficiently to feel the sore spot on her leg.

"I guess I kicked you harder than I thought."

"I think you gave me a bruise."

"Well, you overstepped!" My unusually angry voice had sent Ivy into the next room.

"That Priscilla chick is a twit. I was just starting to have some fun."

"I have to work with that twit." My voice wavers.

"You're really pissed."

"I am pissed. Why were you acting so weird?"

"Weird? I like to push the envelope, you know that. I'm used to parties with a little more pizzazz."

"Then maybe you should go back to your fancy-ass city." I storm into the bedroom and slam the door. After what seems like an eternity of lying on the bed with my wet eyes wide open, I return to the living room. She's in her recliner staring into space.

I sit on the edge of the arm. "I'm sorry. You were right. You were just being yourself."

She leans against me. "I'm sorry too. I didn't intend to make a scene." She adds warily, "I guess you can take me out of the city, but you can't take the city out of me."

"Why should you have to? As soon as we have a free weekend we'll 'blow this burg,' as you say, and you can get your city fix."

*   *   *

"What's up, Ms. DeGiulio?" Mario saunters into my first period class and flings his backpack on to the lab desk. Wrinkled papers spew out of the open zipper.

"Welcome back." I help him pick up the scattered mess. Mario is one of those kids who means well but can never seem to get it together. My heart warms when his girlfriend, Hannah, a meticulous young lady, straightens his notebooks. I guess it's true: opposites attract.

I pass out fresh lab books and start to outline the new unit on sustainable energy. The expressions on their faces range from tentative enthusiasm to total boredom. I love my job.

When the final bell tolls, the building empties, and the members of the Grub Club gather for their first meeting of the year.

"My New Year's resolution is to be on time for detention," Brad announces.

"That's the dumbest thing I've ever heard." Crystal bops him on the back of the head. "Here's a thought—don't be late for school in the first place, and you won't have detention to begin with."

"But I need my beauty sleep," Brad whines, rubbing his head.

"That's so lame." Tracy comes strolling in on Devin's arm.

I credit Devin with the initial success of the club. Last fall he convinced his buddies Jay and Brad to check it out. Jay invited his cousin Shelley, who talked to her friends Caila and Meg. Tracy tags along because she hangs with Devin, and Crystal attends because she has a thing for Brad.

"Wicked cool!" Jay exclaims when Crystal unfurls the blueprints for the Memorial Day float.

I hand around an official-looking paper with line items and intimidating numbers. "Mrs. McNamara needs us to make notes of any changes we want so she can complete the final draft. This is a copy of the budget."

"Whoa, that's a lot of cash!" Jay stammers.

"Lumber is very expensive, dingdong," Meg piques.

"Yeah," Brad jokes, "what do ya think, those two-by-fours grow on trees?"

Shelley rolls her eyes. "Jeez, Brad, you're such an idiot."

I suggest that we brainstorm ways to raise more money. I remind them that we can start with the fifty dollars that we made from our Christmas cactus sale.

"How about corporate sponsors?" Devin asks. "I bet Dannie, I mean Ms. Stevens, would make a donation. We could use the side of the float for advertisements."

"That's a great idea." I don't need to say anything more because the other kids, who will not be outdone, soon have a substantial list of local businesses to approach for contributions.

*   *   *

I'm late getting home. The house is dark and there's a note on the refrigerator:

Delivering Chinese delicacies and dog treats to Willie and Eliot.
Come when you can.

Willie's policy is that if his door is unlocked, we should knock and then walk in. When I enter I hear laughter. Dannie and Willie are camped out on his couch, clacking chopsticks in and out of takeout containers, carrying on like a couple of coeds.

"It's you." Dannie stands to greet me with a hug and a kiss. She hands me a container of chow mein. "Dig in. Willie is divulging some very surprising adventures from his youth."

"I guess we all do outlandish things when we're young," Willie says, scratching Eliot behind the ears. "Speaking of wayward youth, how was your first day back at the salt mines?"

"The Grub Club made some real progress with plans for the float." I share a few other sound bites from my day. I conclude optimistically, "Even though for some of the students the learning curve is steep and chaotic, most of the time I think the future of the world is in capable hands."

Dannie sucks down a lo mien noodle. "When I was that age I was a real bozo. I won't elaborate because I don't want to tarnish my fine reputation."

"Too late," I tease.

"Well, I know I'd never want to go back," Willie states emphatically. "Ninety-five is my best year yet."

*   *   *

"Did he look all right to you?" Dannie asks when we're getting ready for bed.

"Who, Willie?" I snuggle up next to her under the covers. "Maybe a little tired," I yawn. "Why?"

"He just didn't seem to have as much energy as usual."

"I hope I have half his energy when I'm that age."

"Even so, I think I'll stop by more often."

"You're really quite fond of Willie, aren't you?" I ask her.

"He's kind of like the father I never had," she says.

*   *   *

January slides by with hardly a chance to blink. My students knuckle down with preparations for the regional science fair; the members of the Grub Club diligently search out float sponsors, and the Yellow Lotus gears up for Saint Valentine's Day. Despite the fact that I now work exclusively in the greenhouse so Dannie can spread out in the spare room, the house is definitely proving its diminutive stature. Occasionally we throw out the idea of expanding—one more room would be nice, maybe a half-bath off the kitchen. But there's never time to do more than just talk about it, so it gets postponed, along with the previously proposed journey to the city.

Dannie funnels all of her time into the Lotus. I know that she's anxious to move on to another project. I try not to think about what that might mean for us. Business at the shop is booming. Lydia finally decided to quit her job at the preschool, and even though she is still tempered toward Dannie, she's begun to take more of an interest in the flower trade. Turns out she has quite a creative streak, and when she comes up with a clever idea for the spring display, I'm more than happy to relinquish my window-dressing assignment.

Like billiard balls, Dannie and I bump into one another as we spin through our daily tasks. Our differences both attract and annoy. Where I tend to evade issues, she's more apt to tackle them head-on—like yanking a Band-Aid off. Her theory is that even though the initial "ouch" can be harsh, the hurt is afforded more opportunity to heal. Most of the time, we find a compromise we can both live with.

*   *   *

Since Saint Valentine's Day falls smack in the middle of the February break, the school hosts its Sweetheart Ball, a.k.a. the Heart to Heart Dance (balls went out with wicked stepmothers), on the Friday evening before the vacation week. Once again I chaperone and Dannie generously assists with the decorations. According to her it's good advertising, but I think she secretly likes to hang with the kids.

"Got a minute?" Bea peers into my homeroom class the morning of the dance.

Her blank face is difficult to read. "Are you and the baby all right?"

"Everything's fine." She pats her tummy. "It's you I'm worried about."

I start to joke about there being no more babies coming from this body, but she stops me.

"It's Priscilla. Once again she's trying to stir up trouble."

"Again?"

"Priscilla revels in instigating disturbances. If there aren't any brewing in the wings, she'll fabricate one just for good measure. Last year she petitioned to have morning prayer reinstated after the pledge of allegiance."

"Since we don't pray in my homeroom she obviously didn't win that one."

"No, Marilyn put her in her place by asking exactly which prayer she had in mind; Islam's five a day, the Hail Mary, or a Buddhist Meditation?"

"So what's her pick now, and what does it have to do with me?"

"This time it's personal. It's you and Dannie."

"Oh."

"Yesterday I overheard her bending Evan's ear about the dance chaperones setting a good example. Evan thought she was talking about dress codes and assured her that no one on his committee would be wearing a halter top or a backless gown."

I laugh, but I know full well that Priscilla's real solicitude has nothing to do with my wardrobe. Ever since New Year's Day, she continually stops me in the hall or tails me into the lunch room to pester me about whatever nonsensical notion is brewing in her brain at the moment. Somehow she always maneuvers the conversation to some question about Dannie.

*   *   *

"She isn't staying, is she?" Priscilla's question is an accusation.

Dannie is arranging buckets of red and white carnations on the buffet table. She's swaying seductively to the sixties tune the DJ is playing.

"Remember this one?" Dannie boogies over to me and spins me around. "Don't worry, Priscilla, I'm just leaving. I wouldn't want to rub off my bad influence on the little ones. Anyway, I'm needed back at the Lotus to help Caleb and Lydia prepare for the Andrews' wedding." She winks at me. "I'll see you later."

Priscilla spins on her heels and turns her attention to the kids spilling into the gymnasium. She scrutinizes their attire. The dress code is clear: breasts, backs and buttocks must be modestly concealed at all times. Of course, some have chosen to challenge this code to its limits. One young lady arrives in a lovely full-length gown with a neckline that plunges dangerously close to her navel. Priscilla tries to force her to wear one of the large tee shirts that she brought just for the occasion.

"I got this one," I say, artistically draping a colorful shawl over the offending orbs. "I always bring extra just in case." I'm rewarded with a grateful look from the girl and the glare of the devil from Priscilla. "You might want to offer the shirt to the young man who just arrived," I say, trying to redeem myself. "He seems to have forgotten his dress shirt." Sure enough, the guy in question had positioned his very black tie right down the center of his very naked, very hairy chest.

I watch the turbulent teens career about the room with awkward abandonment and I'm suddenly cognizant of the fact that I may have more in common with my pubescent pupils than I do with my own peers. I experience only sympathy when I see a very determined Priscilla waddle after Devin and Tracy and physically remove Devin's hand from Tracy's bottom.

The DJ plays his final tune and the dance is over. "See you next Thursday, Ms. DeGiulio." Shelley and Crystal wave as they join the departing throng.

"Nine o'clock sharp," I remind them.

One of the more ingenious money raising ideas the members of the Grub Club came up with was hiring themselves out to do odd jobs during the vacation week. We'll be convening at Uncle Willie's the day after Valentine's Day to remove so-called rummage from his house.

*   *   *

For Dannie, Valentine's Day dawns excruciatingly early. I give her a sleepy kiss good-bye, and promise to make her favorite curry dish for dinner. She promises not to be too late.

"Not to worry," I say tracing the crease in her brow. I know she's stressed about the extra delivery of roses coming in on time for all those last-minute romantic gestures of the day. "Curry only gets tastier the longer it sits."

I treat myself to a lazy lounge in bed with a mystery novel where the entire cast of human characters acts like idiots and the cat is ultimately the one who solves the crime.

"You could have wrapped that up before chapter four," I say to Ivy, who is watching as I stir honey into my tea. She follows me out to the greenhouse and together we stare in amazement at the awesome sight. Every available surface is covered with crystal vases filled with long stemmed red roses. The fragrance is almost overpowering. "Thank you, Dannie," I murmur, careening around the room and tickling my nose with the soft, velvety petals, "for being your wonderful, over-the-top self."

I sip my tea and think about the silver pendant in the neatly wrapped box waiting on the table for Dannie. When I'd told the local jeweler that I was looking for a gift for my partner he'd immediately brought out trays of tie clips, cuff links, and heavy gold rings. I shook my head and pointed to the more feminine selections.

"Ah," he said. "I see. No problem."

Except then the choices increased tenfold. A locket seemed too juvenile, and the rings . . . I don't know, too permanent? But as soon as I saw the circular pendant I knew it was just right. It resembled a ring on a chain with Dannie's birthstone suspended in the center like a floating star.

*   *   *

"Men are such silly creatures," Dannie says, spooning out mango chutney onto her curry. I pass her the bowl of cashews and raisins. "The later they come into the shop the more flowers they tend to buy."

"Are you saying that there's a direct correlation between pangs of guilt and petals of roses?" I slyly indicate the vase in the center of the table and think about the other five still in the green house.

Dannie coughs. "I'm no man, and I assert no guilty conscience. Besides, I get an employee discount." She plucks a flower from the vase. "Every rose I sold today reminded me of you." She slips a small velvet-covered box from her pocket and places it in front of me.

"Well now," I say coyly, sliding a similar jeweler's box in her direction. "Great minds must think alike."

"It's more coincidental than mystical," she confesses. "I was delivering a get-well bouquet across the street when I happened to see you walk out of the jewelry store. The gentleman at the sales counter was more than cooperative in advising me of the perfect gift to compliment the one my partner had just purchased. Allow me." She sweeps aside my hair and fastens the silver pendant around my neck—identical to the one I'd given her, except the floating star is my own birthstone. "I like not flying solo on Valentine's Day."

I nod. "Or any other day for that matter."

CHAPTER 10

THE FOLLOWING MORNING, Willie welcomes our unlikely troop of laborers with coffee and donuts. Julian has offered us the use of his van to cart away the anticipated recyclables to the Salvation Army.

"Are you sure you want to part with this?" I ask more than once when Willie designates the removal of an antique dresser, a pedestal table, and many of the other relics that look to me like museum-quality pieces.

"Haven't touched them in years—'bout time someone else did."

"Jeez, this thing is heavy," Brad puffs. "What is it?"

"That, son, is a commode." He swings open the single door. It's chock full of old magazines.

"A what? Oh, you mean a magazine holder." Brad stoops down and pulls out a dog-eared periodical. "Wow, these are really old. Look at the date on this one—1965." He makes it sound like it was the year of the dinosaur. Willie and I just smile at each other. I was in grade school that year, and I suspect that he was at the height of his teaching career.

"Not for magazines, silly," Crystal informs Brad. "It's where they put the toilet."

"No way."

"Seriously." Crystal smirks as she pulls out the porcelain chamber pot that is wedged behind the *National Geographic*s.

"It saved us from making a trip to the outhouse on those cold winter nights," Willie chuckles. "Not much use for anything now I guess, except maybe a planter."

"Great idea." I take the offensive vessel from Crystal.

"Whatever," Jay says in disgust. "Just make sure you wash it out good before you fill it with dirt."

Everyone laughs.

By lunchtime the kids are tired. Dannie delivers pizza, we pack up one last load and quit for the day.

Munching on sweet green pepper and gooey mozzarella cheese, I survey our progress.

"You've made more than a dent," Willie says, handing me a check. "Thank you."

Even I'm taken aback by the amount written in his neat hand. I pass the very generous check around. The kids are dumbfounded.

"Hot damn," Meg cries. "For an old guy you're all right."

"You're not so bad yourself. Now be sure to build a grand float for the parade."

"As our biggest sponsor, I think that you should ride on the float with us." Caila says.

"I'd be honored."

*   *   *

The end of February brings one more blast of snow, dropping eight inches in the wee hours of a Friday morning. School is canceled, giving us all a long weekend. Dannie takes the day off from work, and we use the cross-country skiis we'd salvaged from Willie's to kick and glide over the snow-packed fields.

"Don't be surprised if I'm home more during the day," she explains as we add a drizzle of mint liqueur into our hot chocolate. "Caleb and Lydia are beginning to pick up steam at the Lotus and I want to clear the way for their eventual takeover."

I'm almost afraid to ask, "But what will you do with yourself?" This is it; she's getting ready to go back to the city.

"I think I'll learn to cook."

* * *

"Dinner is ready."

"Did anyone ever tell you how sexy you look in an apron?" I say. I wipe a flour smudge from her chin.

"No one's ever seen me in an apron before." She removes a steamy, hot pasta casserole from the oven. "This cooking thing isn't as difficult as I thought it would be." She places the casserole into a thermal carrier.

"Hey, where are you going with that?"

"We're eating at Willie's. One more set of taste buds to test a Julian original."

And so it goes: nearly every night, we dine at Willie's, as Dannie experiments with yet another of Julian's mouth-watering recipes. Willie is thrilled, and not just because of the free meals. I can see that he has genuine affection for Dannie.

On the evening of the ides of March, after stuffing ourselves with a triple-cheese and veggie lasagna, Willie surprises us by producing a plate of his very own homemade chocolate frosted cupcakes. It's his birthday, and unlike last year when there was a big bash to commemorate his ninety-fifth, this year he prefers to quietly celebrate with his two favorite neighbors.

"We're your only neighbors," we remind him. We serenade him with the traditional birthday tune.

"How many more verses are there to this crazy song?" he asks, slightly flushed after we've finished: "*You look like a monkey and you act like one too.*"

"Willie is such a peach," I say. "You are so good for each other." We wave to Willie and Eliot as we head for home. The air temperature is surprisingly warm. "I smell an early spring." I hook my arm through Dannie's.

The light we'd left on in the kitchen spills out of the window and onto the barren flower beds. "Soon it will be time to clear out the dead stalks and turn the soil." I reach down and flake away a corner from the blanket of leaves that covers the sleeping perennials.

"It's all new to me," Dannie says. "The closest I've come to any real attempt at propagation is when I tried to root an avocado pit in a jelly jar." She chatters on. "I don't suppose we need to hire a pair of oxen to till the soil. Maybe we should plant some of those mystery vegetables Julian calls for in his recipes, like okra, kale, and rutabaga."

"You mean the ones you had to research on the Internet?" I tease. "And for your information, they've replaced oxen with a newfangled machine called a rototiller."

We enter the greenhouse and admire the young seedlings of tomatoes, peppers, and squash in their peat pots. I pluck Joe's journal from the top shelf. "It's all in here," I tell her. "What he planted, when he planted it, and how he cared for it."

"God bless Uncle Joe."

*   *   *

The gnarly vines are so dense that my pathway is nearly obscured. It's a massive jungle of green beans, corn husks, and zucchini blossoms. The tomato plants that tower over my head are loaded with fruit the size of baseballs. I reach up to pick one, anticipating its sweet, tangy juice.

Slap! Something forces my hand down. A thick mat of fur chokes my nostrils. I push it away. I'm startled into consciousness when five pinpoint claws prick at my face. It's Ivy.

"Ouch! Stop that! It's way too early." I push her off again. Not to be deterred, she stomps on my chest. I roll out of bed, stumble into the kitchen, and throw kibble into her dish. She ignores the fresh food, streaks right past her dish, and races into the greenhouse. I hear the sound of manic clawing and distressed whining. It's Eliot, trying to stuff himself through Ivy's door flap.

I open the door. "What are you doing out so early?" Instead of coming inside, Eliot barks repeatedly and tears off into the field. When I hesitate he charges back, barks again, and nips at my pajama pants.

"I get it." I throw on my coat, shove my bare feet into my boots and follow.

One, two, three rings. "Come on Dannie, pick up." On the fifth ring, I hear her groggy answer, "You'd better not be a credit card company," she yawns, "'Cause if you are . . ."

I cut her off. "It's me," my voice falters.

"Fern? Where are you?"

"I'm at Willie's."

*   *   *

One week later, on a magnificent, cloudless day as the crocus and daffodils peek up from the ground, we scatter the ashes of Dr. William Thomas Jenkins, nature enthusiast, world-class educator, and neighbor extraordinaire, across the land he loved and lived on his entire life.

The outpouring of gratitude from former students and colleagues is astounding. E-mails from around the world flood the school computers with exalted words of appreciation for this special man who had touched their lives and made such a difference. Teaching is one of those professions where the remunerations for services rendered seldom equal the dedication of one's entire career. However, I am certain that the resounding praise from those who gathered that day in the school's auditorium for Willie's memorial celebration reached beyond the boundaries of life and death.

"I vote we name our Memorial Day float the Uncle Willie's Emissary of Eco—Consciousness," Devin announces when he calls the Grub Club meeting to order on the following afternoon.

"Hey, Einstein, where do you come up with these hundred-dollar words?" Tracy asks.

Devin's voice catches slightly, "Uncle Willie didn't just teach me how to prune apple trees."

The decision is unanimous to name the float in memory of Willie, and it's suggested that Eliot be given a seat of honor to ride in on the day of the parade.

*   *   *

I'm not sure who is in the worse funk, Ivy or Dannie. Ivy misses Eliot, who is now staying with Marilyn and Tim, and Dannie misses Willie.

"I don't know if I can do this," she says, stirring a pot of homemade chili.

At first I think she's talking about the excessive amount of chili powder Julian has called for, but then I see the sadness on her face. I take the spoon from her hand. "I'll finish this."

"I know he had a good, long life," she sighs. "It just sucks that I didn't show up until the end of it."

I try to console her. "He loved you, Dannie. His eyes always sparkled when you went to visit him, and not just because you brought great food. You brought laughter, and that's about the best gift anyone can give."

Most days the regularity of my classes keeps me focused, but Dannie just mopes around the house.

"The Lotus doesn't need me anymore," is all she answers when I ask if she's ready to go back to work.

"Maybe it's time to begin a new project." The pain of seeing her in such misery overrules any worry that a new project might take her away from me. But she's not interested. She spends most of her days in front of the television, flipping channels, and staring at old catalogs. Many nights she doesn't even bother coming to bed; she just falls asleep in her chair.

I'm hopeful that our plans to visit my folks in Florida during the April break will not only provide a change of scenery but will also spark some inspiration. For the most part I leave her alone, recognizing that everyone grieves differently.

Meanwhile I halfheartedly join forces with my colleagues in preparation for the annual April first fund-raising festival. Nicknamed the Festival of Fools, it had its humble roots as a simple bake sale, but it's morphed so many times over the years that it now resembles a state fair and requires months of planning.

The Grub Club is selling African violets and is so well organized that I'm assigned to help Priscilla at the book table.

I complain to Bea. "Why can't I sell balloons at the minicarnival?"

"No one wants to work with Priscilla," Bea says. "We've all had to do it, now it's your turn."

Since this extravaganza is highly anticipated by the entire community, donations have been pouring in for weeks. Priscilla and I sort through bags and boxes of hard—and softcover volumes. She tries not to cringe when she touches the seedy romance novels, I attempt to be philosophical as I stack the works of science fiction, and we both do our best not to hurl the hunting manuals into the trash. Somebody will want to buy them, and it's for a good cause.

"How goes the toil with the literary leviathan?" Dannie asks me when I come home. She's actually in the kitchen making a grilled cheese sandwich.

Is it my imagination or does she seem a little cheerier? "Literary leviathan, that's a good one. Let's just say that I'm doing my best to coddle my colicky colleague." I'm pleased when Dannie offers me a thin smile in response.

Ironically, it's the ponderous Priscilla who provides the impetus that ultimately frees Dannie from her despondency. As we're shelving a collection of P. D. James mysteries, she boasts about her most recent visit with Marilyn and Tim.

"That poor old dog won't eat or drink," she says, "he's wasting away. Maybe they should put him out of his misery."

It's a good thing that I have such great respect for P. D. James or I might have become her next murder suspect with her novel, *Devices and Desires*, a most convenient murder weapon.

Instead I stop by the principal's office on my way home. My serendipitous proposal is instantly approved.

"We're home!" My words are drowned out as Eliot thunders his way onto the couch, slathering a very surprised and very pleased Dannie with thousands of slobbery kisses. Why hadn't I thought of this before? Marilyn and Tim had insisted that Eliot should stay with us permanently. They knew how much he missed Willie, how much he missed the woods, even how much he missed Ivy, but apparently none of us realized how much he missed Dannie.

Dare I say it? *Thank you, Priscilla*. Although she continues to reject the enticement to explore another business venture, Dannie makes the effort to get up and dressed every day and take Eliot for long walks in the woods. She tosses countless sticks for him to fetch, and bathes and grooms him like a show dog.

"Are the two of you coming to the festival tomorrow?" I ask.

"Perhaps." She's brushing Eliot's shiny coat.

"I miss you." I try not to sound wistful, but it seems like ages since we've touched each other.

"I know. I'm sorry."

CHAPTER 11

S HE'S GONE.
Eliot and I went to the city. Need some space. Don't worry.
I'll be in touch. STOP! The message scrawled across the scrap of paper stuck under the *I love NY* magnet is as sterile and flat as a telegram from a stranger.

"Coward!" I shout. I wing the magnet across the room. It smashes on to the floor and shatters into a million pieces. "You'll be in touch? You mean like before, when you got bored with your lavish life and decided to show up on my humble doorstep? I don't think so. If you want space, you can bloody well have it!" In a blind fury I tear around the house and snatch up her junk and clutter. Her books, her papers, her clothes; everything that even whispers her presence, I fling into the spare bedroom, den, her office—whatever the hell it is. BANG!

"This house isn't big enough for the two of us anyway." My tirade recedes as my anguish wanes and I collapse onto the couch. Ivy, her body tightly bundled up on the fireplace mantle, stares at me, her eyes dilated in fear. When I approach her with a desperate look of apology, she merely blinks and turns away.

I go into the bathroom to wash my face, and there on the back of the toilet, staring at me like an evil eye, is Dannie's birthstone pendant. "Did it mean anything to you?" I seal it into an envelope and pen across the flap, *You forgot something.*

*   *   *

"Fern DeGiulio, come on down!" Like an out-of-body experience, I observe myself screaming and running toward contestant's row. I win the washer/dryer, dash up to the stage, and bear-hug an ancient Bob Barker.

"Congratulations," he says into his microphone. "Now all you have to do is choose the correct price for the corresponding prize and you will win both the sleep sofa and the trip for two to Australia."

It all seems too easy. The audience goes wild when I get it right.

"Now." Bob puts his arm on my shoulders. "Tell us who that special someone is who will be going to Australia with you."

"Oh," I stammer. "I don't know." A loud buzzer goes off and the crowd hisses and boos.

"Well that's just too darn bad." Bob grins at me like the Cheshire cat. "No partner, no trip."

I wake up to the clatter of heavy rain pelting against the windows, and a hell of a headache. Ivy leaps onto the bed, spraying me with mud and water, toweling her filthy paws and wet fur on the sheets. The room is dank with the smell of damp silk and wet cat.

"Oh, Ivy," I wail. "Yuck!"

One does not give a cat a bath, so I scoop her up and dump her disgusting self onto Dannie's fine leather chair.

When I open the freezer in search of the extra can of coffee, I behold instead the half gallon of coffee ice cream—why not? Three spoonfuls into the carton and I'm shivering uncontrollably. Using a partially burnt log in the pile of ashes, I manage to light a pitiful fire. Ivy completes her bath and settles down for her first nap of the day. The rain that had been pounding the earth for most of the night ceases, and the sun makes a lame attempt to clear away the clouds. My extreme anger shifts to an exposed hurt. How could she just leave me like that? I imagine her flippant response: "Commitment is just not my bag." I was a fool to think that our love was enough to keep her satisfied for very long.

I groan. "Oh god." My stomach is so bloated with ice cream and nervous knots that I think I'm going to be sick. I double over and bump my head on the coffee table. A thick layer of dust invades my nostrils. "This is not helpful."

And so I purge—not my body but my house. From floor to ceiling, I brush out nasty spiderwebs, mop up killer dust bunnies, and polish every wooden surface within an inch of its life. When I finish scouring the kitchen, I am physically exhausted but emotionally cleansed.

To make amends for the unorthodox breakfast I ate, I fix myself a spinach salad for lunch. The sun is now high in the sky, and the fresh air beckons me outside. Ivy bounces over to a patch of garden and begins to scratch in the damp dirt. The intoxicating aroma of moist earth implores, "It's spring—the season you've been pining for—come play."

My tired, stiff muscles scream in warning, "If you do, you'll be sorry." I sit on the greenhouse threshold, slow my breathing, and decide to defer doing anything more to another day.

With the approaching twilight, my loneliness and disappointment become amplified. Being alone in bed is excruciating. I wake up several times in the night clinging to Dannie's pillow, soaking the satin fabric with tears. I stagger into an early morning and force myself to get ready for school. How will I ever get through the day?

*   *   *

Bea's belly enters my classroom before she does. "What gives, oh bleary-eyed one?"

"Some Mondays seem to last a lifetime," I sigh. "I canceled this afternoon's meeting of the Grub Club. I just can't face it."

"The kids are worried about you. They say you nearly blew up the school during sixth period."

"I think that may be a bit of an exaggeration."

"Maybe so, but I don't think that the kids were exaggerating when they said you were acting weird. What's wrong?"

"Not here."

"Come over to the house then. Seth is at a book signing and won't be back until late. We can comfort ourselves with leftover macaroni and cheese and you can tell me the whole sad story."

"Do you think you should call her?" She asks after I've finished spilling my guts, and gorging myself with a second helping of creamy pasta.

"Not yet."

"You'll know when the time is right." She places my hand on her swollen tummy. "Hey, check out this baby action!" The traveling bump protruding just beneath her tightly stretched skin sends me back twenty-three years, and I can't help but touch my own abdomen, the pleasant memory of baby 'Ria as vivid and poignant as the present moment.

"'Ria." I say her name out loud. That's who I need to call.

Her answering machine picks up. I decide not to go into details, but simply ask her if there's any way she can take a few days off and meet me in Florida. "I'll be on my own," I add, knowing that will further entice her.

*　　*　　*

The inertia of the first few days without Dannie gradually lifts and I begin to embrace the season of my heart—spring. Mother Earth bursts forth with new life, and everywhere I look I'm rewarded with hope and expectation. I bury my lapses of self-pity beneath a surface of busy-ness.

I'm touched by the genuine concern my students have for me after Monday's near explosion. They try their best to cheer me up. At our next meeting, all the members of the Grub club show up with their thumbs painted green. They insist on painting my own opposing digits to match. We all have a good laugh.

"My Grandmother says that laughter is the best medicine," Shelley tells me. "And since she claims she's never been sick a day in her life, she must be right."

The only student who knows what's really bothering me is Devin. He'd become privy to Dannie's absence when he rode his bike to the house to see Eliot.

"Sometimes life just sucks," he'd commiserated.

*　　*　　*

I continue to throw my energies into my gardening. I follow Joe's journal to the letter, each day hauling the trays of seedlings beyond the protection of the greenhouse walls and taking them back in again at night to harden them before they are planted into the ground. Mulching the rotting detritus back into the soil of the gardens that encircle the perimeter of my home nourishes my own emaciated emotions like a healing elixir. My spirits are buoyed by the neatly laid rows of tomatoes and peppers and the mounded hills of zucchini.

It's only the long, lonely evenings that threaten to drag me down. I concentrate on correcting papers while I eat dinner so that I don't notice the empty place across from me at the table. I discipline myself to stay awake until the eleven o'clock news by watching reruns on retro TV of Perry Mason and Nancy Drew mysteries. Countless times I pick up the phone, sometimes I even dial, but I never wait for the connection to be completed.

'Ria is thrilled to be going to Florida. She proffers extreme diplomacy when I explain that Dannie's truancy is due to an unexpected trip to the city. (Not a total lie.) She e-mails a detailed mother-daughter itinerary of spree shopping and beach hopping that makes my head spin.

While I'm away, Bea and Seth have agreed to look in on Ivy and water my plants. With the baby due in less than a month, their only plans are to stay close to home, finish decorating the nursery, and soak up the last few weeks of being just the two of them.

*　　*　　*

In my classroom, spring fever hits the students like the bubonic plague. Thank god Pete and I have scheduled another art and nature field trip.

The clocks are not yet registering daylight savings time, so it's very early when we whip the sleeping younguns off their morning busses and into the vans. Before we disembark, I lay out the rules of engagement.

"What exactly do you mean by absolute silence?" Caila wants to know. "And why is it so important?"

"Because it's the middle of the night," Brad complains. "And any sane animal is still asleep. I should still be asleep."

"Actually," I counter, "early morning is the best time to see the most activity. The nocturnal creatures are rambling off to their dens, and the diurnal animals are scrounging up their morning meal."

Tracy yawns. "I always knew that I was nocturnal."

We creep off the bus and make our way across the fields. Three deer bound out of the tall grass flashing their white tails, giving credence to my tutelage. We've been studying bird migration, so I point out the flock of tree swallows flitting about, nabbing at unsuspecting bugs, their white bellies and iridescent indigo scissor wings dancing above the overgrown meadow. With quiet stealth, we tiptoe on the trail.

Whoop, whoop, whoop, whoop . . . a powerful surge of air current whips over our heads. In tandem, two long necks stretch out from white feathery bodies. The pair of swans wing their way toward the pond. They land smooth and sure, like the bow of a canoe coasting toward the shoreline, barely cutting the water's surface. The kids sketch the regal couple as they paddle around the edge of the pond, once again scoping out the perfect place to make their nest.

No problem with commitment there, I think. *Swans mate for life*.

CHAPTER 12

"READY TO GO?" Seth is at my door. He's driving me to the airport.

"I think so." I hand him my suitcase, take one last look around, and give Ivy a reassuring rub behind her ears. "Don't worry, I'll be back in a few days."

On board the plane, I recline my seat and release an audible sigh. The tears that gather in my eyes are an unwelcome reminder that the wall I've constructed to contain my melancholy is nothing more than a wisp of fabric.

Every time I think I've finally resigned myself to Dannie's desertion, something sets me off.

"Received an e-mail from the boss," Caleb told me when I had stopped at the Lotus to order flowers for Marilyn's birthday. "I guess she's having a great time in the Big Apple."

At least I know she's still alive. "Did she say when she'd be back?"

"Not really," Lydia said. "But she instructed us to carry on as if we owned the place."

I could barely acknowledge their well wishes for my trip to Florida.

*　　*　　*

Despite the fact that my folks have resided in the sunshine state for more than a decade, I have always thought of Florida as a temporary destination for tourists and snowbirds. For me the moist tropical air, the exotic flora and fauna, the pancake-flat landscape are as alien as the moon. At least there's no trace of Dannie. She's never been to Florida, never wanted to; the only reason she even considered going to "the land of the blue-hairs" was because she loved me. Well, I guess that was a crock.

'Ria's flight isn't scheduled to arrive for another hour, so I claim my luggage and roam the terminal like a lone tortoise in a sea of frantic hares. Dutiful parents of every shape and size scurry past me trying to keep up with their progeny, who are all suffering from Mickey Mouse mania.

My lovely daughter jettisons off the gangplank like a pinball on a spring. She's arm in arm with a very tall, somewhat dark, definitely handsome young man. They are so caught up in their animated conversation that they nearly walk right past me.

"Mom!" She engulfs me in an ecstatic embrace. "This is Roberto." She trills the *r* delicately off her tongue. "He's visiting his **abuelita**, his grandmother. And you'll never guess," she pauses to catch her breath, "she lives in the very same complex as Gram and Gramps."

"What a wonderful coincidence," I say, shaking Roberto's hand, the prospect of my anticipated time with 'Ria quickly vanishing. I watch the joyful infatuation play out on both of their faces.

With great reluctance, we part company at the rent-a-car lot. Not to worry, the happy couple have already conspired a dinner date for the following evening.

"What did you do to your hair?" I ask as we drive up the highway ramp. Her cherished length of arrow-straight chestnut mane has been cropped short.

"It was time to start looking like a grown up," she says. "Very chic, don't you think?" She flicks the stylish bob about her face. "One of the women in the office had a cosmetic party, and I had a total makeover. They have all of these new products now, you know, foundations and creams that keep your skin looking youthful. You should try it."

"Are you saying I look old? Just last summer you complimented me on my healthy glow."

We stop at a traffic light and 'Ria touches my shoulder. "Seriously Mom, when was the last time you had your hair done?"

I self-consciously tuck my dull, shaggy bangs behind my ears. "I guess I just haven't felt up to it."

"She left you, didn't she?"

I can only nod my head in the affirmative as we pull the car into a visitor's parking space at the Palm Tree Retirement community.

"You're here!" Mom and Dad usher us into their beachfront villa. Dad insists on carrying our luggage to the spare bedroom. "Chivalry is alive and well," he proclaims with a grin. "However, tips are strongly encouraged."

Mom has laid out a spread fit for a small army. "Airlines are notoriously cheap these days," she complains, "with their skimpy beverages and peanut rations."

We stuff ourselves with cream cheese and olive sandwiches on neatly trimmed, crustless rye, mounds of fresh tropical fruit served from a watermelon that looks like it was cut in half with a pair of pinking shears, and an unending supply of Mom's homemade coconut macaroons.

"Don't forget that your dad will be grilling marinated vegetables and shrimp for dinner," she reminds us as 'Ria and I set out to take our full tummies for a walk on the beach.

"Some things never change," I puff, hastily shuffling through the hot sand toward the incoming surf. My toes rejoice as the waves lap between them, eroding away the fine granules from beneath my feet and pulling me slightly off balance.

'Ria picks up a flat stone and skips it deftly into the foamy water. "Maybe she was simply something you needed to get out of your system."

"What?"

"I've been reading about postmenopausal women, especially those in unhappy marriages, who seek out other women because they are looking for a safe relationship."

"Oh, 'Ria," I say, treading carefully. "I know that this has been a shock for you, but I am not having some kind of a menopausal moment. This is who I am, who I've always been."

"I don't believe you," she rushes on. "I know you and Dad had issues, but there are plenty of other men out there, men your age. There's no reason why you can't find one who enjoys the same things that you do, maybe even another teacher. You are still plenty young enough to marry again and share your life with someone else."

My daughter is in denial and I'm not sure that I have the strength to deal with it. Not now. It was difficult enough when I had to tell her that I couldn't be with her father anymore. How could she comprehend that I'm not interested in being with a man, any man at all?

"Roberto was telling me about this great bar where the not yet retired hang out," she continues. "Maybe you should come with us."

For the first time in my life, I sense a chasm greater than the ocean itself forming between me and my only child. Unlike the brief contentions we'd experienced when she was a teenager, I realize that this one could be irreparably damaging.

I put my hands on either side of her face and look deeply into her eyes. "I love you." My own eyes glisten. "I love that you have found Roberto, I love that you want the same thing for me, but we both need more time to think, to talk, to figure this out, and I know we can, I know we will."

"I love you too." She doesn't say the *but*, however the word hangs between us like an open wound in the salty air.

We stroll past families packing up for the day. I envy the simplicity of their tasks: shaking sand from their belongings, telling their kids to take one last run into the water to rinse off. Their only concern is where they'll be going for dinner or what movie they will watch.

*　　*　　*

"'Ria sleeping in this morning?" Mom joins me on the deck, carrying a tray laden with coffee, fresh squeezed orange juice, and a basket of kiwi muffins. She sits, carefully arranging her cotton caftan over her knees. "Beautiful."

I think she's referring to the magnificent sunrise peaking over the horizon, but she's gazing at my sarong. I look away from her inquiring eyes; she's well aware of the revealing tale behind the delicate fabric.

"You miss her, don't you?"

"Terribly."

Mom palms a square envelope from her pocket. "This came for you in yesterday's mail."

I take it out of her hand. It's from Dannie. Mom murmurs something about fixing breakfast for Dad and leaves me alone.

I contemplate the rising ball of fire-throwing, flaming diamonds on the incoming tide. By noon the sun will be unbearably hot—the only relief will be to migrate into the ocean or retreat into the air-conditioned villa. I tuck Dannie's unopened letter into the back pocket of my shorts and throw myself into a vigorous walk on the beach. Tied loosely about my shoulders, the sarong billows in the breeze like an unattended sail. All around me are the sounds and smells of nearby households rehearsing their morning routines.

"Ouch." My toe collides with a pile of stones, probably collected by a child the day before. Another wave scatters a few more at my feet and I'm reminded of Anne Morrow Lindbergh's *Gift from the Sea*. "What message do you have for me?" I ask the multicolored mound. I choose some of the smaller stones at random, spread out my sarong on dry sand, and scrutinize my treasures. Millions of years tumbling through rough water, bumping and rubbing up against millions of other stones, have removed their sharp edges—what remains is smooth and flawless. One in particular catches my eye. About the size of a robin's egg, it has a milky-white ribbon laced through a deep shade of apricot. The two distinct minerals have been fused together into a beautiful mosaic.

I retrieve the cream-colored envelope from my pocket, slide my finger under the sealed flap, and remove the single sheet of fine linen stationary.

Sweet Fern,

It's been eons since I've penned a letter by hand, but an e-mail didn't seem right, and I figured you'd probably hang up on me if I called. I'll admit that mailing this to your mom and dad's when I knew you'd be there was a bit underhanded, but . . .

I know—I screwed up—again. All my life, the people I've cared about have discarded, disowned, or died on me—except you. I guess in some warped way I decided to leave you first. Crazy, I know.

I wish I could be like you, steady as a rock, sure of where I belonged and what I wanted—but I'm not. I'm complicated, messy—unpredictable. You smooth out my ragged edges, and I probably make your life a living hell.

I just wanted you to know that I'm sorry. I wish I could be a good partner, and for what it's worth, I do love you. To quote a very wise and wonderful woman I met last summer, "I don't know how to do this."

Dannie

I sit for a long while, sifting through the rocks on the sarong like I'm panning for gold nuggets. I hold the mosaic stone against my cheek. I read Dannie's letter again and again, each time formulating a different response.

*   *   *

When I return from my walk, Dad apprises me that 'Ria is on the phone with her young man.

"Making plans for this evening no doubt." I smile warily. "What are you up to today?"

"I'm giving a lecture on rock formations to an Elderhostel group."

"Can I come?"

"Not this time. Actually, I think your mom has something up her sleeve for you female types."

Indeed, Mom had thoughtfully signed the three of us up for a Painting with Penelope class.

"She just lost her husband of fifty years and needs a boost," Mom explains. "Besides, it'll be something fun we can all do together."

Penelope is in her midseventies, doing her darnedest to look half her age. Yikes—the makeup, the hair, the embarrassing display of wrinkled cleavage.

"Welcome to acrylics made easy: a no-fail formula," she says as we take our places at the wooden easels. The room is full of old women and one man, Frank who could be an ancient version of Davy. Mom knows everyone and proudly introduces 'Ria and I. We are treated like guests of honor, fresh blood.

"If you follow my instructions," Penelope assures us sweetly, "I guarantee you'll go home with a perfect rendition of an enchanting sunset on a seascape paradise."

At first I conscientiously copy her every brush stroke, duplicating her peachy-pink underpainting, swirling on aquamarine waves that roll uniformly onto a bronze sandy beach. But when she directs us to carefully place delicate dabs of white on the edge of each incoming wave, I get impatient. As if it has a mind of its own, my brush begins to dance on the canvas, splashing dangerous whitecaps all over the foaming surf. Like a rebellious teen, I can't stop myself, and I outline the silhouettes of two female figures wading into the whirling sea. I stifle a giggle as I paint one figure's hand copping a feel of the other's naked bottom. I tap my own back side, fondling Dannie's letter, still in my pocket. Unpredictable, moody, complicated? Oh yes, but she's also exciting, playful, and unbelievably sexy.

At the end of the class, Penelope has us walk around the room to peruse our finished work. It's like viewing an animated film frame by frame. Same picture over and over again with only the slightest variation—until they get to mine. There are a few gasps, 'Ria groans, my mom winks, and Frank cheers, "You go girl!"

Needless to say, I opt not to accompany 'Ria and Roberto for dinner. Instead I eat a scrumptious dinner of grilled salmon and rice with Mom and Dad. After dessert Mom hands me the phone and practically orders Dad to escort her to the minigolf course.

"Isn't Fern going to join us?"

"Fern has an important phone call to make."

She picks up on the second ring, jarring my nerves because I'm expecting, maybe even hoping, for the omniscient voice of her answering machine.

"Dannie?"

"It's you."

"I read your letter."

CHAPTER 13

MY ADRENALINE IS off the charts. I want to punch out the windows in the aircraft and flap my arms to accelerate the flight home. I let out a joyous gurgle. The man dozing next to me opens his eyes.

"Sorry."

"No problem." His voice holds no annoyance. "I'm glad someone is happy." He settles back into his nap.

"Please come home." The three words I'd spoken to Dannie on the phone whir through my mind like the roar of a jet engine.

I remembered the caution in her response. "Are you sure?"

"Yes."

I hear her exhale into the phone. "So how are things in the Deep South? How are Mom and Dad? How is 'Ria?"

"Unbelievably hot, predictably great, and," I suck in my breath. "'Ria is abominably smitten with some guy named Roberto. She's also trying desperately to change me back."

"Ah."

I swallow hard. "I can't talk about it right now. How are things in New York? How's Eliot? How are you?"

"The first two are traveling at hypersonic speeds and I'm doing my best to keep up. There have been some interesting developments with me, but I think I'll wait until we get home to tell you."

The words *we* and *home* never sounded so good.

"Well?" Mom asks when they return from their minigolf game.

I nod and smile.

Dad puts his arm around me and says, "That's my girl." Up to this point, he's been politely silent about my love life. "I knew the two of you could work it out." He pats his stomach. "Now, how about we pop some popcorn and watch a Pink Panther movie?"

I'm in bed by the time 'Ria returns from her date with Roberto, but I manage to cock a sleepy ear and listen to her bestow him with near Prince Charming status. I only hope he doesn't fall off his stallion too soon.

Perhaps it's fortuitous that 'Ria is caught up in her own love life for the remainder of our trip, because it gives me an excuse not to mention my reconciliation with Dannie. Our one and only mother-daughter outing is a trip to the mall—I keep a hair appointment while she shops for a new outfit to wear for the upcoming dinner with Roberto's *abuelita*.

'Lita, as she is known by her ten grandchildren, welcomes us like long lost relatives. Roberto whisks 'Ria away for a romantic ramble on the beach and the two grandmothers, both phenomenal cooks, join forces in the kitchen. Dad and I park ourselves in the pink and white wicker chairs on the patio facing the ocean and watch a kamikaze squadron of seagulls screech down on some poor little boy eating a bag of french fries. I fear he may be snatched up as well until a teenager—I trust it's his sister and not his mother—yanks him out of the way. How she heard his cry for help is a mystery, because her iPod resembles an umbilical cord permanently attached to her ears.

"Are all your students as plugged in as that young lady?" Dad asks.

"Not during school hours, but the speed at which they reattach themselves when they walk out of the building is beyond frightening."

He shakes his head. "Live communication is becoming a lost art. I myself prefer good old-fashioned body language." The creases around Dad's eyes speak volumes, the wrinkles between his brows signal a look of concern. "Will you be all right?" he asks. "I can't say that I totally understand why Dannie is the one." He looks at me, slightly embarrassed. "And partnerships can a tricky business. Your mother and I have been together for decades, and we still have our challenges."

"Dannie and I will be just fine, but I'm not so sure about 'Ria." Is this really my dad that I'm sharing this with? Gardening, woodworking, rock formations, sure—but relationships? Definitely a new one for both of us. "When Ed left, 'Ria and I were inseparable. We could talk about anything, and we generally agreed about everything."

Dad was thoughtful for a moment. "Inseparable is not so healthy. Total agreement must be a recent myth because I remember many a frantic phone call from you when 'Ria was a teenager. Adult relationships with one's offspring can be mighty perplexing until you get the hang of it. I know I'm still learning."

I kiss him lightly on the cheek "Thanks, Dad. You're the wisest in the world."

"OK then." He clears his throat. "Now let's talk about how you plan to keep the woodchucks out of your vegetable garden this summer."

*   *   *

It's Seth who picks me up from the airport. I know that Dannie hadn't said anything about meeting me, but I'd secretly hoped. I try to cover my disappointment by asking how Bea is doing.

"Let's see," Seth grips the steering wheel. "This week we've had heartburn, leg cramps, and false labor pains. This morning she wept for nearly thirty minutes because she couldn't put her shoes on."

I try to reassure him. "Soon."

"Not soon enough."

*   *   *

"I'm home." Ivy simply stares into space—who the hell are you?

I choose to disregard the absence of one yellow Mini Cooper in the driveway and revel instead in Mother Nature's recent achievements. In less than a week, the changes in my yard are remarkable. The tightly fisted apple blossoms have burst open, the purple petals on the pansies have unfurled, and the grass must have grown at least two inches. Ivy continues to ignore my presence while she tracks a tiger beetle along the walkway; however, she races to her food dish when I refill it with kibble. I guess I'm forgiven.

I had hoped to see some evidence of Dannie's homecoming, but with the exception of her recliner, the place is devoid of her stuff. I try to stay calm when I poke my head into the den and find it completely empty. She's changed her mind, again. I hurry into the bedroom. Her clothes are not in the closet and there's no toothbrush in the bathroom. Taped to the mirror above the sink is a note:

Fern,
I'm at Uncle Willie's—come as soon
as you can. xxxooo Dannie.

Willie's? Sure enough, there's her Mini Cooper parked in front. My knock on the door is answered by Eliot's familiar bark. The door opens and there she is.

"What?" I begin, only to be swept up in a enveloping embrace.

"You're here!" She whirls me into what had once been Willie's living room. "What do you think?"

I honestly don't know what to think. The room has been transformed into some sort of reception area. A wall-to-wall carpet cushions my feet as she leads me over to the grouping of leather chairs around an oval coffee table. Interior design magazines, paint charts, and swatches of fabric are scattered across the glass top. In the far corner of the room is a folding table heaped with file folders and a tangled mass of wires and cables. A phone, a computer, and a copy machine peek out from under the rubble.

"Not totally organized yet." She gestures to the fireplace where a gas insert has been installed. "Ambiance and heat without the ashes. Want to see my office?"

"Your office?"

"It's the creative nerve center of Cottage Industries, Incorporated." I follow her into what was once Willie's bedroom. Her king-size rolltop desk presides in the center of the room—its loyal subjects, a pair of wingback chairs. Hugging one wall are her bookshelves, and on the other, a long, narrow table cluttered with even more electronic devices. "This is where my clients and I will confer."

Comprehension begins to permeate my foggy brain. "A consulting firm? But isn't that what you have in New York?"

"New York is too far away," she says. "Here I can help launch small country businesses. Help the economy of Glendale and the surrounding towns. And it's all thanks to Uncle Willie. I couldn't believe it when his estate lawyer called me and told me that the dear, sweet man had bequeathed the property to me." She steps back and regards me with an inquisitive expression. "Well, what do you think?"

"So you'll work and sleep here?"

"Sleep here?" She crosses her arms. "I thought I'd be sleeping at home with you."

"But all your stuff is here."

"Now that's your fault." She wags her finger at me. "When Eliot and I came home we discovered that someone had handily sequestered all of my belongings into one room. It was just easier to have the movers pack up the entire den. My clothes are out in the car; that is, unless you've changed your mind?"

"No I haven't changed my mind. I thought maybe you'd changed your mind."

"Well, it seems to me that the only thing that's changed then is your hair." She points to the magenta highlights radiating from my recently coiffed head.

* * *

During the remaining days of the spring break, we reclaim and reorganize our life together. We take advantage of Devin and Jay's youthful brawn to rototill a plot for the vegetable garden, and their techno brains to bring Dannie's computers online.

"What's Tracy up to this week?" I ask Devin when we stop for some well-deserved lemonade.

He shrugs, "Working I guess."

"Oh?" I sense a subplot in his answer.

"We've decided to take a break," he says. "You know, maybe see other people, that sort of thing."

"Are you OK with that?"

I take it from his nonchalant reply, "Whatever," that the subject is closed.

*　　*　　*

On Sunday evening, we treat ourselves to a night on the town. We indulge in a bit of nostalgia by returning to the restaurant with the world's finest Italian cuisine.

"Just think," I say, "only nine months ago we were sitting in this very place eating and drinking with that crazy crew from the Water's Edge." I lift my glass of wine. "To Davy, Karin, Sue, and John, wherever they may be."

"Here, here," Dannie clinks my glass with her own. Her tone sobers. "I heard you talking on the phone to 'Ria this afternoon."

"She knows that we're back together. She's not happy, but she conceded that it's my life and I can do what I want. It hurts."

"I know, but she's right. It is your life." After the waitress has taken our order, Dannie changes the subject. "I spoke to the movers in New York. They'll be transporting my things from the condo next Wednesday."

"Are you sure you want to do this?" I ask, looking at her closely. She'd decided to put her condo on the market and move the remainder of her possessions to Glendale. "It feels so permanent."

"It does, doesn't it. A good feeling, I hope?"

"A very good feeling."

After dinner we stroll around the park. The amphitheater is empty. "No symphony to serenade us tonight."

Dannie pinches my earlobe. "If it's music you're after, I can croon in your ear."

"You may have many talents my love, but singing isn't one of them."

She feigns distress. "I'm deeply crushed. But tell me more about my many talents."

"When we get home."

"Which one?"

"Either, as long as both of us are in residence." I keep my voice light but there is apprehension behind what I say next. "Don't run away again."

Dannie searches my face. "I'm not sure that I can make any guarantees, but I'll always let you know where you can find me."

"As long as I know that you want to be found."

CHAPTER 14

"TOTALLY AWESOME!" CRYSTAL gasps. "I've never had a teacher with red hair before." Brad has his arm around Crystal's waist when they enter my classroom.

Crystal corrects him. "It's not red, it's magenta."

"Whatever."

The Grub Club is finalizing plans for the Memorial Day float. "So we'll all convene at Caila's place on Saturday morning?" I wonder if I'm being too optimistic about the early hour, but they all nod their heads enthusiastically. My guess is that they're all as excited as I am to see the finished product. Thanks to Caila's dad, we have a hay wagon to use for the base of the float, and Jay's grandfather's John Deere to pull it. True to their word, the kids had found plenty of sponsors. The Glendale lumber company provided materials for the one-room "gridless house" in the center of the float, the solar panels were on loan from Capture the Sun, Inc., and the Yellow Lotus had donated green T-shirts and an assortment of plants to augment the ones the kids had grown themselves.

To their credit, all the kids except Tracy, who had to work, show up on Saturday by 9:30 a.m. Even Bea, with eight months of baby housed in her farmer jeans, arrives to help supervise.

"I may not be able to do any of the heavy lifting," she proclaims, "but I can still wield a hammer."

Julian swings by at noon with a tray of sandwiches.

"Hummus and olives on spinach roll-ups," Meg swoons. "My favorite. Your dad's the best." She smiles broadly at Devin. He blushes. So that's how it is.

Jay eyes the roll-ups with suspicion. "I sure hope there's something normal to eat."

I present him with two inches of rare meat slapped into a bulky roll. "Roast beef normal enough?"

"That's more like it. None of that healthy sissy crap—I need real food for this body."

Meg shoves his arm. "Come see me after your first heart attack."

"Say hello to Jonas for me," I tell Julian after I thank him for the lunch.

He clears his throat. "Actually I'm not working at the Water's Edge anymore. In fact I'm . . ."

"Sorry to interrupt, Dad," Devin sidles up to us, "but I don't want to be late for practice."

"Soccer?" I ask, still trying to process Julian's news.

"No, lacrosse," he shouts as they take off in the van.

*   *   *

Two women with two animals occupying two houses on ten acres turns out to be a formula for success.

"Earthmother to Don-elle Trump," I say into the handheld device. "The soup is on the table."

"Be there in five," she answers.

The two-way radio had been a housewarming gift from Tim and Marilyn. They shamelessly admitted that it was one of the secrets to their marital success.

"Do you think we're ready for this baby shower?" I ask, adding another dollop of whipped cream onto my rice pudding. We're sitting under the apple trees. Eliot and Ivy are curled up at our feet.

"Absolutely."

Eliot snorts and quivers. Ivy stretches one of her paws out to deter a regiment of ants marching past her nose. They climb up and over the fury appendage without missing a step and journey on their way.

"What a life," Dannie sighs.

"And it's all ours."

*   *   *

"Want to hold her?" Before I say a word, Mary plops the five-month-old on to my lap and walks away. I guess by number four you no longer have separation anxiety. As for little Sasha, she's sound asleep and has no compunction about snuggling deeper into my embrace.

Dannie pulls up a chair beside me. "Now don't you look all cozy and maternal." She waves her hand around. "I think we've done good. Julian's finger sandwiches, fancy cakes, and cheese puffs are a big hit, and Lydia has outdone herself with the decorations."

"Everyone seems to be enjoying themselves," I agree.

"Oh, piffle, here comes trouble." Dannie nods. "Not to worry, I'll take care of her."

"Don't piss her off," I beseech, bracing myself for the onslaught that is Priscilla.

Dannie shakes her head. "Not her, the baby." She gathers Sasha out of my arms and cradles her onto her shoulder like it's the most natural thing in the world.

"What," she exclaims when my mouth drops open, "you don't think I know what to do with a baby?" Swaying slowly from side to side she glides away.

"Unbelievable."

"I know," Priscilla concurs. "We never thought that Beatrice would even get married, never mind have children."

"What? Oh, right I forgot, Bea grew up in Glendale didn't she?" To my dismay, Priscilla sits down by my side and continues on in her conspiratorial tone, "Such a tomboy."

I'm in no mood for her petty platitudes. "I'll just go see if the punch bowl needs topping up." I start to stand but she puts her hand on my arm. "Quite an extravagant spread, it's so kind of you to host this auspicious occasion."

Her ability to make an ordinary compliment sound so sinister never ceases to amaze me.

"Bea's a good friend to both Dannie and me, and we were glad to do it. Besides, Julian is the one who provided the "spread," as you call it."

"Speaking of Ms. Stevens and your handsome young Julian," she lowers her voice. "I saw them yesterday morning at the Main Street Café. They seemed quite besotted with each other. They had their heads so close together that they didn't even notice me."

"Oh." I honestly couldn't think of a thing to say.

"Just thought you'd like to know." Having delivered her weighty testimony, she starts to leave. This time I'm the one to stop her.

"Not that it's any of your beeswax, Priscilla, but Julian is launching his own catering business, and he's hired Dannie as his consultant. She'll make his business a success just like she did with the Lotus for Lydia and Caleb. And yes, Priscilla, Dannie and I do live together and we are very much in love, so just get over it."

"Time to open the gifts!" Marilyn organizes us into a semicircle around Bea. The room is filled with oohs and aahs as she unwraps the terry cloth bibs, the hand-knitted blankets, and the miniature booties—each one more adorable than the one before.

*   *   *

"It's a boy!" Seth shouts into the phone. "Eight pounds eleven ounces."

Dannie and I are savoring leftover baby shower danish before we go to work. "Congratulations," I manage to say, gulping down my mouthful of pastry. "How's Bea?"

"She's magnificent. Baby Shane is magnificent. The doctors are magnificent."

"I get it," I break in, realizing that he's high on daddy adrenaline. "Shall I give the good word to everyone at school?"

"Yes, that would be mag—"

"I know, magnificent. Please give the magnificent Bea our love and let us know when we can visit."

The arrival of Bea's baby is the buzz of the day, and I'm not the only one who finds it a challenge to concentrate, especially when Bea and Seth e-mail a picture of little Shane to my cell phone. His face is all scrunched up, and he has a tuft of strawberry blond fuzz on the top of his head. A mohawk, the kids say, pronouncing him the cutest baby in the world. Shane's red hair segues nicely into a discussion about dominant and recessive genes.

*　　*　　*

"*I love a parade*," Dannie warbles at a decibel that sends Eliot into a howl and Ivy scrambling for cover. It's early, too early, but the parade participants are required to gather in the Shop and Save parking lot at the insane hour of 6:00 a.m.

Eventually the pandemonium of people, bands, and floats comes to some semblance of order. Marilyn and Tim climb into the back of a hybrid convertible; the bass drum thumps out a moderate tempo, the snare drums reply with an earsplitting riff, and we fan out like a gigantic accordion.

I display more pretense than expertise as I putt-putt the John Deere at a slow crawl, carefully pulling my precious cargo down the street. The kids have done a phenomenal job, and I hope that their float wins first place.

Crowd participation is over the top. Folks jam the sidewalks holding up posters, waving banners, and wearing tee shirts that endorse all manner of earth friendly mantras. GO GREEN. SAVE OUR PLANET. BRING YOUR OWN BAGS. Pastor Chad is standing at attention on the steps of the church holding a placard inscribed *W.W.J.D.?* What would Jesus do? At his elbow is the ever helpful Priscilla flourishing the directive, *COMPOST DAILY*.

The kids throw up a cheer for Lydia and Caleb, who are poised in front of the Yellow Lotus. Eliot barks a greeting from the top of his mountain of blue recycle bins. I spot Jonas sporting a sign suggesting that an excellent way to conserve water is to shower with a friend. Next to him is a woman dressed all in brown with branches sprouting from her hat. Printed across her chest: *Have you hugged a tree today?* Walking up and down the parade route is a man wearing a sandwich board declaring: *Replant or the end is near.*

We round the corner for the final lap. I can smell the aroma of buttery popcorn and barbeque chicken wings drifting out from the vendors in the park. All along the sidewalk are families and friends waving and shouting as their loved ones march by. I scan the unfamiliar faces until I find them—my family. Bea and Seth are at the curb. Snuggled against Bea's chest is a peacefully sleeping Shane, and smiling broadly at their side is Dannie. She salutes.

I salute back and blow her a kiss.

Made in the USA
Lexington, KY
14 October 2011